Vixen

Charles Ray

North Potomac, MD

This book is a work of fiction. Names, except for most geographical place names, events, and persons are either fictional or used fictionally. The events in this book are a product of the author's imagination. Any resemblance to places, events, or persons, living or dead, is purely coincidental.

If you'd like information about other works by this author, contact him at charlesray.author@gmail.com

Authors, especially independent authors survive on word of mouth buzz about their books. One way to achieve this is through reviews. If you like what you read, please consider leaving a brief review on the site where you bought it.

Printed in the United States of America

Copyright © 2017 Charles Ray

All rights reserved.

ISBN: 069291160X
ISBN-13: 978-0692911600

DEDICATION

Next to playing cowboys and Indians, the most popular game for youngsters when I was growing up, especially young boys, was playing pirate. For reasons that it never occurred to me to ask at the time, girls were never encouraged to play pirate—or cowboys and Indians either, for that matter. Well, sorry about that, but, this book is not dedicated to you young men, but to all the young women who also dreamed of a life of adventure on the open sea, in outer space, or just across town. Don't stop dreaming, and don't let anyone kill your dreams.

Vixen

April, 1791, on board the British galleon, City of Dover, 200 miles east of the port of Boston

The little girl wiped at the lock of red hair covering her left eye and plastered to her ivory cheek by the incessant salty spray that was whipped across the deck by the wind blowing from the south. At mid-morning, it should have been a bright day, but a gauzy veil of haze coated the sky, turning the sun behind the galleon, *City of Dover,* into an ineffectual disk of yellowish white, casting barely enough light to create her shadow on the gleaming, dark brown oak planks of the deck.

Despite the stinging spray, she kept her eyes on the horizon beyond the prominent bow of *Dover,* even knowing that it would be at least another week, perhaps ten days before she would see anything. For now, the only thing to see was the undulating surface of the north Atlantic, a dull, gray-blue flecked with occasional white froth as waves broke over some subsurface imperfection; a color that seemed to merge with the blue-gray of the sky, a uniform color, unbroken by the white of clouds that were masked by the haze that had been hanging over them for the last five days.

At least, she thought, the ocean was calm, or as calm as the north Atlantic ever gets. Until midnight the previous night, she'd hardly been able to come on deck because the ocean was, as Captain Beadle, master of *Dover*, was fond of saying, 'pitching a right fine fit.' Waves, tons of blue-black water fringed with white froth, swept across the decks, even the raised quarter deck in the stern, and anything—or anyone—unlucky enough to be on the deck at the time and not secured to something like a mast, would be swept into the sea, probably never to be seen again. Only the officers and men of the watch had been allowed above decks, and then only working in teams. The break in the weather had been welcomed by everyone, but especially the little redhead.

She rested her forearms on the polished wood of the rail and rested her pointed chin on her arms. Even though she was only eight, she was tall for her age, so was able to see over the rail without having to resort to the risky maneuver of standing on tiptoe.

Her mother and father were in their cabin, one deck below, not far from the captain's cabin, as befitted her father's status as the new British consul in Boston. He was probably reading yet again one of the many foolscaps given him by the foreign office, describing the customs, culture, and economy of the young country that had once been a jewel in the British Empire's crown, but had forced a separation through armed conflict that rocked the crown to its knees. Despite the war, and disagreements that still existed because of England's refusal to pay damages, and the continued presence of British forces on the new country's western frontier, commercial relations between Britain and its former colony were again vibrant—especially with the states of the northeast where mercantile interests sought to ply their goods in British and European markets, and prized certain imports from their former colonial master. In fact, her father had informed her with a wry grin, these selfsame mercantile interests had, in many instances, continued to trade with England even during the war. While those in leadership positions in the government of the new United States of America had no doubt known this, it was commonly believed that because they knew they would need the support of those with wealth in order for the new country to survive, these traders were not treated with the same degree of harshness that many of the so-called traitors, the Tories, had suffered.

"There is a special fondness for things English in Boston and many of the other areas of the north of the country," her father had said. "This might seem strange, given that Boston was the birthplace of the insurrection against the crown, but after they gained their independence, many of the northerners were bypassed in favor of the Virginians who at present dominate the central government. Of course, they shouldn't have been surprised at that, them and their 'one man, one vote' philosophy, even if they only count white men of property, and mostly of English lineage."

"Why is that, father?" the girl had asked, instantly

regretting it, because her father could go on for hours about the foibles of foreigners and Englishmen alike, especially as it pertained to wealth and power, while all she wanted to do was explore the ship.

"Virginia is the most populous of the thirteen states, and is the leader of the southern delegates, so that state has the most influence in central government affairs. Their president, Mr. Washington, is a Virginia planter from a wealthy family, and many of the men in his cabinet are intimate acquaintances of similar background. People like Mr. Adams and Mr. Franklin, both northerners, despite the key roles they played in gaining support from France and achieving their independence were relegated to minor roles."

None of this, though, was of interest to an inquisitive eight-year-old anxious to go exploring, so she asked no more questions, and her father eventually lost interest in talking to her in favor of another of his dispatches.

` Her mother, on the other hand, would probably be abed with another of her 'headaches.' She'd been having them since they boarded the carriage in south London that bore them south to the port of Dover, from whence the ship took its name and its leave from England. As long as she was quiet and didn't disturb her mother's rest, she was ignored. The only time her mother had engaged her in conversation for any length of time was during the fourth day of the voyage when she suggested that it might be better if she spent more time in the cabin, and less wandering around among the riff raff that made up the ship's crew.

This was not for her, though. Confined to a musty cabin, lit only by the glow of a foul-smelling whale oil lamp—another of the colonial, no American, exports from the northeastern port cities and their great whaling fleets—was not her idea of how to spend an ocean voyage. It was her first ever, and who knew when such an opportunity would again present itself? When the storm struck, and the captain insisted that his passengers remain in their cabin until further instructed, she was sure she would go crazy. When the portly Beadle rapped on their cabin door and announced that the seas were as calm as a Yorkshire meadow, she almost knocked her father over in her race for the door, and the quarterdeck.

Sailors didn't normally favor having women and children aboard ship, believing that it brought bad luck. Because of her father's position, and the hefty sum the foreign office had paid for their passage, her mother was tolerated, especially since she rarely left her cabin. Wary of her at first, the sailors, to a man, quickly came to accept and then welcome the little redheaded girl. She didn't act like a little girl in the first place, and she had a quick mind, asking dozens of questions about the ship, remembering everything she was told, and by the time they'd been at sea for five days knew it better than Tim Worthy, the cabin boy, who always looked a bit green under the gills whenever the ship rolled or pitched. Not her, though. She found her sea legs within hours of the big vessel pulling away from the docks, and by the time they were a day's sail from the port of Dover, was traversing the deck as surefootedly as the most seasoned seaman aboard.

Even Captain Beadle, a crusty man with a generous paunch and a fringe of white hair ringing his head, but missing the top, who was known to blister the paint of the quarter deck hull with his language when angered, had taken to the precocious youngster and her almost preternatural ability to absorb sailing lore. Had she been a boy, he said to her one day when she was standing beside him near the helm, she would one day make a fine sailor.

"Why can't I be a sailor?" she'd asked.

"Well, dearie," he'd said. "It's just not done. Women aren't cut out to be sailors. Having a woman aboard a ship'd bring no end of trouble, y'see."

She did not see, but he refused to be any more forthcoming, so she'd let the matter drop.

Today, the first day on deck after five days cooped up in the cabin with her father ignoring her to read his briefing papers, and her mother whining that the tossing and rolling of the ship was only making her headache worse, she only wanted to be alone and enjoy the view, what there was of it, without being bothered by the presence of anyone else.

Something about the sea fascinated her. She could not put a name to the attraction; the vastness—the way it never seemed to end as it stretched off to infinity all around you—or, perhaps the power that was evident in the way it tossed the enormous galleon around like a cork in a rapidly flowing stream. Whatever it was, it called to her.

"Mornin', missy, nice to see ye out 'n about today," the crusty voice said from her left, causing her to start and jerk around toward it.

She immediately relaxed and smiled. It was only Old Jack, as he insisted on being called, the ship's cook. Bent at the shoulders, with gnarled hands barely able any longer to grasp the great carving knives he kept in a chest in the galley, with stringy white hair that flapped about in the wind blowing across the deck like the tattered threads of a curtain in an open window, and only two brown and crooked teeth left in his mouth, Old Jack would have frightened most children, but the redheaded girl loved to listen to his stories of his many years at sea, and he, in turn, found something endearing in her bright blue eyes, her quick wit, and her apparent fearlessness. Whenever he wasn't preparing a meal for the ever-hungry crew, or for the captain and his special passengers, and the weather was clement enough to allow her to be on the deck, he would join her.

"Good morning, Old Jack," she said. "It is nice to be able to come up here."

"I'll wager ye will be happy to see Old Jack receding in the dust behind ye."

She shook her head vigorously. "No, I've enjoyed talking to you." She looked around, her eyes filled with wonder. "And, I've really enjoyed being on *The City of Dover*."

The man peered down into her eyes. She was, he could tell, absolutely sincere. What a strange and amazing child, he thought.

"Aye, I can see ye do, lass. But, ye know, even the most hardened sailor longs to have solid earth under his feet again after many weeks at sea. Ye mark my words, ye'll be happy to set foot in Boston Harbor."

She reached out and grasped his knotted hand. "I'll miss you, Old Jack."

"Aye, missy, 'n Old Jack's goin' ter miss ye as well."

She turned back to the railing, and he was about to

return to the galley, when a soft gasp escaped her throat.

"What be it, missy?" he asked.

She pointed across the railing, toward the north, her pink lips opening and closing, but at first, no sound coming out. Then, she found her voice. "It's another ship," she said.

Old Jack moved to the railing and stared off in the direction she was pointing, shaking his head. Then his rheumy eyes went wide and his nostrils flared.

"By Jove, lassie, ye've got the eyes of an eagle. I don't think the lookout's even seen it yet. Ye're right, it be a ship." Then, he got a look of dread in his eyes. "Lassie, ye'd better get below to yer cabin."

"Why?" she asked. "That ship looks like it's coming this way. It'll pass right across our bow. I'd love to see that."

Now, the man was trembling. "Listen to me, missy, ye've got to git below. Above decks isna a fittin' place for ye right now."

She looked intently up at him. She didn't have to crane too hard, for Old Jack was only a couple hand spans taller than she was. She read the fear written plainly on his weather-beaten face.

"What is it, Old Jack? What's going on?"

Something in the calm way she asked, compelled the old man to answer.

"I recognize yon ship, lassie, though I never thought to see 'er up close in me lifetime; but them three masts and that extra-long bowspirit be unmistakable," he said. "Yon ship belong to the dread pirate, John Cleague. He be known as the Devil's Ally, 'cause he have a practice of killin' his victims after robbin' 'em."

She could feel some of his dread, but there was something else she felt, a sensation she did not fully understand—excitement.

"Very well, Old Jack, I'll go below," she said. "You'd better go and warn the captain. Do you think they'll attack us?"

"Aye, they'll try, but the old lady's got a lot of speed in her. We be only a week or so out of Boston, so if the wind stays with us, we might be able to out run him until we come across an American warship."

There was no conviction in his voice, she sensed it. Yet, she still felt that . . . excitement. The old man turned and hobbled as fast as his arthritic legs would carry him toward the captain's quarters, poking the shoulders of the sailors as he passed them, and yelling into their faces. In short order, there was a sense of barely controlled panic on the deck. No one noticed the redheaded girl secrete herself behind a stack of kegs lashed to the aft mast.

Wedged into the crevice formed between two kegs, she was only able to see upwards where the billowing sails blocked all but a sliver of the leaden sky. But, she could hear everything. At first, it was just the slap of feet on the wooden deck and an occasional shout as the captain called out orders to the seamen. She could feel the pitch and roll of the galleon as it crested a swell and plunged down into the trough between the swells.

Then, things began to change. The bucking and tossing of the ship became wilder, and the sails flapped louder. She heard the sound of running feet going to and fro past her hiding place. But, it was the tenor in the voices that gave her a feeling of icy coldness in the pit of her stomach.

"Captain, they be getting' closer," a frantic voice said.

"Full sail," Beadle's voice boomed, clear even over the noise of the sails and hissing wind. "Bring 'er three points to port. Mayhap we can catch the southbound current."

She felt the ship sway sharply as his command was obeyed.

"We got 'er runnin' flat out, cap'n, but that bastard's still gainin' on us."

"Jack, are you sure that's John Cleague's ship?" the captain asked.

"Aye, cap'n" Old Jack said. "As sure as I be standin' here before you. I'd know that black hull anywhere."

"What're we gonna do, captain?" another voice asked.

"We keep tryin' to outrun 'em. In the meantime, break out the muskets and cutlasses, and have crews man the demi-culverins."

"But, cap'n, them two little popguns ain't no match fer the ten cannons Cleague's got on that cursed ship of his," Old Jack said. "And, as fer the muskets and cutlasses, this bunch go up agin Cleague's cutthroats with 'em, we might's well use 'em on ourselves . . . we'll be just as dead, but a damn sight quicker'n we'll be when he gits his hands on us."

"This pirate, Cleague," Beadle said. "I understand he takes no prisoners for ransom?"

"That be right. I hear he think it be too much bother. He also don't leave no witnesses to his actions. Only a few men have ever met him at sea and lived to tell the tale, and that's 'cause they jumped overboard afore the ships closed, and was able to cling to the wreckage after Cleague sailed away with his booty."

"Well, Jack, as I see it, we have no choice but to try and run. Failing that, we will give the best we got. If we die, let's try and take a few of the bloody bastards with us."

The little girl could scarcely believe what she was hearing. Pirates! And, this close to their destination. Her pulse pounded in her ears, threatening to drown out the sound of frantic activity all around her.

The time seemed to drag on forever. And, then she heard a far-off boom, followed a few seconds later by a crash and the sound of men screaming in pain.

"They're closin', break out the muskets and cutlasses," Beadle shouted. "Prepare to repel boarders."

There were more booming sounds, some very nearby; more crashing of timbers and screaming, some cut off sharply. Then, she heard a grating sound and the galleon heeled sharply to the right. Had the casks not been tied securely to the mast, she thought, they, and she, would surely have been dumped into the sea.

She heard shouting and screaming, the clanking sound of steel against steel, and the sharp crack of musket fire.

It seemed to go on forever. The smell of gunpowder stung her eyes and another metallic smell that she didn't recognize made her feel as she wanted to vomit. But, she continued to crouch behind the casks with her eyes tightly shut and her hands clamped over her ears to try and drown out the horrible sounds.

And then, just as suddenly as it began, it ended. The only sound was the flapping of the sails and the gentle hiss of the wind which she could hear but, huddled down beneath the casks, couldn't feel. The *Dover* rocked gently from side to side.

A shadow blocked the light from above, and looking up, she saw broad shoulders covered in a black coat with wide leather straps crisscrossing over the back.

"Is she secure?" A booming voice rang out.

From the nearness, she knew it came from the man with the broad shoulders standing just inches from where she hid. She took shallow breaths, but was sure the man could hear the wild beating of her heart.

"All secure, cap'n," a voice called from far away. "Ain't a man . . . or woman left alive."

"Good. Strip the valuables and let's get back aboard *The Vixen*. I don't want to linger long here, just in case the damn American navy's got frigates patrollin' out this far. It ain't much of a navy, mind ye, but a frigate with twenty-two guns has a lot of fight in it, and I don't go into a fight I'm not sure I can win, so get a move on."

The girl heard footsteps hurrying away, but the broad shoulders continued to block her view. Sweat was trickling down her brow and into her eyes, stinging them. Her hair was plastered to her skull and face, and her clothing, an impractical dress that her mother insisted she wear whenever she left the cabin, was soaked with sweat and smelled of gunpowder and sweat, and stuck to her body in some most uncomfortable places.

The most troubling thing, though, was the strong cloud of gunpowder that hung over the ship. Tendrils of the grayish mist had invaded the space with her, and it was causing her nose to itch something awful.

She could feel a sneeze building up in her nose and her throat was constricting. She tried as hard as she could to hold it in, wanting to remain hidden until the pirates finished their looting and departed. She wasn't sure what she'd do then—especially if it was true what she'd heard, they'd killed everyone. Everyone included her mother and father. She choked back a sob at the thought, but knew that her father would have told her to keep a 'stiff upper lip, and soldier on.' Even though he'd never served in the army himself, he always used terms like that, which meant little to her, but she always tried to please him, because he would then let her do things that her mother blanched at, calling them 'unfit for a proper young lady.'

Just when she thought the pirates would go away, a voice she'd not heard before, a young person by the sound, rang out. "We're all done, cap'n, you want us to fire it now?"

Fire it, she thought. *I wonder if that's some kind of weapon. But, why should they want to be firing it after the battle is over?*

"Aye, Diego lad," the deep voice of the man with broad shoulders said. "You men get the torches and some whale oil. I want this ship burnin' like a right proper bonfire in the next ten minutes, so get to it."

Ship? Burning? Oh no, she thought. *That is most definitely not good.*

Distracted by the fear of being trapped aboard a burning ship, she loosened the muscles in her throat, and an explosive sneeze that had been trapped in her nose for several minutes exploded with a noise like loose gunpowder when it's been touched by a burning taper.

"Well, well," the deep voice said. "What do we have here? A stowaway, perhaps?"

She looked up. The broad-shouldered man had turned and peered over the cask behind which she was hiding. His face was partially in shadow, but what she could see sent chills down her spine. He had a face that was mostly angles; a broad brow with bushy black brows over large eyes that were as dark as pools of ink, and a wide nose that had a bump halfway down its length. Beneath the nose was a bushy mustache that looked like a large black caterpillar, followed by thick, cracked lips, and a black beard that was braided into two forks that stood at a sharp angle from each other.

She wasn't sure she believed in the devil, but if there was indeed such a being, this is what he would undoubtedly look like.

She only vaguely registered the other men standing around, or moving quickly to the railing with burdens on their shoulders which they passed on to men standing at the railing of a ship that was secured to *Dover* by grappling hooks. The only detail she saw clearly was that while the railings of *Dover* were a light brown, those of the ship attached to her were as black as the darkest night.

As the broad-shouldered man reached a grimy looking hand down toward her, she jumped up and scurried past him. She didn't get far, however, quickly finding herself wrapped in the arms of a foul-smelling man with most of his teeth missing, and one eye that looked up while the other one remained immobile. She began to pummel him, hitting him on his already smashed-looking nose, and eliciting a howl of pain. He dropped her, but she was quickly pinioned by another equally foul-smelling man, this one with skin the color of mahogany, and a shaved head that glistened in the gray light. He pressed her so that her arms were pinned at her sides. She leaned forward and sank her teeth into his shoulder, tasting salt, a fish-like flavor, and the metallic taste of blood. The dark man, no more than a boy really, winced, but didn't loosen his hold on her. He did, however, twist her around so that her back was to him, and kept his arms low enough that she could no longer bite any portion of his anatomy.

"Aie-aiee, captain, this one she have bite like she-leopard," the dark man said. "Should I slit her throat and throw her overboard, or just throw her and let sharks eat her alive."

The girl almost screamed. But, she held it in and stared at the big man.

"You killed my mother and father," she said. There was a little tremor in her voice. "You might as well kill me."

The big man tugged at his beard and looked at her, his expression at first unreadable. And then, he laughed. "Nay, M'nondo," he said. "This one has spirit. More'n any of the jackals aboard this ship. I think I'll be keepin' her as a pet. Take her to my cabin."

As she was being taken away her mind raced, torn by what had just happened. She wasn't being killed, but would be kept as a . . . pet. The pet of a pirate. Suddenly, she felt cold all over. Her mind began to speculate on what that meant, and nothing was positive. The more she thought, the colder she got until she fainted from exhaustion and fear.

Charles Ray

Chapter One

June 1811, on board *The Vixen*, in the North Atlantic Ocean, 200 miles east of the Port of Boston

Elizabeth Parker hated the North Atlantic. She hated it in winter and she hated it in summer. It is an angry ocean, slate grey in winter and deep blue, almost black, in summer, it returned her hate with full force whenever she dared traverse its broad expanse.

It seemed to be especially angry now, its brine-laden water, as cold as the snow on the highest mountain peak, rising as high as the midpoint of the foremast, and then crashing in a loud, thunderous roar over the decks of *The Vixen*, threatening to rip the sails from the masts and spars and washing her and her crew overboard.

The crashing, tossing waves, and the icy winds sweeping down from the north, tossed *The Vixen* around like a tiny twig in a rushing stream. The timbers of the ship's hull groaned and creaked, making a mournful sound that created in her mind the image of tormented souls wandering in limbo, wailing for release.

But, despite nature's best efforts, and the angry spitefulness of the ocean, *The Vixen* held together, and continued to make headway toward its destination, a spot due east of the American coastline, approximately 200 miles from the port of Boston. It was a place that held special significance for her, a place that she'd visited each year, only this year, she was, due to circumstances beyond her control, she was two months overdue. No matter, she thought. Out here on the ocean, time only matters when you're closing in on another ship, and then it's measured in minutes, not days. *Old Black John would've said, ye gits there when ye gits there, and ain't no use in frettin' about it.* So be it. They would be in about the right place in another hour of sailing. Not that you could find a precise spot in a trackless ocean, but she had a sense about it, as did her foster father and mentor, and each year, from the time she was nine years old, they'd come here and dropped a bunch of tropical flowers into the ocean, At least they had until five years ago when they'd been cornered by the American frigate, *Intrepid*, and Black John had been captured in the ensuing skirmish. She and the rest of the crew had managed to escape, but it had come at a price. The captain of the American vessel, rather than taking John back to a port for trial, had personally beheaded him and tossed his body into the shark-infested waters. What the bastard had done with the head, she never knew.

But, one day, she would know. And John's head would have company.

She stared out at the unseen horizon, noticing that

the pitching of the ship seemed less severe with each passing minute. Good, she thought, the storm is finally abating. We'll be able to sail in, drop the damn flowers, and sail out. She was only doing it because it's what John would've wanted, what he would have insisted upon. He'd made her come to this spot in the ocean every April for a good chunk of the previous twenty years. At some point, she was sure, he'd explained the reason for it, but it had become fuzzy over the years, and she no longer remembered.

She sensed rather than heard the man moving up behind and to her left, a skill that had saved her life on more than one occasion. On this occasion, though, she did not draw the long, razor-sharp sword from its scabbard at her left side. She recognized the smell of the man as soon as he was within sword range— M'nondo, her friend and constant companion for two decades, a man who was more like a brother than a subordinate crew member.

Ten years older than Elizabeth, a good six inches taller, and a hundred pounds heavier, with his shaven head, skin the color of polished oak, and decorative scars on both of his broad cheeks, M'nondo was an imposing figure. Her foster father and mentor, Captain John Cleague, had assigned M'nondo, a newly-arrived slave at a South Carolina rice plantation who escaped by stealing a small boat and rowing out to sea, preferring to die rather than live in chains, who had then been picked up by *The Vixen*, which just happened to be sailing off the coast of South Carolina at the time. Impressed by the man's bravery, and foolhardiness, Cleague, rather than leave him to die, had invited him to join the crew of *The Vixen* as a seaman. There would be no pay, for *The Vixen,* with its hull painted inky black, was not your run of the mill merchant ship, but a pirate ship, and as a crew member, M'nondo was entitled to a share in all loot captured, which he viewed as far more preferable to either being a slave or starving to death in a leaky boat.

Elizabeth had hazy memories of M'nondo hugging her, and her biting him, but could not remember the incident in any detail, nor the circumstances that would make her want to hurt her lifelong companion.

"Looks like the storm is about to break," he said in his deep, resonant voice as he came alongside her.

"Aye, and we should be at the position in another hour," she said. "Then, we can throw the damn flowers overboard, and go looking for some fat merchantman."

"That would be pleasant. Pickings have been slim of late. However, you should take this ceremony more seriously. You know how much it meant to Captain John."

She wiped at a stray lock of bright red hair, darkened now by the ocean spray, that had plastered itself to her red eyebrows and cheek. "I know, M'nondo, but I just never understood *why* it was so damned important."

The only reaction the man showed to her use of profanity, which he was, even after two decades, shocked at, was a slight lifting of his brows. He ran a thumb over the scars on his left cheek and looked down at her, his deep brown eyes gazing warmly at the woman who, in addition to being his captain, was like the younger sister he'd never had.

"Maybe someday you'll . . . remember," he said. His

deep voice was soft, almost drowned out by the wind that swept across the deck of the brigantine, and the flapping of the square sails on the main and fore masts. "It's important to you, too."

She looked up at him, a question in her gaze. "Why in the name of seven hells should it mean anything to me?"

He locked gaze with her.

"That is something you must discover for yourself, Elizabeth."

A look of worry flickered on her face. He never called her by her first name except in the privacy of her cabin. For him to do it on the open deck, despite the fact that no one else from the crew was near enough to hear over the wind, told her that he had something important on his mind. But, she knew enough not to press him on it. A stoic who seldom smiled, M'nondo was one hell of a warrior. Even in the heat of battle, when other men succumbed to the bloodlust, and grew wild-eyed, he went about his business with an expression as calm as if he was picking flowers. His expression now, though, was anything but stoic. She wondered what was on his mind, but knew that if he wanted her to know, he would tell her—in his own good time.

"Well, I reckon if I'm to know, I'll know when it's time for me to know." She adjusted the sword at her waist. "For now, though, let's just get this flower ceremony over with. There's bound to be booty awaiting us in the waters south of here."

His face dropped back into its usual stony expression. He looked out across the gray waters.

"Aye, captain," he said. "The sea's beginning to

calm, and we are almost there. I'll go and see that the flowers are made ready."

He saluted by touching a fingertip to his right brow, followed by his right hand over his heart and a slight bow, turned, and as silently as he'd come, moved away. Elizabeth turned her gaze back to the sea that stretched out before the ship. The waves were no longer crashing over the deck, and the swells that lifted *The Vixen* were no longer plunging her down into the troughs, but lowering her gently in a rocking motion that was more to her liking.

The North Atlantic was fickle like that. One minute it was tossing you around like a leaf in the wind, and the next it was rocking you as gently as a mother rocks a newborn. *Damn, I'll be glad when this is over and we're back on the hunt.*

A shout from the lookout, perched near the top of the main mast, pulled her from her reverie.

"Sails to the nor'east!" Ahmed Hamas, dark brown-skinned man from somewhere in North Africa, shouted. "Looks to be a frigate."

Without hesitation and with a sure-footedness that came from a life mostly spent aboard vessels at sea, she ran toward the quarter deck, where the helmsman and Diego Garcia, her first officer, were scanning the horizon to the northeast in an effort to see what had so alarmed the lookout. Garcia, darker brown than usual from their extended stay in the seas off Haiti, gave her a scathing glance as she arrived. She chose to ignore it, although it was beginning to grate. Even after all this time, he resented the fact that the crew had chosen her as captain after Cleague's death and not him. They had only reluctantly accepted him as first officer, and then only after Elizabeth had insisted. One of the most important things she'd learned from John Cleague, among the many things he'd taught her, was to always keep your enemies where you can see them, and there was no doubt in her mind that Diego, one-time cabin boy to John Cleague, the most feared pirate in the Caribbean, who had worked his way up in the crew hierarchy, some said through a lot of skullduggery and double dealing, was her enemy. One day, she would have to deal with that little problem. But, that would have to wait for another day. For now, she had a ship to save.

"Do we know if it's American or English?" she asked.

Garcia looked at her down the length of his aquiline nose, and ran a hand through his glossy black hair before answering. His shirt was open almost to the waist, exposing a slender, but muscular form that, along with his exotic good looks, had set many a maiden's heart aflutter in some of the ports they'd sailed into. She hated to admit it, but she'd on occasion even found herself having certain thoughts when she watched him walk across the deck, but then, she'd mentally slap herself on the side of her head with the thought, *a fer de lance is beautiful, too, but deadly if you try to pick it up.* Whenever she had such thoughts, she would go off by herself and find some willing islander who was more than willing to comply with the tall redheaded woman's wishes, especially as she usually accompanied her requests with a handful of gold coins. Her crew thought her celibate and an ice maiden, with the exception of M'nondo, who she was sure knew of her nocturnal wanderings in certain ports, but had never said or done anything about it.

But, today was also not the time for thinking of things carnal. There was an unidentified ship on the horizon, and her damned handsome as a Greek god first mate was toying with her by delaying giving an answer to her question.

"Dammit, number one." She put her face just inches from his as she spoke. "I asked a question. Is it American or British?"

Garcia, half an inch shorter, but bulkier, blanched at the tone and volume of her voice, but he took a step back as well. "Sorry, *captain,* I was just waiting for you to take the helm so I could go and find out."

She definitely didn't like his arrogant tone, and made a mental note to speak with him about it later.

"Very well, then," she said. "Get about it."

She moved in next to the helmsman, a skinny Irishman with reddish brown hair and freckles, named Michael O'Reilly.

"Orders, cap'n?" he asked.

"Steady as she goes," Elizabeth said. "Until we know what we're dealing with."

"Aye, cap'n, steady as she goes."

Like most of the rest of the crew, O'Reilly had been with *The Vixen* for years under Cleague's command, and had known Elizabeth, a gangly girl who could fight, curse, and sail as well as any man among them, for most of her life. He respected her and her ability to guide the ship through storm or battle, and unlike Garcia, did not resent being under her command.

"Be ready to move the old girl on a farthing at my command, though," she said. "If that's one of the American navy frigates, we could be in for a rough day."

"Aye, cap'n."

The Vixen and the fledgling American navy had a long and bloody history. Cleague had preyed on all merchantmen who plied the ocean from Newfoundland to the northeast coast of South America, but the young country, anxious to build its economy after gaining its independence from England took a dimmer view of piracy than the old European monarchies, who saw it as one of the costs of doing business, and who often recruited pirate captains to serve their interests in their endless wars. It had been an American vessel that had surprised them off the coast of South Carolina and had chased them almost all the way back to the islands in the Caribbean where they would've been able to outmaneuver the larger frigate with its deeper draft. A fluke in the wind had caused the frigate to gain on them and a boarding party of marine infantry had come aboard *The Vixen*. In the ensuing fracas, which they got out of through sheer luck, Captain Cleague had been hit over the head with a musket butt and taken prisoner. Elizabeth, serving unofficially as his first officer at the time, was giving the order to turn the ship about to go to his rescue when his booming voice came across the gap between the ships, ordering her to head for home. Everything in her screamed to ignore and disobey him, but she knew he was right. She had a duty to the ship and crew. So, she gave the order to go to full sail and head full speed toward the shallow waters of the string of islands that run from the coast of Florida to Haiti, knowing the frigate wouldn't be able to pursue.

The last thing she saw as they began to pull away,

was the damned American captain swinging his cutlass, and Cleague's head tumbling from his shoulders. She was too far away to see his expression, but she imagined that he was smiling as the blade struck.

From that day, she'd sworn that someday, somehow, she would avenge Cleague. She did it in small ways every chance she got, showing a preference for American merchant ships, although she didn't pass up others, and harassing the smaller navy vessels, sloops and brigantines, but it was not enough. She had one particular ship and one particular captain at the top of her list. One day, she thought, one day.

At that moment, Garcia came back to the quarterdeck. He looked slightly pale, as if he'd seen a ghost.

"What is it?" she asked curtly. "Did you identify whether the ship the lookout saw was American or not?"

"I did, captain, and it is American."

"How well armed?"

"Appears to be 22 cannons, and I'm sure they have a detachment of marine infantry snipers aboard."

She shrugged. "Ah well, I guess we'll give them a pass. No sense biting off more than we can chew. Helm, hard left rudder, get us headed due south. Number one, get those sails rigged for a flat out run for the islands."

"Hard left rudder, aye, cap'n." O'Reilly said.

Garcia didn't move. He stared blankly at her.

"Didn't you hear what I said, Garcia? Move your ass, now!"

"C-captain, it's *Intrepid*."

Her eyes went wide and her nostrils flared. "Are you sure?"

"Absolutely, captain. I took a look through the spyglass, and could read her name on the bow as plain as day."

"Belay my last order, helm," she said. "Right full rudder. Bring us around to an intercept course."

Charles Ray

Chapter Two

June 1811, on board *U.S.S. Intrepid,* in the North Atlantic Ocean, 120 miles east of the Port of Boston

"Mister Worth, you are out of order," Captain Beauregard Dangerfield said, his broad nostrils flaring and his eyes blazing. He waved a pudgy pink finger under Lieutenant Colin Worth's nose.

"Sir, I was just saying that I believed a week on bread and water was a bit harsh for the crime of having a button on a shirt undone," Colin said.

They were in the captain's stateroom

Dangerfield, a pudgy man who, despite his best efforts looked like he'd slept in his blue uniform jacket which was half a size too small, glared at the man standing before him. Not only had he questioned Dangerfield's judgment by having the nerve to object to a punishment he'd decided to administer, but the man looked so damn fit and proper in his uniform, making Dangerfield look even worse. And, to add insult to injury, he was a full six inches taller, forcing the pudgy naval officer to look up at him.

"You are aware, are you not, Mister Worth, that as captain of *Intrepid*, my word is law, and is not to be gainsaid by anyone else on board, not by anyone, is that clear?"

Colin looked down at the man. With his florid face, the broken veins in his nose from too much drinking, and his pear-shaped body, he looked more like an innkeeper than a ship's captain, and when he spewed his venomous words, the smell of garlic from his breath made Colin's eyes water. He'd only been aboard *Intrepid* six months, but under Dangerfield's command, it felt like six years. But, he was stuck. Remaining aboard the frigate and enduring the unending abuse from the little weasel was the only way he would ever have his own ship.

"Aye, sir," he said. "And, I do apologize for getting out of line."

His hopes that his shy smile and obsequious words would placate Dangerfield were dashed almost immediately.

"I do wish I could believe you, Worth, but I do not. I know you were sent here to undermine me. I never wanted you as my executive officer, but the North Atlantic Fleet commander insisted. You must know, however, that your conduct today was . . . is very close to mutiny."

The shock Colin felt was like a body blow. "Mutiny? No, captain," he said. "I was merely expressing an opinion."

"An unwelcome opinion, Worth. I know you snobby types from Boston. How you look down your aristocratic noses at those you consider your inferiors. Well, I may be a Virginian, but I'm bloody well just as good as one of you damn Boston Brahams any day of the week."

Colin had never heard the term before, although he knew that many of the southerners had issues with northerners, Bostonians in particular, but if Dangerfield meant what he thought he meant by it, he was way off the mark. Colin was the son of a shopkeeper who had to work from sunup to sundown just to make ends meet. His father, Hiram, had wanted Colin to take over the shop from him, but at the age of eighteen, he'd run away, making his way to the harbor, where he begged and cajoled until one of the merchantmen had taken him on as an apprentice seaman. Four years later, now an experienced mariner, he'd enrolled in the fledgling American navy just in time to join the fleet for the final battles against Tripoli's Barbary pirates. He'd distinguished himself in one of the assaults on the harbor at Tripoli and had been promoted to ensign. At twenty-two, he was older than most of the others of his rank, but his hard work and good nature quickly won him friends, and by the time he turned twenty-eight, he'd received his second promotion, to lieutenant, and was assigned to *Intrepid* as executive officer, a sure sign that he was being groomed for higher level duties.

From the first moment he met Captain Beauregard Dangerfield, however, he began feeling a sense of dread, of his luck having run its course. Dangerfield seemed dead set on this being the end of Colin Worth's career.

"I can assure you, sir," Colin said, adopting as placating a tone as he could manage. "I do not judge a man by where he comes from."

"I don't like your tone, sir," Dangerfield said, moving in close and causing Colin to hold his breath to avoid the garlic fumes. "I've a mind when we get back to port to bring you up on charges of insubordination."

Colin looked confused. True, he knew Dangerfield wouldn't like anyone disagreeing with him, but the captain of the first ship he'd served on had told him that it was an officer's duty to inform his commander when he was about to make a mistake. Apparently, Dangerfield came from a different school of leadership. But, insubordination? It was ridiculous on the face of it, and the fact that the helmsman and quartermaster, and the offending seaman, had all been witness to the encounter would support Colin's contention that he'd not been insubordinate.

"But, captain, I was not being insubordinate, I was merely expressing my opinion based upon things I hear from the crew."

"Aha, I knew it." Spittle flew from Dangerfield's lips. "You're conspiring with the crew against me. That, Mister Worth is mutiny."

Colin's mouth flew open. He was too stunned to speak. Dangerfield strode to the door and flung it open. Outside the door stood two corporals from the marine infantry contingent, two of the biggest and meanest of a bunch of big and mean men.

"Corporal," Dangerfield said to the man in front. "Lieutenant Worth is hereby placed under arrest for mutiny. Escort him to the brig and see that he's securely locked up."

The huge, but baby-faced marine looked confused. "Sir?"

"I do believe I spoke clearly, corporal. Is there something about my order that you don't understand?"

The man's face turned red. "Uh, no sir, I understand, sir."

"Then, you will execute that order immediately."

The abashed looking corporal stepped forward, reaching for Colin's sword. Colin stiffened and laid his hand on the hilt. The second corporal brought the musket he carried up, preparing to aim it. At that moment, the ship's quartermaster, Lieutenant-junior grade) Albert Comstock, a short, bowlegged man, who, though Colin's age was already going bald on top, burst into the passageway leading to the captain's cabin. His face was flushed.

"Captain," he said. "You need to come up to the quarterdeck immediately."

"What is it, Comstock? I'm attending to urgent business here."

"Lookout spotted a ship off the port bow, sir," Comstock said. He paused and took several deep breaths. "It looks to be a pirate ship, sir."

"How far away is it?"

"Approximately fourteen miles, sir, and it appears to be sailing toward us."

"Well, let them come. Go back and have the gun crews stand by, and I'll be with you shortly as soon as I attend to this little matter." He gave Colin a sly look.

"Sir . . . the ship's got a black hull.:

Dangerfield was in the process of turning away. At those words, he froze in place, his face turning red. "A black hull, you say?"

"Aye, sir."

"By damn, it's *The Vixen.* I knew someday I'd get that bastard in my sights. Comstock, go to the quarterdeck and bring the ship to general quarters. Get the cannons and the snipers ready for action."

"Sir," Colin said. "Our orders were to proceed to Charleston and join a fleet preparing to patrol off the southern coast to be on the lookout for British warships. Do you think it wise to divert for one ship?"

Dangerfield gave him an icy stare. "You just can't help yourself, can you? Forever resisting me." He turned back to Comstock. "You have your orders, Comstock. Go and carry them out immediately. I'll be right behind you."

Comstock looked confused, his eyes shifting from Dangerfield to Colin.

"*Lieutenant* Comstock, did you hear what I just told you?"

"Aye, aye, sir."

"Then, be about your business."

With one last pleading look at Colin, the little officer turned on his heels and fled back up the passageway. Dangerfield, an enigmatic look on his face turned back to Colin. "Well, Lieutenant, it seems there's been a change of plans. I'm not having you put in the brig after all."

Colin felt a sense of relief, but at the same time a sense of foreboding.

"Thank you, sir," he said. "I'll head for the quarterdeck and help with preparing the crew for action."

Dangerfield laughed. It was a mirthless laugh that gave Colin chills.

"Oh no, lieutenant. You'll not be going to the quarterdeck. Corporal, take Worth here to the boat in the bow. Give him water and rations for three, no, make that four, days, and put him overboard."

"Sir?" the marine asked, with a look of shock on his face.

"You're putting me off the ship, out here in the middle of the ocean?" Colin couldn't believe what he'd just heard. "You can't do that."

"I can, Worth, and I will. If you're lucky, maybe a merchantman will pick you up before your water runs out. If not, well, I'd like to say it was nice knowing you, but we both know that would be a lie. Corporal, you have your orders."

Charles Ray

Chapter Three

"Captain, I really don't think that would be a wise idea," Garcia said. "That frigate has us outgunned and outmanned."

"I agree with Diego," M'nondo, who had just joined them on the quarterdeck, said. "I know how you feel about this particular ship, but now would not be a good time to indulge your thirst for revenge."

Elizabeth paused. She'd been ready to round on Garcia for arguing with her, but M'nondo's serious expression caused her to bite back the words she was about to utter. She was furious with both of them, but most of all, she was furious with herself. She was furious because they were both right. She would be sailing her ship and crew to certain destruction if she engaged the heavily-armed American frigate here in the open sea. Even though *The Vixen* had the advantage in speed and maneuverability, the guns on *Intrepid* had a greater range than their small cannons, and would quickly pound them into floating wreckage. She took a deep breath.

"Very well. You're both right. Thank you for helping me avoid what might have been a fatal mistake. Helmsman, take evasive action. Full right rudder, and take her northeast as fast as you can. Once we're out of her line of sight, we'll duck back in toward the coast and sneak south toward the Bahamas."

Garcia and M'nondo both nodded.

"That's a good idea, captain," M'nondo said. "They won't be expecting that, and even if they do spot us as we head south, they'll not likely follow for too long, for fear of being caught out by an English warship or two."

Even Garcia was nodding enthusiastically. She felt the blood flowing hotly through her body, and a sense of excitement. This was what she loved most of all. She had a fine ship and a crew that was second to none, even including Garcia. When the stakes were high, the one thing she could depend on was every man aboard the ship pulling together like many fingers on one hand.

"Then, make it so, number two," she said to Garcia.

The ship heeled sharply to the right as the helmsman made the ordered course correction. Garcia moved purposively about the deck, yelling orders in a calm voice, and soon all sails were filled with air and the ship leapt forward as if a giant hand had reached down and snagged her in its grip.

The chase was on.

Her plan was simple, but risky. They would continue to head north, sometimes northeast, but mostly northwest, straining to keep ahead of the pursuing frigate until nightfall, some four hours distant, at which time, they would change course, aiming east for a few miles and then cut south for a night run down the coast, hoping they wouldn't run into another ship, or heaven forbid, an armada, before reaching the relative safety of the Bahama island chain, where even if the American ship followed, they would be about as easy to find as a single weed in an unplowed field.

The sky was dark, almost purple, and the sun had disappeared below the western horizon. Elizabeth had all ship's lights doused, making it impossible for the ship to be seen from anywhere over one hundred yards. The only sound, besides that of the hissing wind and the pounding ocean, was the flapping of the sails and the creaking of the hull's timbers.

Everyone, Elizabeth included, was bone tired and tense. They'd quickly lost sight of their pursuer, but she knew he was still out there. The fat man who captained her wouldn't give up that easy. By getting away, she'd injured his pride. *That's not all I'll injure, you bastard. Maybe not today, but the time will come.*

When it was finally so dark she couldn't see the bow, she ordered a change of course to the east, running until she estimated they were about a hundred miles from the coast, and then due south.

She had some of the sails furled for the southward voyage. Stealth, not speed, was called for during this leg of the journey. Now, the waiting game began. After so many hours at full speed, the slower speed made it feel as if they were simply floating along with the current. When they'd not been challenged, or shot at after the passage of three hours, she finally let herself relax against the railing. Her body felt as she'd just completed a match against a master wrestler. Every muscle in her body ached, and she had a stabbing pain behind her eyes. She had to fight to keep her eyes open, so badly did she want to sleep. But, now was not the time for sleep. That would come later. To keep herself awake, she imagined the inventive tortures she'd inflict upon the captain of *Intrepid* when she finally had him in her grasp.

Chapter Four

June 1811, in a ship's boat somewhere in the Atlantic Ocean off the east coast of America

It was dark, so dark, he could hardly see his hand when he held it in front of his face. He'd lost track of the hours since he'd been dumped into the ship's boat along with a single cask of water and a muslin bag of hardtack biscuits and dried beef, and then dumped unceremoniously overboard. The bastards had taken the boat's oars, leaving him to the mercy of the currents. At first, he sat there watching as *Intrepid* sailed away. He watched until she was nothing but a small dot on the horizon, and then she was gone. All around him was nothing but the rolling, gray-blue sea that seemed to curve upwards to join with the slate-blue sky. Except for the sloshing of the ocean against the sides of the boat and the sound of his ragged breathing, it was silent, a silence that was deafening.

He got his bearings by watching the sky and noticing which section darkened first, reckoning that to be east, and realized that he was drifting northward with the prevailing current. If luck, and his food and water, held out, he might—just might—drift into a shipping lane and be seen by a merchantman, or even another navy ship. His hope was that it would be a naval vessel, because he could hardly wait to tell his story to the naval authorities.

By the time darkness fell, though, he began to lose hope. In the dark, he couldn't get his bearings, so he wouldn't know if he drifted too far east and got caught in the southward flowing current. He also had no way of estimating his speed. It could take days, even weeks, for him to be seen, and he doubted that his provisions, especially the water, would last that long. With nothing to protect him from the sun during the day, he would quickly become dehydrated, and when his water was gone, it would only be a matter of hours, a day at most, before he died from dehydration. His other fear was that one of the freakish summer storms that made the Atlantic such an inhospitable place would suddenly pop up. It wouldn't take much of a gale or a rogue wave to reduce his little boat to kindling, and even though he was a good swimmer, he knew that if he went into the water it would be over.

When a person has become accustomed to having many others around, such as in the close confines of a naval vessel, being totally alone can be unsettling. Even when you don't want to talk to another person, their very presence is comforting. When you're alone *and* in total darkness, it's beyond unsettling, and when you're alone, in the dark, and have no idea where you are, it can, Colin soon realized, drive you insane.

Because he couldn't see anything but the hazy outline of the boat and his legs stretched out in front of him, and them only because of the white pants he wore—at least, he assumed the fuzzy gray stick-line things he saw were his legs; after a few hours, he was no longer certain of anything, he could feel everything, and hear everything. He could feel the gentle rocking of the boat, for which he was thankful, for that meant the sea was relatively calm. He could hear the sound of the ocean as it beat against the boat, and the splash of the hull as he dropped from the top of a swell into the trough. When that happened, he could also feel the sensation of falling from a great height.

His mind began playing tricks on him. At one point, he thought he saw a light in the distance, and was convinced that it was a ship and his rescue was imminent. After ten minutes of shouting, until he was hoarse, the light simply disappeared. Another time, he heard the flapping of sails filled with wind, and the creaking of wooden timbers of a ship's hull. This time, he was too hoarse to shout, so he waited. The sound went on, it seemed like, forever, and then, as suddenly as it had started, it ceased.

That was when he knew he was slowly going insane. His first instinct was to curl up in the bottom of the boat and try to shut his ears, eyes and mind, and hope the hallucinations would go away. Then, he considered just slipping over the gunwale and dropping into the sea. He'd heard that drowning wasn't an unpleasant death. But, of course, no one he knew who had drowned had ever come back to corroborate that, and having witnessed death in many forms since leaving Boston as a young lad, he was convinced that the only painless death was the one that sneaked up on you in your dotage when you were fast asleep.

No, he thought, he could not . . . he *would* not give up. He had a reason to live. If he never did anything else with his life, he would make Dangerfield pay for sending him over the side and leaving him to die. He didn't know when, and he didn't know how, but he *knew* he would.

The bastard had lied about giving him four days' rations. When he'd opened the muslin bag, it contained eight biscuits and four wrinkled pieces of beef that looked like it was six months old or older. If he rationed himself, one meal per day, biscuits one day and beef the next, he could survive twelve days. That is, provided the cask of water held out. The one thing he could ill afford to skimp on was water. If he didn't drink enough, it mattered not that he was eating. The wind and sun would leech the moisture from his body, and he would die from dehydration and exposure.

The night went on, and he tried sleeping, but each time he closed his eyes, he remembered the demented look in Dangerfield's eyes when he'd ordered the marines to put him off the ship, and his eyes would snap open. And, even though he could see no one, he felt those cold, dead eyes boring into him.

Finally, he took his jacket off and wrapped it around his upper body and lay back against the stern, and let the boat carry him where it will.

When the sky began to change from pure ebony to purple to a pinkish gray to the east, to his right, which indicated that thankfully he was still drifting north, he sat up.

As he'd done the previous day, he scanned the sea all around him. At the horizon to his northeast, or what he assumed was the horizon, for the sea and sky seemed to merge and everything looked fuzzy, he thought he saw something, but ignored it, putting it down as another hallucination. His scan completed, he thought about eating, but the thought made him nauseous and his stomach cramped. His rational mind knew this was because, not having eaten for nearly twelve hours, the stomach cramps were from hunger, but his rational mind was slowly, but inexorably, been pushed aside by something in his mind that was far from rational.

He lay back and looked up at the sky. What he saw should have worried him, but his rational brain was on vacation. Above him and to the west was a bank of wispy pearly white clouds with scaly formations; lobster clouds, signaling that rain was on the way. His lizard brain, that small, peanut-sized portion of the brain at the base of the skull, welcomed it, because it meant he would be able to fill his cask with fresh water. Maybe water would fill the boat, not enough, he hoped to sink it, but enough to give him an extra cushion of potable water.

Satisfied, he continued to lie there, gazing upward.

He was so intent on his study of the clouds he didn't hear the slap of water against a larger object, or the flutter and flapping of large sails at first. When he did, he first put it down to another hallucination. But then, it kept getting louder and louder. None of his hallucinations had done that before. He pushed himself up to a sitting position and stared ahead.

He blinked. He shook his head, rubbed his eyes, and looked again.

It was a ship, and it was bearing straight down upon him. It was still a long way off, but not so far that he couldn't make out the small, dark figures in the bow, and others in the riggings.

Colin wasn't particularly religious, but at that moment, he gave a silent prayer of thanks. *I am not to die alone out here after all.*

The ship drew closer, close enough for him to get a clear look and make out details, and what he saw made him regret his hasty prayer.

The ship heading for him was a two-masted brigantine, a category of ship that was popular in two hundred years earlier, but had been supplanted by the larger, sturdier galleons for heavy work, and sloops for light cargo. But, it was the hull that caught his eye.

It was as black as the night.

Chapter Five

Fleeing from *Intrepid* Elizabeth had run *The Vixen* north, almost to Nova Scotia, before deciding to turn to port and head for a position about a hundred miles off the coast for their southern run. Crew members not directly involved in navigating the ship were put on watch in the bow, along both rails and in the stern, to keep an eye out for *Intrepid*, or any other vessel, American or British ships out of Canada, both of which represented a danger to them, the Americans because their growing overseas trade was threatened by piracy, and the English because they resented anyone else having primacy on the high seas.

Just as they made the turn to the southwest,

hoping to make a wide enough turn to avoid their pursuer, but not so wide as to attract any vessels that might be sailing close to the coastline, they were aided by a sudden squall that seemed to come out of nowhere. While she was accustomed to the Atlantic's sudden mood swings in winter, and would have normally been upset at a storm appearing without even a minute's notice, she thanked the saints who look out for sailors for this one, for it helped to further cloak their movements.

Despite having seen no sign of *Intrepid* since losing sight of it off Boston, tensions on the quarterdeck were high, and Elizabeth didn't relax the watch rules. She knew well that it was complacency on the part of the pirates rather than the skill of the navies pursuing them that led many a pirate to end his career taking a long trip at the end of a short rope. That was definitely part of her career plan. No, a quiet retirement on one of the idyllic islands of the Caribbean, sitting in the sun sipping rum, eating fruit, and watching the dancing waves crashing over pure white sand; that was how she planned to end her days.

She sensed when M'nondo, standing so that she was sandwiched between him and the helmsman, looked down at her, but said nothing. It was a game they'd played for as long as she could remember. He would stare at her for a long time to try and get her to say something. In the early days, sensing his gaze upon her, even from behind sometimes, had been unsettling. But, she'd learned to accept it—this connection they had with each other—and she worked on her self-control until, now, she could withstand many, many minutes of the warm sensation of his gaze upon her neck. Rather than being put off by it, M'nondo seemed to enjoy her newfound power. He smiled down at her.

"Captain," he said. "You look as if your mind is not with us in this world."

Only then did she look at him, her smile signaling that she'd won—yet again. He smiled back.

"It was, M'nondo. I was thinking about our island."

That was how she thought of it. It would be *their* island, because he had been such a part of her life for such a long time, she couldn't imagine life without his comforting presence. Despite their differences in appearance; her, tall and slender with porcelain skin and flame-red hair; him, skin as dark as polished mahogany, taller than her by the span of a couple of hands, and muscles like corded rope in arms, legs, and chest, a head that he shaved regularly with a razor-sharp machete—and, of course, those intricate scars on his cheeks; they were as close as any siblings could ever be. When one hurt, the other felt it, even at a distance. They often, when alone, completed each other's sentences, but often, they would sit together in her cabin for hours, saying nothing, simply enjoying each other's presence.

"Yes, when will we go to this place you dream of, *Esi*?" he asked, using the word meaning 'Sunday' in Fante, the language of the tribe he'd been stolen from on the Gold Coast of Africa. It was a nickname he'd given her because it had been on a Sunday when she'd finally spoken to him after they'd taken her from . . . that other place.

"Soon, *Kofi*, soon," she replied, calling him 'Friday,' for reasons she no longer remembered, but he always chuckled when she said it. "I'm thinking, mayhap, if we make a good haul or two when we reach the islands, it might be a good time to go looking for it. What do you say?"

For a long time, he said nothing. Standing as still as a carved ebony statue, he stared off at the horizon which was just beginning to show the first light of the day. She looked up at him, and noticed that when he stared like that he didn't even blink. Then, he turned to face her, his scarred, but otherwise unlined face had a worried look on it.

"I don't know if this would be a good time, even if we do make several rich hauls," he said.

"And why, pray tell, do you say that? I've been thinking that one of the smaller islands in the south Bahama chain, or maybe the Turks, would be a perfect place to retire right now.""

"You have surely heard the rumors, *Esi,* just as I have. The English fleet is all over the Bahamas, as far south as the Turks, and they have been seizing ships and impressing seamen."

She made a 'hmph!' sound and smiled up at him. "There's nothing new about that, and you know it. The damned English have been doing that for the longest time, as far back as either of us can remember."

"Aye, they have," he said. "But, lately they have been seizing American ships and seamen. The Americans, still bearing some ill will toward their former colonial masters, are very upset. There is rumor of war."

She shook her head, causing her red tresses to wave back and forth across her eyes, reminding her that she needed to tie it back. It wouldn't do to have it do that in the middle of a fight. "Then, let them. The damned insufferable English and those upstart Americans deserve each other."

His face took on an even more serious demeanor. "I remember a saying in my village, 'when the elephants fight, the grass gets trampled.' In this fight between the English and Americans, I would not want us to be the grass."

"The English have been boarding American ships and impressing their sailors for over five years. Why do you think the Americans have waited until now to think about war?"

"I overheard a man in a tavern in Dominca last month say that the new American president, James Madison, wants to show that he's as tough as Jefferson, the man he replaced. Jefferson was president when their navy defeated the Bey of Tripoli, and the man said the whole damn country is now consumed with war fever."

That was something with which she could not disagree. When encountered at sea, at least, the pesky Americans, and their young navy, were as aggressive as bulldogs, often going above and beyond to engage what they perceived as enemy vessels, and were reluctant to break off engagements once started. So unlike the Europeans, even the snobby English, who still fought wars like the gentlemen knights of old, often content to inflict a bit of pain upon an opponent and then retiring to fight another day. There was, though, one exception to that; and that was the English response to ships participating in the slave trade. Ever since banning the slave trade in 1807, British ships had been quite active, especially in the

Middle Passage, that stretch of the Atlantic between the coast of West Africa and the east coast of South America, in pursuing the wallowing slave ships, their holds often crammed bulkhead to bulkhead with chained human bodies stacked like barrels of ale or cordwood. In those cases, English ships did not break off contact until the slaver was run to ground, or sunk. Elizabeth shuddered at the thought. The trade in human beings was far worse than piracy in her opinion. Sure, pirates were known to kill their victims, but those victims were more often than not armed and capable of fighting back. The slaves were in chains, beaten, kept on short rations, and given no opportunity to defend themselves. She'd even heard tales of slaver captains having their cargo dumped overboard whenever an English warship was sighted, preferring to lose the investment than face time in an English prison, or worse.

"Aye, *Kofi*, you're right," she said. "The Bahamas and Turks are probably not a good idea right now. What about the Antilles, though? Some of the windward islands are just as beautiful as those in the Bahamas."

He fingered the scars on his cheeks again, deep in thought.

"That sounds like a good idea. Of course, we would still need to be careful. Spain's colonies in that area are up in arms. Ever since Argentina declared its independence from Spain last year, there's been movement all over. In Venezuela, this Simon de Bolivar started a guerilla war last year, and word is he's beating them at every turn. I fear the fever of independence might have also infected the Antilles."

"Mayhap, mayhap not," she said. "Don't forget, the Antilles belong to the Dutch, and far's I know, their colonies seem pretty content."

M'nondo closed his eyes. His face looked pained.

"That, I doubt. Quiet, maybe, content, never," he said, his eyes still clinched shut. "No man can be truly content when he is under the control of another." His eyes snapped open. "But, I think you are right. The Antilles would be a nice place to retire."

Her smile was warm but reserved. Although she didn't fully understand him at times, she had learned to trust M'nondo's insights, and if he was troubled, it signaled that trouble was on the horizon. The rest of the crew sensed it as well, which was why, during their flight from the American warship, the crew had never panicked. They only had to look at M'nondo, standing as calm and still as a statue carved from dark wood on the quarterdeck next to the captain—her—who was too busy giving orders to be nervous, and they knew they would be okay.

"The dawn's breaking," she said, looking east, where the first pink rays of sun were struggling vainly to break through the low cloud cover. "Looks, though, like it will be cloudy. That's good. Make it hard for another ship to spot us."

"True, but it will also make it hard for us to spot another ship," M'nondo said. "Never forget, little sister, each coin has two sides."

Any sting of approbation in his words was erased by the slight crinkling at the corners of his thick lips, indicating that he was suppressing a smile. She frowned at him with her lips, but her eyes smiled. *That one to you, big brother. I'd fire something witty back, but I'm too damned tired at the moment.*

"Well," she said. "Let's just keep sailing south and see what happens."

Chapter Six

"What do you mean we've lost them?" Dangerfield's face was red, and despite the chill in the air, he was sweating so heavily there were dark, moon-shaped stains under the armpits of his blue jacket.

Albert Comstock stood between Dangerfield and the sailor at the helm. He too was sweating, and not from the heat. With the unexplained disappearance of Colin Worth, Dangerfield had assigned him duties as executive officer, a position he was honest enough with himself to admit he was totally unqualified for. And, even had he been qualified, being the number two for a man like Dangerfield was not on his list of desired positions. In fact, at that moment, he was seriously considering resigning his commission as soon as they reached port—if the blustering maniac glaring at him didn't get them sunk first.

"We've been sailing north for over a day, captain," he said, with as much calmness as he could muster. "We've seen no sign of them."

"They can't be that fast, Dangerfield said. "Can't we put on more speed?"

The helmsman, a young sailor who was at moment wishing he'd been assigned galley duty instead, grasped the wheel so tightly his hands turned pasty white.

"S-sir," Comstock said. "We're at flank speed now. I'm afraid that's all she has in her. I t-think we should turn back for Boston."

"No, lieutenant. We will continue to pursue. That black bastard's not getting away from me this time."

"B-but, sir, we'll be in Canadian waters soon if we stay on this heading."

"Damn your eyes, boy, I don't want to hear your lame excuses. I want to catch that pirate. If you're not up to the job, I can always replace you."

Comstock's face puckered up, and he looked-felt-as if he would start crying. He took a deep breath. It wouldn't do for the rating at the helm to see him looking so weak. He had problems enough getting the men to take him seriously without *that* burden. *If Colin was here, he'd know what to do. He'd face the captain down over his irrational behavior. On the other hand, look what happened when he did that. I wonder if he actually deserted like the captain said. Oh God, what am I to do?* The young officer took a deep breath. He was not the confrontational type, but he didn't want to have to explain how he, the acting executive officer, allowed the captain to commit an unprovoked act of war, which is exactly what it would be if they sailed uninvited into Canadian—English-waters. There had to be a way out of this, maybe, if he played to the man's insufferable ego.

"C-captain, sir," he said. "I've doubled the lookouts since we started the pursuit. If we'd come within hailing distance of that ship, even at night, it would've been spotted. Either it's deep in Canadian waters, and consequently out of our reach . . . for now, or, more likely, in the night it sailed far to the east or west and doubled back."

Dangerfield's eyes narrowed to slits, and then he smiled.

"By Jove, lieutenant, I do believe you're right," he said. "I'll bet that's exactly what that bastard did. He's probably near on to Boston by now." He stared out toward the northern horizon, his hands clasped behind his back. "Very well, helmsman, bring us about, and make all speed south. Get us within a hundred fifty miles of the coast and keep it steady south, do you have that?"

The young sailor, goggle-eyed, looked from Dangerfield to Comstock. The latter inclined his head ever so slightly. "Aye, sir," the sailor replied. "Bring 'er about and full speed due south, sir!"

With a smug, self-satisfied look on his face, Dangerfield stood like a solid oak pole as the ship began to heel making the sharp turn, while Comstock swayed like a stalk of wheat in a storm.

Dangerfield didn't notice. He was too busy peering

into the distance.

"I'll get you now, you bloody bastard," he said. "It's been five years, but it feels like yesterday. But, soon, very soon, you'll pay. Your head will join that fucking Cleague's at the bottom of the ocean where you belong."

Chapter Seven

**June 1811, in a ship's boat somewhere in the
Atlantic Ocean off the east coast of America**

As quickly as it had appeared, the black ship
disappeared. One moment it was bearing down upon
him, so close he would have sworn he could hear the
ocean slapping against its wooden sides. The next, the
only thing he saw was the endless, gray ocean. That's
when he knew he was going insane.

"NO-O-O-O-O," he screamed at the ocean. *This
can't be happening. I was not meant to die out here,
alone and unmourned.* "No, I will not die. I will live." He
raised his fist to the heavens. "Do you hear me? I will
live!"

He had enough sanity left to know that railing and
thrashing about in the boat would only hasten the

depletion of his body's meager resources, and shouting would cause him to dehydrate more rapidly. He pulled his jacket off and slumped down, pulling it up over his head to protect himself as much as possible from the bright light. Even though the sun hadn't made an appearance yet, he knew that the light reflecting off the ocean's surface could do just as much damage, including blinding him.

Not that it really mattered. There was nothing to see but water. So bloody much water, and all he had to drink was half a cask of tepid water. He'd been a seafarer long enough to know that drinking the sea water would hasten his madness and death, and that death would be gruesome. What would it be like, he wondered, to die of thirst? It couldn't be more pleasant. But then, he knew of no pleasant ways to die.

No, I must stop thinking like that. I must not think of death. It comes to all eventually, but I will neither welcome nor hasten it. I will conserve my energy and think of my revenge.

With that thought, he lay back, pulled the jacket over his head and closed his eyes. There was nothing to see, and nothing to do. He had no oars with which to row, nothing to fashion into a sail or rudder, so he was at the mercy of the currents. They would take him where they would take him, so he might as well sleep and conserve what energy he had left. It took some time, but he soon fell into a fitful sleep.

The dreams began immediately. Dangerfield, with a vicious leer stood over him, looking down as if from a great height.

"You're dead," he said. "You should've known better

than to cross me. No one crosses me and gets away with it."

"I'll get you," Colin said in a cracked voice. "You won't get away with this. When I get back to Boston, everyone will know what you did."

Dangerfield laughed. "Look around you, boyo. What do you see? Dirt to the right of you, dirt to the left of you, and nothing but the blue sky above. Take a good look at that sky, because this is the last time you'll see it. Once they throw the dirt in atop your worthless, shriveled carcass, you'll be gone for good. You hear, me, boyo? Gone for good."

"No," Colin cried. "No, that can't be. I can't be here. I was lost at sea. No, I'm not dead, I'm stranded, but not dead."

"You're dead, boyo, dead, dead, dead." Dangerfield laughed, and it was the laugh of a madman. "Look at the sky, boyo. Feel it's warmth on your skin for the last time, for the last time . . . ."

The voice trailed off, and Colin opened his eyes. It was dark, but he *could* feel warmth on his skin. He thrashed about, causing the jacket to slip from his face, and the light of the sun, now high overhead, nearly blinded him before he thought to shut his eyes.

Damn, I go crazy if I stay awake, and I go crazy when I sleep. Might as well stay awake and face my demons head on. Lord, I'm so hungry. But, I have to ration what little food I have. I have to make it last.

As he thought this, he heard a splash that was different from the splash of the water against the side of the boat. Peering over the gunwale, he saw a flash of silver followed by a splash. It took seconds for his mind to register what he was seeing. A school of fish was swimming along beside and beneath his boat. They were small, no more than six to eight inches long, but, they represented food if only he could catch a few.

Slowly, so as not to scare them away, he leaned on the gunwale, bracing himself on his chest, and slowly dipped his hands into the icy cold water. He stared so hard his eyes began to burn, but he kept his focus on the darting silver shapes. When one appeared close, he grabbed. Missed. He waited patiently, looking, waiting, and sure enough, another one swam close. He let his arms trail through the water, keeping them relaxed. The curious fish swam closer until its mouth was less than an inch from Colin's fingers. As it edged closer, its mouth open, he grabbed. *Huzzah!* He got it. The fish was a good eight inches long and looked meaty. It squirmed and flapped in his hand as he lifted it out of the water and dropped it in the bottom of the boat. Letting it flap about, he turned and put his hands in the water again. After an hour, his hands were wrinkled, stinging, and turning gray from being immersed in the salt water so long, and he was sweating from the sun's heat, but he'd managed to catch five fish. That would save the dried beef for at least a day, maybe even two. He'd let the fish dry in the sun, and eat them for supper.

As he looked down at the fish, now still and glassy-eyed on the bottom of the boat, his mood lightened.

Hours later, he realized that he hadn't moved. He still sat, his head and arms exposed to the searing rays of the midday sun. He could feel the sting of sunburn on the back of his neck, and his arms looked like a lobster just taken from a pot of boiling water. He touched his forearm. His brain vaguely registered that it hurt, but it was as if he was touching someone else. He brought his hands up and held them in front of his eyes. Strange, he thought, there are four hands. I should only have two. He touched a finger to his nose. It felt like he'd been stabbed with a hot poker. He felt his cheeks. The same intense burning sensation.

He knew this was bad somehow, but his brain couldn't make the necessary connections to realize that he was suffering from heat exhaustion and dehydration, having neglected to drink any water since waking up. His jacket lay in a crumpled heap in the bottom of the boat, but he only looked at it. There was something about it he tried to remember, but he couldn't form the thought. He looked around him. Everything was a uniform blue-gray and seemed to be moving. It should be green. Grass is green, not blue. And, why is it moving. I'm moving, too. Why am I moving? Where am I? Who am I/

He opened his mouth to speak, but his tongue was swollen and his mouth felt as dry as the sands of the Sahara. He tried blinking, but his eyes felt scratchy. His breathing came in heavy rasps as if a tight band was wound around his chest.

At his feet lay . . . fish, yes, fish. He recognized them, but had no clue why they were there and what he was to do with them.

He sat down, his legs splayed out in front him. He looked at his boots, so far away at the end of legs that might as well have belonged to someone else.

He looked toward the bow of the boat, and then slowly twisted his head and shoulders until he could see the stern, which was bare of rudder. Some instinct told him that the square part of the boat was the best place to be, so he inched slowly, dragging his buttocks across the rough boards of the bottom of the boat until his back rested against the stern.

Soon, sleep, merciful sleep, this time without dreams, claimed him.

Chapter Eight

June 1811, on board *The Vixen*, in the North Atlantic Ocean, 100 miles east and 50 miles south of Portland, Maine

"Cap'n, small boat about two hundred yards off the starboard bow," Ahmed said from his position atop the main mast. "It 'pears to be a ship's boat."

Elizabeth had been watching the sea to their stern, keeping a lookout just in case *Intrepid* had figure out her little stratagem. She whirled and looked in the direction the dusky little man was pointing. Sure enough, though it rode low in the water, disappearing as it went into the troughs between swells, she recognized the lines of a small boat, similar to the two she had lashed to her own decks for use in emergencies, or to go ashore at smaller islands that didn't have docking facilities.

"Is it manned?" she asked.

"Can't be sure, cap'n. Looks to be mayhap one body aboard, but the way he's lyin', he's likely dead."

Her first instinct was to keep sailing. But, Cleague, though a pirate, had schooled her relentlessly in the courtesies of the sea. Unless a boat was a target, in which case you attacked it; or a bigger- and better-armed warship, then you ran for your life; you never ignored another mariner in peril. If the poor soul on that boat was dead, they could at least wrap the body in some of their spare canvas and give him a decent burial at sea—while underway, of course. And, the odds were, depending upon how long the poor sod had been floating in an open boat, and what his condition had been when he started his ill-fated journey, he—and, she just assumed it was a man, because no woman would be left abandoned in a boat—was a goner.

"Bring us alongside for a better look," she said to O'Reilly at the helm.

"Aye, cap'n," the Irishman said.

Bringing a brigantine, or any large ship to a near stop, and matching position with a drifting derelict, is a tricky maneuver when the sea is dead calm. When it's generating six-foot swells, and said derelict is drifting in the direction opposite the direction you're going, it's the devil's own to do. But, O'Reilly was up to the task.

Within ten minutes, they'd pulled alongside the boat and dropped grappling hooks and two of the wirier pirates to secure it to the side of *The Vixen*.

When they dropped into the boat, they thought the

grayish form lying in the stern was a dead man, but when Cacao Rodriguez, a Colombian so named for his addiction to the nut of the cacao plant prodded him with a naked foot, the figure grunted.

"*Madre de Dios*, he's alive," he said, jumping back and stumbling into Martine Devereux, a mulatto gambler from Louisiana who had made his way to the Bahamas to avoid a group of disgruntled gentlemen who had accused him of dealing from the bottom in a card game where he'd relieved them of most of what was in their purses. They had planned on doing some very ungentlemanly things to his anatomy. He had signed on to Elizabeth's crew because he needed the money, and was willing to do just about anything for it.

"*Merde*, Cacao," he said. "You almost knock me clean out of the boat. Watch what you do."

"*Pardon, amigo, pero esto* . . . I mean, this *hombre*, he is alive."

Elizabeth leaned over the rail. "What's going on down there?"

Ma capitaine," Devereux said. "*Le homme ici est ne pas mort,* uh, this man, he is not dead."

"Yes, Martine, I understand enough French, no need to translate." With a crew made up of rogues from many nations and tribes, Elizabeth had been forced to learn a few words and phrases in six or seven languages, although she usually insisted that every man on board learned passable English. "You sure he's not dead?"

"*Si, capitan*," Rodriguez said. "Unless the dead can speak. He talk like crazy man, but he talk."

She felt M'nondo's presence at her side. "I wonder

how long he's been adrift in that boat, and why?" she said.

"We will not learn this standing here," he said, still beating her at the war of words game they played. "He still might not survive, but if he is to do so, we must bring him aboard *Vixen*."

"I know that," she said, tossing her head and sending her red locks flying.

M'nondo only smiled enigmatically. She looked down at the bobbing boat. Devereux and Rodriguez were standing, looking down at the supine figure propped against the stern, swaying with the boat and looking puzzled.

"What in blazes are you two doing there?" Elizabeth shouted. "We can't sit here like a fat goose all day."

"Uh, *mon capitaine*, there is something I feel you must know before we bring this man aboard," Devereux called up.

Frustrated, she blew air through her nose, took a deep breath, and, doing what M'nondo had taught her, counted each of the fingers on her hand, starting with the little finger on the left, wiggling each as she did. Her emotions centered, she leaned back over the rail.

"Well, are you going to make me wait all day before you tell me, or will you bloody well get on with it."

"It is the water cask, *capitan*," Rodriquez said. "It has the name of a ship burned into the side."

"And?" She rolled her eyes, causing M'nondo to chuckle softly.

"The name, *capitan*, is *Intrepid*.

She suddenly felt cold and hot at the same time. It was as if the blood throughout her body had frozen and someone had doused her with flaming coals. She felt her breath catch in her throat. Grasping the rail, she leaned forward, her lips curled down in a feral grimace. As she was about to open her mouth, M'nondo laid a calloused hand on her hand gripping the rail.

"I know what you are thinking, *Esi*," he said quietly for her ears only. "You are thinking this man is from the ship that has caused you much pain, and the thing to do is feed him to the sharks. But, you are not thinking clearly."

She took another deep breath. "I am thinking very clearly. That bastard's from *Intrepid*, and he deserves to be in the belly of a shark."

His hand tightened on hers. "Before you give that order, ask yourself. why is he here, alone in a boat, and from what I can see without enough rations to survive for very long? Would it not be better to hope that he survives so that you can question him about your *real* enemy, the captain, the man who—"

"Shit, as usual, you're right." She jerked her hand away. "You're bloody insufferable sometimes, you know."

He smiled. "Of course, I know. That is what a big brother is supposed to be, is it not."

She rolled her eyes and leaned back over the rail.

"Bring him aboard," she said. "Secure him in the hold and see that his injuries are attended to. Let me know as soon as he's able to talk."

Her orders given, she turned away from the rail and headed for the quarterdeck.

M'nondo watched her walk away. A look of concern clouded his features.

Charles Ray

Chapter Nine

Below decks on *The Vixen*

His eyes opened, but all they saw at first was darkness, not the black darkness of night, but the gray, hazy light of twilight. *Night has fallen, and I'm still alive*, was his first thought.

He shifted his body, and heard a metallic clink. He blinked a few times to clear the fuzziness before his eyes, and then lifted—tried to life—his hand to rub at them, but, it stopped a after a few inches, and he felt a tightness gripping his wrist. Blinking again, he looked and saw that a black iron manacle encircled his raised wrist. His head jerked to the side, and he saw that it was the same for the other wrist. Further inspection showed that his ankles were similarly encircled.

What the bloody hell. Where am I, and why am I in chains?

He flailed arms and legs, setting up a racket that

startled the rats lurking in the shadows of the compartment and sending them scuttling for even darker corners, but no one seemed to notice.

"Hey, is there anyone here? Where am I, and why do you have me in chains?"

His vision was beginning to clear and he was becoming more aware of his surroundings. The one thing he noticed that bothered him was that he could feel a rising and falling sensation that could only come from being on a ship at sea.

If I'm on a moving ship there has to be crew here. Why doesn't someone respond?

Then, he realized that clinking the chains would probably not draw any attention, what with all the noise associated with a sailing ship, including flapping sails and clinking chains.

"Hey! Is anyone there. Damn your eyes, I know you're there and you can hear me. Show yourself, or are you afraid to?"

Whether such a bold challenge was wise or not, he was past the point of caring. He wanted, no he needed, to talk to someone, anyone. He'd had enough time alone in the bloody boat. Now, he craved human contact, even if it was with his captors, whomever they might be.

But, no one was responding. Was he in such a distance part of the ship that he couldn't be heard? Or, was this some form of torture? As it had when he was alone in the boat, his mind began to create scenarios, and each was scarier than the one before.

When he had all but given up hope, he heard a creaking sound. Craning his neck around, he noticed a rectangular portion of the bulkhead swinging inward. A large, dark man filled the opening. His shirt was open almost to his waist, revealing a muscled chest the color of dark wood and glistening with sweat or oil. In the dim light of the passageway, he couldn't make out the details of the man's face, other than his head was bald and also glistened. There was a smaller figure behind the giant, but all he could see was a slim leg in gray trousers and thigh-high boots of polished leather.

Then, the giant moved aside, and Colin's breath caught in his throat. The small figure, even in the dim light he could see the fiery red hair and the way the trousers and jacket hugged every curve of a most beguiling female form.

The slender, but almost as tall as the giant, woman advanced into the small space in which he was confined, and stood looking down at him, her hands on curvy hips that Colin had to make an effort not to stare at. He let his gaze travel from the hips, up past a narrow waist, on to a not ungenerous pair of breasts that pushed at the dingy white muslin shirt, to the oval, ivory hued face framed by luxurious red hair that fell in wavy lines to shoulders that were a bit broad for a woman, but not, he decided unfeminine at all. All in all, not an unpleasant sight to wake up to. The dark giant moved in behind the woman and stood immobile, his right hand resting on the hilt of a wickedly sharp looking saber.

Straining against his chains to sit up, Colin stared up at his two visitors. The woman looked down at him with bright blue eyes that seemed to pierce right through his chest. She didn't look angry, but she also didn't look too welcoming. The man seemed to be looking through Colin, at something on the bulkhead behind him. He stood as immobile as a statue. Neither said anything.

"Who the bloody hell are you people, and why do you have me chained here like an animal?" he said in his best command voice, undercut a bit due to his hoarseness.

"I'll ask the questions here," the redheaded woman said. Her voice was as beautiful as her face, but the tone was one of command.

Colin had never seen a woman on a ship before, except for the occasional passenger on a merchantman, usually the wife or daughter of the ship's owner, which was the only way to overcome the sailors' superstition about women or children aboard ship being bad luck. This woman, though, not only looked at home here, but she seemed to be someone of importance. He wondered if she was the captain's wife or perhaps his comfort woman. But, that made no sense. The captain having a woman to share his stateroom could lead to dissension among the crew unless she was shared, and he couldn't imagine *this* woman being passed around like a flagon of rum.

"Well," he said. "Ask your bloody questions and be done with it."

He thought he saw a flicker of emotion in the dark man's eyes, but it was gone so quick, he figured it might have just been a trick of the light—or lack of light.

"For a man in chains, you have a lot of grit," the woman said. "But, you know, a moving mouth can easily catch a closed fist. I'd advise you to keep a civil tongue in your head, lest you wish to lose both your tongue and your head."

Colin knew when to back down, or at least, now he did. It was his quickness to speak his mind that had ended him up marooned in the ocean. *Well, I don't have to be hit over the head with a stave to get the message.* "My apologies, madam," he said. "I guess being marooned has robbed me of my manners. Please, ask of me what you will."

The woman smiled. "I'm not madam," she said. "You may, if you need to call me anything, just call me captain."

Colin's mouth dropped open and he stared at her with what he knew was a stupid expression, and then he compounded that stupidity by speaking, "Captain, as captain of this ship, or whatever it is?"

The flash of anger in her eyes told him he'd put his foot in his mouth yet again, but it was too late. He couldn't call the words or the unbelieving expression back.

Then, she laughed. Her face lit up when she laughed, and caused his heart to race. *Stop it, Colin, you fool. You just might be looking at your executioner. This is no time to be thinking of things of the flesh.* That, of course, was like telling someone not to think of a yellow whale. Once the thought is planted, it grows of its own accord.

"I forget sometimes, you Americans are as bad as the English when it comes to how you view women. To you, they're either ornaments or property, or a combination of both," she said. Disdain dripped from her mouth with every word. "I just so happen to be master of this ship, and have been for the past five years."

Oh Lord, how do I get my foot out of my mouth. "My apologies, captain. It's just that you look too young to be a ship's captain."

She regarded him through narrow slits, her head cocked to one side, as if examining him.

"Too young, eh? And, it's not that I'm a woman that makes you doubt that I'm captain of this vessel?"

He looked at her looking at him, and he knew that she was testing him. He considered telling her that it *was* just her apparent youth, but then thought better of it. Something in her eyes told him that she would know if he lied.

"No, captain, I'll be honest and admit that I never thought I'd see a woman as captain of a ship. I've hardly ever seen a woman *on* a ship. How did you come to your position?"

"I told you that I would be the one to ask questions." Her tone this time, though, was not so harsh. "But, I'll answer that one. I grew up aboard this vessel. When my foster father, the former captain . . . died, the men accepted me as his heir and the new captain."

"It must be difficult for a fragile woman to deal with such a rough world," Colin said.

The dark man coughed and quickly covered his mouth with his hand. The redhead shot him a dark look.

"I assure you, whatever your name is, I am anything but fragile. And, by the way, just what *is* your name?"

"I'll tell you mine, captain, if you'll tell me yours."

She frowned so hard her eyebrows almost met in the middle of her forehead. Colin found the sight endearing, despite the circumstances, and couldn't hold back a smile.

"Don't' play games with me, sir," she said, fire in her eyes. "Or I shall be forced to wipe that arrogant smile off your face."

"Again, captain, my apologies. It's just that if I'm to give you information, it seems only fair that I know to whom I'm giving it."

She seemed to be mentally debating it. She glanced at the dark man who nodded slightly.

"Very well," she said. "I'm Captain Elizabeth Parker. Now, what's your name?"

"Colin Worth, captain," he said.

"Your jacket looks like it had the markings of an officer on it."

"Yes, I'm afraid they became unattached when I was trying to fish for my supper."

"You are an American by your accent?

"Aye, I'm originally from Boston."

"So, you're in the American navy? What is your rank, and what was your ship?"

At that point, Colin clamped his mouth shut. He didn't know who she was. She could very well be an English privateer or spy, looking for information about the navy's plans and maneuvers. Would they drain him of information and then toss him back into the sea? Could he live with himself if he betrayed his country or his shipmates? If there'd been a way to bring harm upon Dangerfield without putting the rest of the ship in peril, he would have seriously considered it. He could not, however, bluntly refuse to answer her question.

"I am a lieutenant," he said.

"And, your ship?"

Should be no harm there. After all, with *Intrepid* off chasing that damned pirate ship, she was well out of harm's way. "I was assigned aboard *U.S.S. Intrepid*."

That seemed to please her. She half-smiled. "And, what was the *U.S.S. Intrepid* doing out here, and why were you put off it alone in that small boat?"

This would take some finesse. "You would have to ask the captain that," he said. "He was not in the habit of sharing more than necessary with us junior officers. As to why I was in that boat, let's just say I had a little disagreement with the captain that got out of hand, and that was my punishment."

Again, that half smile and a knowing nod.

"What was your disagreement about?" she asked.

He looked down at the deck plates, concentrating on the wood grain, and didn't answer for many heartbeats. Finally, he looked up at her waiting patiently for his answer.

"If you don't mind, captain, I'd rather not talk about that . . . at least not now."

She tensed and her right hand went to her sword. He gulped. Had he pushed her too far? Was she now going to run him through. The dark man coughed, and she relaxed.

"Very well, Lieutenant Colin Worth," she said. "That will be all for now. But, rest assured, we will talk more later."

Without further word, she turned and walked out, the dark giant silently following.

Colin let out a huge sigh of relief and sank back against the bulkhead. As perverse as it was, he was looking forward to their next encounter.

Chapter Ten

July 1811, Headquarters, North Atlantic Fleet, U.S. Navy, Boston, Massachusetts

"It is always regrettable to lose a man, captain," said the man in the exquisitely tailored blue waistcoat with the golden epaulets of a naval captain on his shoulders. "Please, tell me again, just what were the circumstances of Lieutenant Worth's loss?" Although his words sounded sincere, Dangerfield could hear the underlying tinge of sarcasm.

Dangerfield himself wore captain's epaulets, but his blue jacket was less fine, and weeks at sea, with the corrosive action of the salt-laden air, his had become tarnished, as had, based on the scornful look in the man conducting his inquisition, his reputation. It was unthinkable that this popinjay would question his word, him a man who had been going to sea since he was just a stripling, who had clawed and scratched his way to ship's command, and guarded the nation's coast despite the stupidity of the congress in disbanding the navy immediately after independence. He'd been one of the first to heed the call when that august body realized the foolishness of its decision and reestablished the navy, and authorized construction of five ships of the line. In the meantime, it was captains like him, sailing vessels, many long past their usable life, who protected the merchantmen and the coast from the depredations of pirates and brigands, and was the first line of defense against the bloody English. Sure, he hadn't been a part of Jefferson's action against the Tripoli pirates. He was sure the damned insufferable Virginian had deliberately had him and his ship omitted from the fleet that rained death and destruction upon the head of the murderous Bey of Tripoli, but he'd protected the coast while the others were away garnering glory.

He wasn't the first captain to lose a man. That went with the profession. Seafaring was a dangerous pursuit.

But, in addition to his obsession with getting the black-hulled ship, his only other real goal in life was to command one of the newly-constructed ships of the line. In order to achieve that dream, unfortunately, he must needs kiss the asses of people like Captain Pompey Montford.

He pulled himself up to his full height and puffed out his chest.

"As I said . . . sir," he began, trying to keep the disdain from leaking through. "It was a rather chaotic period. We were in pursuit of this pirate ship, which I suspect of raiding merchant ships off the coast of Maine. I believe young Mister Worth might have gone over the rail during a somewhat extreme maneuver and been missed until the pirate got away and we were able to account for the crew."

Montford's cold, penetrating blue eyes bored into Dangerfield.

"Were there any other losses?"

"No, praise the Lord. We were extremely fortunate in that regard."

After shuffling the papers on the table before him, Montford cleared his throat.

"So, Captain Dangerfield, what shall we do with *Intrepid* now?"

You mean, what do we do with Dangerfield now? I know that you and the rest of the bloody, fucking snobs in this headquarters would like nothing more than for it to have been me reported missing. Well, you sons of syphilitic whores, I'll be here when you're all gone.

"If it please, sir." He put every ounce of obsequiousness that he could manage into his tone. "I would like permission to go after and punish that pirate. We must avenge the loss of such a fine officer as Mister Worth."

"I don't know, captain. This is a difficult time. With the English harassing our shipping and impressing our men into the royal navy, relations are quite tense. There is talk of the president asking congress for a declaration of war."

"Surely Madison wouldn't be so foolish as to do that," Dangerfield said. "Our navy is just building up. We're no match for the English fleet right now. It would be suicide."

Montford scowled reprovingly. "Careful what you say about the president, Dangerfield."

Realizing he'd gone too far, Dangerfield hastily cleared his throat.

"Uh, I meant no disrespect, sir. It's just that I worry that we might expose the navy to a risk it has yet to prepare for. We need a few years to whip everyone into shape . . . and then—"

"Yes, yes, you make a valid point." Montford waved a hand in a gesture of dismissal. "But, back to your request to go after this pirate; why should we allow your ship to be pulled away from coastal patrol for this mission?"

Dangerfield saw his opening and dove for it. "We wouldn't be taken away from coastal patrol, sir," he said. "Since we can assume this pirate will be prowling our coast, lying in wait for some fat merchant ship to come along, it is in patrolling the coast from Maine to Florida that I think we shall find her." Then, he went in for the kill. "These damn pirates, preying on our merchant shipping and wreaking havoc on our commerce, are a threat every bit as potent as the English. If we do not wipe them off the face of the earth, they could ruin us economically."

The way Montfort's eyes narrowed, Dangerfield knew he'd struck a nerve. The one thing that was uppermost in the minds of every official in the government was the economy. The fledgling American government had to print money to pay the $400 million it cost to field the continental army, leading to massive inflation. In addition, trade lost due to boycotts before and during the war wasn't completely offset by trade with the islands of the Caribbean and the French, and the government was struggling to repay the loans it had received from European countries like France, Spain and the Netherlands. Anything that threatened the country's economic revival got attention from senior officials, and Montfort was no exception. Dangerfield could see that the man was calculating the risk should he deny the request for *Intrepid* to go after the pirates and subsequently some rich merchant's cargo was plundered.

"You'll not forget that your primary mission is to be on the lookout for English warships," he said.

"Of course, I won't forget," Dangerfield said, knowing that this is precisely what he would do as soon as *Intrepid* was underway. Let all those other fools spend their time sailing about looking for trouble with the English fleet, and probably getting their asses shot off in the process. He had a much bigger prize in mind, and a matter of wounded pride. "My first duty is always to the mission assigned to me by fleet headquarters."

"Very well then, Captain Dangerfield. You may pursue this pirate, and I wish you and your crew God speed."

Dangerfield bowed slightly at the waist rather than saluting the man, who was his senior only because of the position he occupied, and who had far less time with a ship under his feet. *And, the devil take all of you bastards*, he thought, as he turned and strode out of the office.

As he made his way out of the headquarters building and to the carriage waiting to take him to his ship waiting at the docks, hopefully re-provisioned and ready to set sail, he had a spring in his step and a smile on his face.

Charles Ray

Chapter Eleven

July 1811, Cat Island in the Bahama island chain

Five days after picking the marooned Lieutenant Colin
Worth out of the Atlantic, *The Vixen* dropped anchor
off Cat Island, a long, narrow island with snow-white
sandy beaches dotted with palm trees that lay about
150 miles east of the main island. It was seldom
visited by European or American merchant ships, but
served as a waystation for small boats plying the
Caribbean's interisland trade, as well as the occasional
pirate or privateer looking for some time ashore. The
small population, a mixture of European and recently-
freed African slaves, asked no questions as long as the
appropriate amount of gold coins were placed on the
table, and the alcohol they distilled from local fruits
was almost as good as the rum made from the cane

that grew on Jamaica.

While her crew battened down the ship, and M'nondo and Garcia assigned watch duties, Elizabeth put on her best leggings and blouse, and a new pair of soft calfskin boots, checked her flame-red hair, and then went below.

Colin hadn't fared to poorly during the voyage. The two of them had played a cat-and-mouse game for the entire five days, with her asking him questions the answers to which she already knew, and him either changing the subject, or telling her just enough, but, not enough to directly endanger his former shipmates. He'd been allowed up on deck for two hours each day, always under the watchful eyes of M'nondo, who kept his hand on the large saber that Colin was beginning to think he slept with, and was fed the same rations as the rest of the crew—minus the occasional cup of rum—so, he'd regained his normal color, and had even added a slight shade from his walks in the sun on the main deck. He was, however, still chained to the bulkhead of the small space under the foredeck for the rest of the time, albeit, the chains had been lengthened to allow him to stand and move as far as the oaken bucket in the far corner which had been provided for him to relieve himself. Emptying it each day at the start of his time on deck was one of the duties he'd been assigned, and he didn't object. The smell of his own waste kept him from sleeping for the first two days. By the third day, he no longer noticed it as much, but was still glad to be rid of it for a good part of the day.

When Elizabeth opened the door, and stepped in, he was sitting with his back against the bulkhead waving his hands about in front of his face. Wide-eyed, she watched him for a moment. He had to know she was there, but he ignored her, continuing to wave his hands about. Finally, she could take it no longer. She stepped forward, stamping her boot against the wood. He continued waving his hands about for a few seconds, and then stopped and let them drop to his side. He looked up at her, a pleasant expression on his face, his smile obscured a bit by the light brown hairs sprouting from his face.

"Don't tell me that you've gone crazy," she said. "I thought your time on deck each day would prevent that."

He smiled. She felt her heart skip a beat, but kept her expression neutral.

"No, captain," he said. "I'm not going crazy, or at least, I don't think I am. I was just imagining myself as the conductor of an orchestra. It helps to pass the time when there's no one to talk to."

She returned his smile. "I'd be willing to talk to you more if only you would answer my questions."

"But, I have answered your questions, and everything I've told you has been the truth."

"I believe you in that regard, but it has also been useless."

"Useless, because you already knew most of the answers," he said.

"Enough to know that, while you didn't lie, you withheld much. Why is that?"

"If you know what I'm withholding," he said, smiling again. "Then, there is no need for me to tell you, now is there?"

This brought a laugh from her, despite her effort

not to. "Well played, lieutenant. I wonder, are you as good a sailor as you are a wordsmith?"

From his sitting position, with his legs drawn up, he bowed as low as he could. "Far better, milady . . . oh, excuse me, captain. I was not from a family wealth enough or connected enough to afford to send me to college. When it comes to words, I am self-taught."

She returned his bow, and then quickly straightened when she realized that the motion of bowing caused her breasts to sway under the loose shirt, and that his eyes were fixed on that part of her anatomy. Her cheeks felt hot.

"You had a good teacher," she said to cover her embarrassment. "Look, I know you withheld certain details about your ship out of loyalty to your crew, and I respect that, believe it or not. Not that it matters, because I already know all I need to know about *Intrepid*. I am curious, though. Whenever I ask you about the dispute with your captain that got you marooned, you refuse to answer. Surely, that doesn't endanger your former shipmates."

He looked down at his feet. "I'd rather not talk about it. It's not important."

But, she was sure it *was* important, at least to him, and she was determined to ferret it out.

"That's not why I'm here now, though. You might have noticed that ship has dropped anchor."

"Yes, I heard it go over. Where are we?"

She cocked her head to one side and smiled down at him. "Have you been to the Bahamas before?"

"No, I've not had the pleasure, but I've heard that it's a tropical paradise."

"If paradise has mosquitoes as big as your thumb,

and lizards that crawl into bed with you at night, then, I suppose that's true," she said. "But, the natives are friendly, the food is not half bad, and the liquid refreshment is in plentiful supply and cheap."

"It sounds like paradise to a sailor, especially one who has been at sea for months."

"Good, I'm glad to hear that." She moved closer to him, so close she could feel the heat from his body. "I've decided to allow you to go ashore with the crew. However, there are conditions."

"And, what might those conditions be?"

"You will be watched at all times. If you try to run away, or to tell anyone who you are and ask for help, M'nondo will remove your head from your body. If you behave, however, I assure you that you will have a good time."

He laughed and slapped his knees. "Except for the part about losing my head, anything would be an improvement over sitting here counting dust motes all day. I accept your terms, captain. There is, however, one problem."

She looked at him, not smiling, not frowning, but wondering what trick he might be about to try and pull. When she didn't say anything, he went on, "Unfortunately, when I was removed from my previous accommodations, I was not allowed to take any of my personal possessions, which included my purse. Unless the island engages in barter, say my services in exchange for their goods, I will be restricted to sitting and watching everyone else have fun."

She let out a breath, sucked in more air, and let that out, and then bent at the waist and laughed. She laughed until she had tears in her eyes, while he sat there looking up at her with a befuddled expression on his face. When she finally regained some measure of control, she took another deep breath and straightened.

"You have no need to worry about that," she said. "For today you'll be my guest. I will pay for your food and drink . . . within reason. I will *not*, however, pay for any dalliances you might to engage in. Is that understood?"

"Yes, captain," he said, bowing his head. "I will eat and drink in moderation, and keep my base animal instincts in check. I appreciate your generosity."

"There's nothing generous about it, lieutenant." She laughed. "When we're back aboard ship, you'll work off every coin I spend."

Chapter Twelve

In addition to releasing him from his chains, Colin was allowed to bath and one of the crew who was about his size gave him a pair of canvas trousers and a cotton shirt to wear. He kept his boots, which didn't identify him as being navy.

He went ashore in a boat with Elizabeth, M'nondo, and several others, including Devereux and Rodriguez, the two men who had taken him from the boat. There was no proper dock, the water being too shallow for all but the small native boats that sailed between and among the islands. Long, fragile looking wooden jetties jutted out from the sand to where the water was less than ten feet deep. They rowed in until the bow scraped the wet sand, got out, tied it to a piling and headed for what passed for a town on the island, a collection of ramshackle huts with palm frond roofs and in some cases, walls that folded up to allow the constant ocean breeze to blow through.

They headed to a place that Elizabeth said had the best fried plantains and beer on the island, which, from what he was seeing, didn't impress Colin, since there weren't all that many places on the island, but since she was paying, he kept his mouth shut.

The place had a crudely-lettered sign that said in big black letters on a rough wooden board over the door, 'Mama Lillie's'. The door was a curtain made of small sea shells that set up a clatter whenever someone entered. The floor was uneven wooden planks, polished by the thousands of feet that had walked across them, and there was a straight shot from the door to a small wooden bar in the back. Down both sides were six square wooden tables, three on each side, each with four chairs. Three of the tables, the two nearest the door and the second the right, were occupied by twelve of the roughest, meanest looking men Colin had ever seen. They were all huddled over pewter mugs and engaged in hushed conversations, which stopped the moment M'nondo pushed the beads aside and entered.

Twelve heads swiveled as they walked past. Twelve sets of eyes bored through them. But, no one spoke.

At the bar, they were met by the biggest woman Colin had ever seen in his life, in fact, the biggest person he'd ever seen. With skin as dark as a fresh-brewed cup of coffee, round cheeks, and thick lips, her head covered in a red, blue and yellow scarf, and her body covered by a one-piece blue and white dress that had enough material to make a four-man tent, the woman, Colin guessed, weighed at least three hundred pounds. As they approached, she waddled from behind the bar and grabbed Elizabeth in a hug that, despite

Elizabeth's height and size, seemed to completely engulf her.

"Leezbeth, so long I don't see you, *ma* cherie," the woman said in a voice that was so young and feminine sounding, Colin had to look closely to make sure it was coming from her. "Mama Lillie, she think you done forget her."

"That would be impossible, Mama Lillie," Elizabeth said as the woman released her. "We sailed far north this time is why it's been so long."

"So, you bring Mama Lillie something special?"

Elizabeth reached inside her blouse and took out a small cloth bundle, which she handed to Mama Lillie. Like a small child at Christmas, she immediately began unwrapping whatever was inside. She opened the cloth and laid it on the bar. She clapped her hands, each as large as a good-sized ham, to her cheeks.

"*Mon Dieu,* it is *tres*, oh, how you say in *anglais* . . . beautiful." She picked the item up and held it up for all to see. It was a simple gold heart on a gold chain, which looked just big enough to fit around the woman's gigantic neck. "Oh, Leezbeth, you make an old woman so happy. How you know this is just what I want?"

Elizabeth smiled. "Oh, I fell in love with it when I saw it in the shop in St. Augustine, so I knew you would like it."

Mama Lillie wipe away the tears that flowed across her cheeks and beamed at Elizabeth. "*Il est donc très beau, tout-petit.* You are so kind to an old woman." Turning away from Elizabeth, she caught sight of Colin. "Ah, and what do we have here, *ma petit*? I have not seen this handsome one before. A new crew member . . . or maybe, something more?"

Elizabeth's cheeks reddened and she coughed. "Mama Lillie," she said. "This is Colin Worth, a new member of my crew."

Mama Lillie pinched Colin's cheek. She ran her pudgy fingers through his growing beard, making clucking sounds as she did. Finally, she stepped back and put her hands on her hips.

"And, a fine one he is, *cherie*. Now, what can Mama Lillie do for you today. I have special *gumbo*, been cookin' since last night." She began pushing Elizabeth and Colin toward the nearest empty table. "You sit yourselves down, and I get it. What you drink, eh? Oh, I know, you like some Jamaican rum. Just got new shipment in. You, handsome Colin, I think you like rum, no? Yes, you like." Without waiting for them to respond, she turned and with surprising agility for someone of her bulk, hustled off behind the bar, through beaded curtains like the ones over the entrance.

"Is she always like this?" Colin asked.

"No," Elizabeth said. "She's really quite calm today."

Everyone at the table laughed.

Colin looked around. "I thought the Bahamas was English territory, but Mama Lillie speaks French."

"She came here from Haiti." M'nondo spoke for the first time. "She was house slave and mistress of Frenchman who owned tavern in Cape Haitien. When the slaves revolted in 1784, he fled here with his gold and Lillie, who was twenty-five at the time. He died shortly after arrival. She stayed and used what was left of his gold to build this place."

Colin chuckled. "Hard to imagine her as someone's . . . mistress."

"Oh, Mama Lillie has gained quite a bit of weight over the years," Elizabeth said. "I think it's her way of keeping the men at bay. I hear that she was quite the beauty at one time."

Colin had to admit that the woman did have a pleasant face, and her personality was . . . quite overwhelming in a pleasant way, but, someone's mistress. The picture that formed in his mind of her in bed . . . he began chuckling again. Elizabeth kicked his ankle.

"Stop that," she said. "She might hear you."

Red-faced, Colin choked back the laughter. As he looked around, he noticed that Devereux and Rodriguez also had their lips pressed tightly. His image was obviously infectious. Only M'nondo did not look like he wanted to smile.

"Yes," he said. "You're absolutely right. I'm sorry."

"What are you sorry for, *mon cherie*?" Mama Lillie, for such a large person, moved as quietly as an Iroquois warrior through the forest. Colin's face reddened. He wondered if she'd heard what he'd said. But, as he looked up, he saw that she was smiling, so he assumed that she hadn't.

"Uh, I was just saying that I'm sorry that I have not had the chance to visit your beautiful island before," he said quickly, looking at the others to see if they would expose his rudeness. He noticed that M'nondo had a slight smile on his dark brown face and a twinkle in his eye. *Dammit, he's enjoying my discomfiture.*

"Yes," M'nondo said. "We were telling him that he

has wasted much of his life traveling to the wrong places. It is a place such as this that he can find true happiness." The big man winked quickly and smiled at Colin.

"*Oui, mais oui,* this is the truth," Mama Lillie said. "Here, a man can find everything he needs in life. Now, you must try my gumbo, but first, the drinks." She set a large bottle of dark brown liquor on the table along with five mugs. "I will allow you to pour for yourselves while I go and get the gumbo."

Without a further word, she turned and walked away. Colin nodded his silent thanks to M'nondo, who merely smiled enigmatically in response.

"Captain," Colin said. "May I pour you the first drink?"

Elizabeth tilted her head at him. "So, you are capable of being chivalrous, after all. By all means."

He poured a generous amount in each mug, and waited for Elizabeth to lift hers.

"Here's to our continuing good fortune," she said, raising her mug toward the center of the table.

Everyone but Colin immediately raised their mugs and clinked them against hers. He felt conflicted. After all, he was their prisoner, so he wasn't sure it was appropriate to wish them good luck in their criminal endeavors. The mugs suspended over the table, all eyes turned to him. M'nondo's brows were raised in a question. *Hell, might as well. Maybe if they have good fortune, they'll let me go.* Smiling, he raised his mug and clinked it against hers. "Here's to good fortune for everyone," he said.

Elizabeth gave him a look, as if she was about to say something, then, she blinked and smiled.

"Here, here," she said. She lifted the mug to her lips, tilted her head back and took a long swallow.

The others copied her. Colin, who had never much liked rum, shrugged and took a big gulp, and almost choked. This was so much stronger than the watered-down rum he'd had with his shipmates in a harbor in a town whose name he no longer remembered. His mouth and throat felt as if he'd swallowed fire. He coughed, sending what was left of the rum in his mouth in a shower toward the center of the table. Coughing, he fought to breathe. M'nondo laughed and slapped him on the back.

"You must take it slow at first, and allow your body to accustom itself."

Colin took several deep breaths until his mouth only felt as if he'd swallowed tar fresh from the boiling pot.

"Thanks," he said hoarsely. "For warning me before I drank it."

They all laughed. He stiffened until he saw that they were not really laughing *at* him, but at his situation. It was no different than the genial teasing newly assigned sailors experienced aboard every ship that he'd served on. For now, they seemed to be accepting him. As he thought about it, he had to admit that if he'd not been the subject of the laughter, he too would probably have found it funny. In fact, it was really funny. He joined them in the laughter, which only incited them to laugh harder, until they were all leaning back in their chairs and laughing so hard tears flowed.

At that moment, Mama Lillie, bearing a large wooden tray upon which were five large polished wooden bowls, and five small pewter bowls balanced on her shoulder, came out of the back. The load looked heavy to Colin, and he marveled at how gracefully and effortlessly she carried it.

She smiled broadly at them as she set two bowls in front of each. From a pocket in her voluminous dress she plucked five large wooden spoons and placed one beside each.

"Fresh gumbo," she said. "Made it from a mess of crabs brought here fresh off the boat, and vegetables I picked from my own garden out back. *Bon appetit.*"

She folder her arms under her huge breasts and stood, watching them with a steely gaze.

Colin looked at the stew-like concoction in the large bowls. He didn't recognize anything, but upon sniffing, decided that it smelled delicious. The small pewter bowls contained boiled white rice. He waited and watched Elizabeth, figuring that she would know how to eat this gumbo concoction, and it would be polite to wait for her, as captain, to begin.

She smiled knowingly at him, as if to say, I know what you're doing. Then, she picked up the small bowl and dumped the rice into the gumbo. She took her spoon and stirred until the rice was completely mixed in. Then, she dipped the spoon into the mixture, filled it and shoved it into her mouth. As she chewed, her expression changed from its normal stoniness to a look of pure rapture. After swallowing, she looked up at Mama Lillie. "Mama, you've outdone yourself this time. This is the best gumbo I have ever tasted, and I've eaten gumbo from here to Martinique."

The big woman nodded, smiled, and turned her attention to Colin. He didn't need words to know what she was doing. She was mentally ordering him to eat.

He returned her smile, and then copied Elizabeth's actions. When the gumbo hit his tongue, he instantly understood her look languorous look. He'd never in his life tasted anything like it. He could taste the fresh crab, and a tangy flavor that must have been onion or garlic, and a spicy taste unlike anything he'd ever experienced. There was also a slowly building sensation of heat that began on the tip of his tongue and spread throughout his mouth. When he swallowed, the heat followed the gumbo down his throat. He could feel it all the way to his stomach. From the way his face felt, he knew that it had turned red.

M'nondo laughed and patted his back again. "You should include more rice until your mouth gets used to the pepper," he said. "After a few more bites, you won't feel it at all."

Colin decided to take his word for it. He had a snappy retort in mind, but the way his mouth was burning, he wasn't sure talking was such a good idea. He used his spoon to scour rice from the bottom of the mixture and put it in his mouth. Very quickly, the burning sensation subsided. *Well, I'll be damned. I learn something new every day.* Armed with this new knowledge, he resumed eating, making sure to have a healthy portion of rice in each spoonful of gumbo. With his mouth no longer feeling like it was on fire, he was able to enjoy the taste of this new and strange food, and he had to concur with Elizabeth; it was one of the best dishes he'd ever had.

Satisfied that he was according her food the proper respect, Mama Lillie smiled.

"You finish up the gumbo, and I got a special treat," she said. "I made some pies from a basket of limes I bought off a trader last week. I mixed lots of fresh cream in, and I think you will like it."

"If you cook it, Mama Lillie," Devereux said. "I know we gonna like it."

She went back to the kitchen, and they resumed eating.

It didn't take long for their bowls, Colin's included, to be scraped clean.

"So," Rodriquez said. "What you think of gumbo?"

Colin rubbed his stomach. "Once the burning stopped, it was . . . great. I've had clam chowder, but this is the first time I ever had seafood prepared this way."

"It's a combination of French and West African cooking," M'nondo said. "Lots of spice and vegetables. Best thing to eat if you have had too much rum."

"That's for sure," Elizabeth said, nodding. "Makes the headaches and cotton mouth go right away."

"I'll have to remember that the next time I'm tempted to drink too much," Colin said. He looked around.

"What you looking for?" Devereux asked.

"Uh, I was just wondering if there was any more of this gumbo."

That got everyone laughing again. The clacking of the curtains in back signaled the return of Mama Lillie. "You bad *enfants* stop laughing at him. He got some good taste, he has." She was carrying a large iron pot and a ladle. She came to Colin's side and ladled a generous helping of the gumbo into his bowl. "You wait, mon *cher*, I bring you more rice."

He waited, but the spicy aroma wafting up from the bowl made it difficult. Soon, though, she was back with another bowl of the white, fluffy rice, which she dumped into his gumbo. While the other four looked on in awe, he made quick work of the second bowl, licking the spoon when there was nothing left in the wooden bowl. Mama Lillie stood at his shoulder, her hands on her hips and a broad smile on her face. When he was finally finished, she patted him on the shoulder.

"Now, everybody ready for sweets?"

"Yes, please," they said in unison.

"I be right back. You finish your rum. The gumbo make it taste better, and it help make the pie taste better."

Colin took tentative sip. It still felt hot on his tongue, but not uncomfortably so, and she'd been right; somehow the flavor of the gumbo, still in his mouth, enhanced the woody, acrid taste of the rum. He took a bigger swallow. *I could quickly become accustomed to this.* As he put his empty mug on the table, he looked around. Everyone was looking at him, smiling broadly.

"What?" he asked.

"You know, I think you make good pirate," Rodriguez said.

"But, I'm an officer in the United States Navy," Colin countered.

Rodriquez shrugged. "Maybe you change jobs some day."

Before Colin could answer, they were distracted by the sound of wood scraping across wood. Then, a shadow fell across the table. Colin looked up to see two of the men who had been sitting at the table to the right of the door, scowling down at them, no, they were looking across the table at Elizabeth. She caressed her mug and returned their gaze, her own expression unreadable.

Colin tensed up. In dozens of taverns in dozens of towns across the globe, from Boston to Dover to Tripoli, he'd seen such scenes play out. Local toughs challenging the new arrivals for dominance, or bored drunks looking for excitement. The two men were large, not fat, although they did each show a bit of paunch, no doubt from overindulging in Mama Lillie's food and ale, and their forearms were corded with muscle from many years of hauling ropes and wrestling with heavy sails. They had wide shoulders, so wide that they wouldn't have been able to enter Mama Lillie's side by side. What caught Colin's eye though, was the look in their bloodshot eyes—the dead, staring look of men for whom life held no mystery or importance, men who would stop eating, slit your throat, and resume eating as if nothing had happened. What Colin and his group had done to attract their attention, he did not know, but attract their attention they had, and now it was about to erupt in fighting. Of that, he had no doubt. The only thing in doubt was who would strike the first blow.

The silence was palpable. The two groups stared at each other. The rest of the place looked on with expressions of eager anticipation.

Mama Lillie came out of the kitchen, took one look at the tableau, and wisely went back to the kitchen.

Elizabeth finally broke the silence. "Is there something we can do for you . . . gentlemen?"

The one nearest to Colin, a bitter-looking man with a jagged, red, puckered scar that ran from the corner of his left eye, down his jaw, and tucked under his unshaven chin, cleared his throat as if he was about to spit.

"You this lady captain we been hearin' so much about?" he asked in a rusty, creaking voice, and a guttural accent that Colin didn't recognize.

"That depends," she replied. "What have you been hearing?"

"I'm hearin' that you mayhap be needin' some new crew for that ship of yours."

"Well now, I fear you've heard wrong. My ship is fully manned."

The other man, a ferret faced individual whose left eye kept flickering from side to side while the right eye remained fixed, staring straight ahead, made a head motion toward the table they'd just vacated. The remaining two men there, and the four from the adjacent table, scraped back their chairs and stood.

"I hear that because of some ill fortune, you mebbe short a few men," he said, in a deep voice. Colin thought his accent sounded like he might be from one of the Gulf coast states of the United States.

"I assure you gentlemen, my crew are all in fine health, and are likely to remain so for the foreseeable future."

"We'll see about that," the first man said.

He took a step forward. His companion moved toward the right a half step.

Colin looked at M'nondo who inclined his head slightly and smiled.

There are a number of ways to deal with bullies.

One is to avoid them. But, this is often not possible. The other is to wait until they start something, and respond with overwhelming force. The best way, Colin had found, though, was to anticipate when a bully was about to attack, and attack first. Hit first, hit fast, and hit hard.

While the two men had been focusing on Elizabeth, he'd wrapped his right hand around his mug, and put his left hand near the now-empty rum bottle. M'nondo, he noticed, had placed his large dark hand on the thick wooden bowl in front of him.

Prior to going to sea, Colin hadn't had much experience fighting beyond the occasional scuffle with some of the boys in his neighborhood. But, years of sailing from port to port, and interacting with the rough sorts who chose life as a mariner, he'd learned well how to take care of himself. One of the things he'd learned was not to make the mistake of watching an opponent's hands, which as often as not would mislead you about his intentions to attack. He'd learned to watch the eyes, for involuntarily they would flicker just before an attacker committed. For that reason, he kept his gaze focused on the man closest to him.

As the man's eyes flickered downward, a movement he himself was probably not aware of, Colin grasped the rum bottle tightly, swept it off the table and downward, and then sharply upward between the man's legs, smashing it with as much force as he could into the soft spot between the man's legs. He felt the give as the bottle crushed the man's testicles, driving them upwards into his lower abdomen. The big man made a wheezing sound and grabbed at his mangled manhood, his eyes going wide as the pain hit. Before he could make more than a mewling sound, which was the beginning of a shriek of pain, Colin stood and slammed the pewter mug into his temple. The big man's eyes rolled back in their sockets and he fell over backward, his head making a solid thudding sound as it hit the wooden floor. M'nondo in the meantime, had grasped the wooden bowl by the rim with his right hand and brought it around in a sweeping motion, slamming it into the face of the second man. The sound of the bones in his nose was like the cracking sound icicles make when they separate from the eaves of a roof, and a bright red stream of blood shot from his nose. M'nondo pulled the bowl back and slapped the man's temple, sending him to join his unconscious comrade on the floor.

The remaining men at the tables near the entrance stood and started moving toward them with murder in their eyes.

"Oh, no you do not, not in my place, mangy *chiens*," Mama Lillie said in a high-pitched shriek, as she came through the beaded curtains brandishing a wooden stave about two inches across and four feet long.

The man unlucky enough to be the fastest, a short, muscular man with reddish-brown skin, lank brown hair, and a mustache that drooped below his chin on both sides, caught the full force of the stave as she swung it. *Whack!* He stopped as if he'd run into the side of a building and went over backwards, tangling up with the two men immediately behind him. Faced with three hundred pounds of angry woman defending her home, the rest of the men froze in place, looking like they'd like to be someplace else.

"How dare you," Mama Lillie said. "You attack my friends, in my place. I have the *pretre de* voodoo pay you a visit, no? How you like maybe wake up tomorrow as a gecko?"

An older looking man in the group raised his hands in a gesture of surrender.

"*Pardon, Maman,* we meant no harm. Black Pete and Morgan just have a little fun, *non.*"

"Jean-Paul, you know I do not allow this in my café," she said. "Why you do such a thing?"

"*Maman,* I tried to talk them out of it. But, you know how they can be. They think they have a little fun with the lady captain, is all."

She looked down at the three unconscious men with an expression of derision.

"Well, I hope when they wake up and the headache gone, they still think it was fun. Now, you and *tes ami* get this *ordures* out of my place, and I do not want to see you in here again. Do you understand?"

"*Oui, Maman.* Okay, you men, help me lift them."

As meekly as schoolboys who have been disciplined for talking in class when they should have been studying, the group of men hefted their limp companions and made haste leaving.

After they were gone, Colin looked at Mama Lillie with awe.

"You would be a good companion to have in a fight," he said.

She smiled at him. "I do not like when people try to hurt my friends," she said. "And, I think you will be good friend, *non*?"

Colin eyed the stave, which she was lightly tapping into her palm as she smiled at him.

"Most assuredly, Mama Lillie," he said. "I hope to be one of your best friends."

"*Tres bien*. Now, sit down and I bring a new bottle of my special rum." She whacked her palm one final time with the stave and waddled toward the back.

When she was gone, Colin sat, shaking his head.

"You look as if you do not believe what you just saw," Elizabeth said. "Did you not think women capable of fighting so?"

"Oh no, I've seen many a mother, human and animal, do amazing things when aroused. I was just wondering . . . she threatened to send a Pret voodoo to turn them into a gecko. What was that, and why did they all turn pale when she said it?"

Elizabeth laughed. "It's *pretre* voodoo," she said. "That's a priest of the black arts brought here to the islands by the slaves from Africa. It's said they can bring the dead back to life to do their bidding, turn them into zombies, or turn a man into any animal they chose."

"And, they really believe that?"

"If you stay in these islands long enough, Colin Worth, you might come to believe as well. I have seen things here that I cannot explain."

"Surely, such things are not possible?"

She shook her head.

"Let's hope you never have to find out.

Well, one thing's for sure," he said. "I will never make Mama Lillie angry."

Charles Ray

Chapter Thirteen

July 1811, *U.S.S. Intrepid* at Great Abaco Island, Bahamas Islands

Eight days after leaving Boston, *Intrepid* sailed into the harbor at Great Abaco Island, a sickle-shaped island, the northernmost of the Bahamas chain of islands. They had sailed a zigzag course from Boston, as far north as southern Maine, and then back down along the coast to Florida. Dangerfield, assuming correctly that *The Vixen* had made a run for the islands of the Caribbean to find safe haven, decided to stop at the most likely ports of call to gather intelligence.

Rather than sail in and tie up at the barely serviceable wharf, he anchored a half mile offshore, and, leaving Comstock in command of the ship, took a squad of six marine infantry and six of his biggest, meanest looking sailors ashore.

While the Bahamas were legally English territory,

they and the rest of the islands in the Caribbean were known to be hospitable to the many pirate gangs that preyed on shipping up and down the Atlantic seaboard, and the English, more concerned with plaguing the American navy and protecting Canada, concentrated their fleet elsewhere.

He was, nonetheless, taking a great chance. A warship or two might just be patrolling the southern waters, and Comstock had unwisely mentioned this just before he boarded the boat that was to take him ashore.

"Mister Comstock," Dangerfield said, his voice dripping venom. "When I want your opinion, I will request it. Until I do, keep your mouth shut and carry out the orders I give you. Is that fully understood?"

"Yes, sir, understood, sir," Comstock said, while silently praying that there were no English warships in the vicinity.

His question, though, put Dangerfield in a foul mood, so the sailors and marines in the boat with him kept their mouths shut and their eyes fixed on the approaching beach where they planned to land.

Dangerfield waited until the boat was well-grounded in the sand, and he was able to step off the bow onto area where the sand was relatively dry and did not dirty his boots. Up where it was completely dry, he waited until his men had secured the boat by rope to a stake they pounded into the sand. Leaving two men to guard the boat, for he didn't trust the locals not to steal it if it was left unattended, he had the rest follow him in two columns and set out to look for a suitable place to conduct inquiries.

As was the usual on most of the islands with more

than fifty inhabitants, he didn't have far to walk. And, even though Dangerfield had removed his uniform and replaced it with the broadcloth attire of a merchant, and had his men dress in clothing commonly worn by merchant seamen, the way they walked in stiff formation cleared a path for them as they trod the sand streets of the little town. People gave way to them, and they earned more than their fair share of stares, pointing, and hostile glares.

The *Boar's Head Inn* was located a five-minute walk from the beach, and the noise coming from inside the adobe and palm frond structure, combined with the reek of stale liquor and sweaty bodies, told him that this would be the place where there would be someone who knew everything that happened on or near Abaco.

The hum of conversation, clink of bottles, and plink of pewter and stone mugs came to an abrupt standstill when Dangerfield pushed open the flimsy batwing doors, and, followed, by his entourage, entered the place. All eyes swiveled in the direction of the door.

Ignoring the stares, Dangerfield strode across the litter-strewn floor to the bar, behind which a beefy man with a crown of stringy black hair encircling his bald top leaned his ample belly against it while he polished at a glass with a dingy looking cloth.

At the bar, Dangerfield pressed his hands on the dark wood top, and then quickly pulled them away, looking at his palms with an expression of disgust.

"How can I help you, friend?" the bartender asked in a guttural German accent.

Dangerfield wiped his palms on his trousers. "I'm looking for a ship," he said.

The bartender's brows rose and he looked behind

him at the rows of bottles on rickety wooden shelves. "Sorry, friend, but we only have drink, boiled eggs, and a little female companionship in the shed out back . . . if that's of interest."

Dangerfield's face wrinkled in disgust and frustration. A wizened old man with a scabby, bald head, and clothes encrusted with dried mud, sitting on a stool to Dangerfield's right, cackled.

"I do not want to *buy* a ship," Dangerfield said. "I'm looking for a ship that might have put in here during the last few days, or perhaps a week ago."

"Lots of ships call here on their way somewhere else." The man kept wiping at the glass, spreading the greasy stains around. "Why you look for it?"

"There is someone on that ship that I seek."

"What is name of this ship?"

"I believe it's called *The Vixen*. If you've seen it you would know it. It has a black hull."

The bartender's brows wiggled and he stopped wiping for a second, then resumed.

"I never see such a ship," he said.

Dangerfield knew instinctively that the man was lying. "Are you sure? I am prepared to make it worth your while."

"I tell you, I never see such a ship. Now, you want drink, or not?"

"Perhaps a glass of your best rum."

"It cost two shillings."

Fortunately, Dangerfield had anticipated this, and since shillings had remained in use in America for a long time after Independence because of the shortage of coins in the newly independent states, he had several hundred dollars' worth of the English coins which he kept in a strongbox aboard *Intrepid*, knowing that the use of American currency in the Caribbean, in addition to creating difficulties in making change, could cause someone to report his presence to English authorities, something he wanted to avoid at all costs. Despite what he'd told that pompous captain back in Boston, *his* mission did not include looking for English ships. He pulled two coins from his pocket, frowning at the outrageous price for what he knew would be rotgut that tasted like whale oil, and slapped them on the bar.

"Make sure the glass is clean," he said.

"What about men who come with you?" the bartender asked.

"They don't want anything."

The man made an 'hmph' sound. "I get good rum from back." Without waiting for Dangerfield's acknowledgement, he turned and disappeared behind a beaded curtain.

The old man poked at Dangerfield's arm with a gnarled hand that showed more dirt than skin.

"Say, mister," he said in a cracked voice. "I hear ye say, ye be lookin' fer *The Vixen*?"

Dangerfield shivered at the filthy creature's touch, but he knew that his chances of getting anything useful from the bartender were slim to none.

"That is correct. Do you know it?"

The old man cackled again. "Hell's bells, ain't a man jack here in the islands whot don't know *The Vixen* 'n 'er cap'n."

"Has it been here lately? Do you know where it went?" Dangerfield felt his pulse racing.

"Well now, mebbe I do, 'n mebbe I don't. What it be

worth to ye?"

Dangerfield thought it over. The old man might just be trying to cadge a few coins for drink. On the other hand, it was just possible that he knew something useful.

"I'll give you ten shillings."

The old man's rheumy eyes lit up. Dangerfield smiled. At an exchange rate of about four shillings to an American dollar, he was offering the old man more money than he could make in six months at honest labor, and judging by his age and condition, more than he could make at dishonest labor.

"Show me yer coin," the old man said.

Dangerfield took ten coins from his pocket and stacked them on the bar, just out of the old man's reach.

"You only get them, though, when you tell me something useful."

The old man opened his mouth, revealing only two brown and crooked teeth. He ran a tongue over his chapped lips.

"Sure now, old Mortimer tell ye good. Ye ast anybody, they tell ye, old Mortimer never lie or cheat. *The Vixen* she sail by here a few day ago, but she don't stop."

"Which way did she go?"

"She sail southeast. I think she be headin' fer the leeward islands, or mebbe the Turks. I hear tell that be where she make port when she ain't out . . . sailin'."

Dangerfield considered it. It made sense. The pirate, after the encounter with a ship of the American navy, would likely go to ground for a while. He decided that ten shillings was a good investment. He shoved the pile of coins toward the old man who snatched them up, biting one before secreting in the pocket of his filthy pants. Dangerfield turned to leave.

"Say, stranger, what about yer rum?" the old man asked.

"Tell the innkeeper that I bought it for you. My compliments."

With a toss of his head, Dangerfield signaled his men that they were leaving. As he went through the door into the blinding sunshine outside, he could hear the old man cackling.

Charles Ray

Chapter Fourteen

July 1811, *U.S.S. Intrepid* at Cat Island, Bahamas Islands

The journey from Great Abaco, southeast took the better part of two days because Dangerfield had them sail in close to every island they neared to see if he could see any sign of *The Vixen*. Cat Island came into view at dusk on the second day. From the sea, it didn't look like much, but he noticed the number of ships either moored at the long, rambling piers, or at anchor in the harbor, and decided this would be a good place to stop and gather more information.

He had his crew drop anchor half a mile offshore and ordered extra watch, and instructed Comstock to prepare a party of four marine infantry, out of uniform and armed with cutlasses and pistols, to accompany him the next day for a trip to the humble little settlement he could see hugging the coast.

The next morning, just as the sun was coming up and casting the tiny island in stark relief, Dangerfield had the four burly men assigned to accompany him eat a quick and early breakfast, and joined them in the ship's boat that was lowered over the side. The four men pulled the oars as he sat in the stern directing them to a suitable landing spot on the beach, far enough from the other boats bobbing in the water near the shore, but not so far as to cause them to have to walk too far in the heat and humidity, which was already evident despite the fact that the sun was no more than two hand spans above the horizon.

Two days of no sightings hadn't made him happy, and when he stepped off the boat and his boots sank two inches into the damp sand, leaving them streaked when he managed to pull them out and get onto dry, but still soft sand which stuck to them, it darkened even more. He took his ire out on the four hapless marines who, despite being larger and fitter, quaked under his tongue lashings.

His anger dissipated a bit by the time they reached the hard-packed dirt that served as a street of sorts in this tropical backwater, so he merely mumbled to himself as he and three marines—one was left to guard the boat—set out toward a collection of thatched huts that seemed to be the business district.

They walked past *Mama Lillie's*, and the sight of the huge, scowling black woman standing beside the door made of what appeared to be seashells, along with the lack of apparent business in the place, caused Dangerfield to increase his walking speed. He could feel the big woman's glare boring into his back until they were nearly a hundred feet away.

A precariously tilting hut, its sides covered with palm bark, with a roof of yellowing palm fronds, and no door, attracted his attention. Ill-dressed and dangerous-looking men filed in and out of the place in a steady flow, and the noise from within its dusky interior was deafening, even outside. This was the place. If anyone on this godforsaken island knows of the comings and goings of a pirate ship, they are sure to be found here.

The marines looked uncertain when his pace slowed as they neared, and they looked ashen when they saw the crudely hand-lettered sign nailed to the bark over the door, **Devuls Den**. Not all that literate themselves, they had no problem understanding what the sign said, or what it represented. Dangerfield also hesitated a couple of heartbeats, knowing that the four of them—well, the three marines, for he wouldn't think of lowering himself to engage in a rowdy tavern brawl—stood little chance against a room full of drunk mariners. For a brief moment, he regretted his decision to avoid drawing too much attention by traveling with a large group as he'd done on Abaco.

But, his mission was important, and he had God on his side—or so he was convinced. He took a deep breath and forged ahead, stepping through the open door and into the dimly-lit interior as if he owned the place. The three men with him entered with much less self-assurance, but with determined looks on their faces.

Unlike Abaco, where every head had turned whenever they appeared, and conversations would stop whenever they entered a drinking establishment or café, no one even looked up as Dangerfield walked toward the platform at the back, which he assumed to be the bar. Behind the bar stood an emaciated young man with glossy black hair plastered to his oval skull. The pasty whiteness of his skin was further accented by jet-black eyes set in circles of light-blue, and a reddish tint to his full, pouting lips. *Sant's preserve us. He's one of those abominations.* Dangerfield was tempted to turn and flee, but he noticed that there were only two customers at the bar being served by the effeminate looking corpse, men with bulky muscles and surly expressions, one with a grimy bandage wrapped over his nose and around his face. *Surely, they are not the type to prefer men.* He walked on, with a bit less bravado in his expression, until he reached the bar.

"May I be of service to you?" the thing, as Dangerfield thought of him, behind the bar asked in a loud voice that despite the man's appearance and a slight lisp, carried clearly over the noise of a dozen loud conversations.

Swallowing his distaste, his downright abhorrence, Dangerfield pressed against the bar and leaned forward to make himself heard. "I'm looking for a ship, *The Vixen*, do you know if she's been here lately."

The dark eyes flared, and the painted lips pursed. *"Mais non, monsieur,"* he said. "I know nothing of *Le Vixen.*"

The way his eyelids flickered, Dangerfield knew he was lying, but he was in no mood to engage the man any more than necessary. It had been that way with everyone they'd encountered, except the old drunk on Abaco, locals, whether or not they were themselves pirates, did not give up other locals to outsiders. He huffed air out of his mouth in disgust, and turned to leave.

"Did I hear you say you be lookin' for *The Vixen?*" the man with the bandaged nose asked. His voice was somewhat muffled and slurred by whatever damage had been done to his nose, but Dangerfield thought he recognized an accent common to the Georgia coastlands.

"I am," he said. "Do you know of her?"

"Aye, I know of her, and Cap'n Parker, her master, know 'em well. Why are you lookin' for 'em?"

"It's a private matter, but I'm prepared to make it worth your while if you can tell me anything about them."

"From your tone, I take it your private matter ain't got nothin' to do with friendship."

The man was nosy and persistent, but he seemed on the verge of providing *some* information. Dangerfield's problem was deciding whether or not it was worth the effort.

"No, it has nothing to do with friendship," he said, and snapped his mouth shut.

"Did the good Cap'n Parker mayhap cheat or swindle you?"

"Something like that."

"Would you mebbe be plannin' on killin' her when you meet up?"

"Yes, I—what, her, what do you mean, her?"

The man's brow creased and his eyes looked suspicious.

"You're looking for *The Vixen*, and you don't know it's master's a woman?" His hand dropped to the hilt of the long-bladed knife at his belt. "What are you playin' at, stranger?"

The sound of chairs scraping against the floor, and the sudden cessation of conversation, almost drove Dangerfield into a fit of panic. But, he was driven in his quest to get revenge, and now that he knew the captain of the ship that had humiliated him was a woman, he was even more determined. He took a deep breath and threw caution to the winds.

"When I last encountered *The Vixen*," he lied. "Her captain was John Cleague, a pirate known as Black John. I captured Cleague, but the rest of his crew escaped. I didn't know his first officer was a woman. I didn't know there *were* any woman pirates."

The bandaged man kept his hand on his knife, but his expression relaxed. "Ain't many. Elizabeth Parker's an exception. She wasn't Cleague's first officer, she was his daughter, or ward, or somethin'. When he was kilt, she took over the ship, and has been in charge since, and iffen you ask me, gettin' a mite too big for them britches she wears."

Interesting, very interesting. So, this woman captain is not a beneficiary of the local solidarity. "I gather that you're not an admirer of Captain Parker?"

"No, I ain't. Far's I'm concerned, we'd all be better off if her'n her whole crew was sent to hell, where they belong, specially that black bastard that's always stuck to her side, and that new fella, the American."

Dangerfield's senses were instantly on alert. "American, you say? She has an American among her crew, someone new?"

"Aye, she has." The man's description sent chills through Dangerfield. It couldn't be, but the man had described Colin Worth down to his devil may care smile.

"When were they here?" Dangerfield asked.

"They sailed just two day ago." The man looked around, his gaze resting on the three nervous marines. "You ain't gon' be able to handle 'em with this few men."

"Never you mind. I have more men . . . and cannons. More than enough to deal with this upstart. Now, where did they go. I'll pay handsomely for the information."

The man smiled, a smile that sent more chills through Dangerfield.

"The only pay you need to give me is to twist your blade when you drive it into that bitch's heart," he said. "Unless, mebbe, you could cut off the heads of that blackamoor, M'nondo's his name, and the new man. I didn't catch his name, but you can't miss him. He looks more like a dandy than a sailor. Iffen you could bring me their heads, I'd consider that fair payment."

Dangerfield couldn't believe his luck. "Consider it done, Mister . . ."

"Morgan, everybody just calls me Morgan, and I'm easy enough to find, just ask the first young'un you see on the street to go find old Morgan."

"Very well, Mr. Morgan," Dangerfield said. "Now, as to the location of *The Vixen*."

"My guess is they be at their hidey hole, a little place called Lost Island." He pointed at the bartender. "Hey, Pierre, gimme a piece of paper and one a them charcoal sticks so I can make a map."

"Would be better if you used ink," Pierre said, frowning. "But, I am think this is not such a good idea."

"I didn't ask you what you think. Just get me the damn ink and paper."

The foppish man, Pierre, frowned, but this Morgan, Dangerfield thought, was obviously someone no one wanted to run afoul of. And, he had a grudge against the captain of *The Vixen* and her captain and crew. He smiled inwardly. His luck was holding. Even better, he noticed that Morgan, for all his crudity and apparent lack of education, was a most capable mapmaker. The sketch he presented was very detailed, with the dot representing Lost Island drawn in heavy strokes to make it stand out. And, it appeared to be no more than a day or two's sail from Cat Island.

As he and his men headed back to the beach, Dangerfield patted his jacket, inside which he'd carefully tucked the neatly folded map. As they walked, the sun seemed to caress his face, and the sound of the surf crashing on the beach was like a great orchestra. The three marines sneaked covert glances at him and looked even more worried than they'd been when he was ranting and mumbling to himself. He had, on his face, a look of pure rapture.

Chapter Fifteen

July 1811, on board *The Vixen* somewhere south of Cat Island

After their altercation in *Mama Lillie's*, Elizabeth decided that they should cut short their stay on Cat Island. She paid for their food and drink, adding a little extra to cover any damage the fight had caused, and they went back to the boat.

They immediately set sail, pointing the bow generally southeast.

Colin, who, after his performance ashore with the two cutthroats who'd accosted him, was no longer chained below decks, but allowed the freedom of the ship, although his sword still had not been returned, came up beside her where she stood at the starboard rail of the quarterdeck, gazing out across the trackless ocean.

"Beautiful, isn't it," he said.

She looked at him, and her heart skipped a beat.

"Yes, it is. But, the sea, as you well know, can be a harsh mistress. One minute, she is loving and kind, and the next, she is an angry goddess trying to smash you to bits and pull you deep into her dark bosom."

"Aye, but is that not what attracts us to her? The mystery, the uncertainty—no, the certainty, that out here, you only get one chance. You can never afford to make a mistake. There is no place that tests a man . . . a person, like the sea."

She marveled at how his face lit up when he spoke of the sea, and how she felt a tingling in her loins when he smiled.

"I never thought of it quite in that way before," she said. "I suppose you're right."

There was a moment of silence between them as both gazed out at the undulating sea, and listened to the whisper of the swells and the slap as they broke against the hull.

"I want to thank you," he said finally.

"Thank me? For what?"

"For not placing me back in chains below deck. For allowing me the freedom to walk about the ship."

She smiled at him. "You earned that much. But, do not forget, your freedom is contingent upon your good behavior. M'nondo's cutlass awaits your neck if you stray."

He cringed and rubbed at his neck, which made her smile more.

"I gave a promise," he said. "And, I always keep my promises."

"Why did you do it?" she asked.

"Do what?"

"Join in our fight at Mama Lillie's place? It was me and my men those two had issues with."

"Unfortunately, sitting where I was, they would have had to go through me to get to you, and I sensed that they wouldn't do that in a gentle manner. So, in a sense, I was merely protecting myself."

"But, you initiated the fighting. You struck first."

"Captain, my dear captain, hasn't anyone ever taught you that the best defense is a good offense. The best way to ensure that a fight is short and that you're the victor is to strike hard and strike first."

"I will have to keep that in mind." She tugged at a stray lock of hair. "It does make sense, though. And, it is without doubt that it was a fight they sought. Well, no mind. You did well. You have the makings of a good pirate."

His cringe made her laugh.

"Excuse me, captain," he said. He bowed slightly. "I have more of the ship to explore."

As he turned to walk away, she could not resist letting her gaze linger on the way his muscles moved beneath his shirt and trousers. Out of the corner of her eye, she saw the glare that Garcia, her first mate, shot Colin's way. *Trouble brewing there. I'll have to watch that closely.* She also noticed that, as Colin started down from the quarterdeck, he met M'nondo who was just coming up. The coldness that her elder brother had shown prior to the stopover at Cat Island was gone. While M'nondo was not what one would call a demonstrative person, his attitude toward Colin was almost as warm as that he showed her.

From where she stood, even though M'nondo spoke in normal tones, through some quirk of nature, she could hear his words clearly.

"You fought well, Colin Worth," he said. "I did not know you were such a warrior."

"Like Mama Lillie said," Colin replied. "I can't sit idly by and watch people hurt my friends."

M'nondo placed a hand on his shoulder. "Spoken like a true warrior, my brother."

Colin blushed. "Thank you, M'nondo. Thank you very much."

Well, so much for my being able to use the threat of M'nondo cutting his head off. Elizabeth turned back to the sea so that no one could see her smile.

Chapter Sixteen

Although Colin hadn't been put back in chains, he hadn't been invited to share the crews' quarters, so when dusk made exploring the ship difficult, he returned to his 'cell.' He was surprised when he got there to see that someone had provided him with a straw mat, a blanket, and a chamber pot. They still hadn't returned his weapons. *Oh well, these things take time. I would probably do the same if roles were reversed.*

He had just settled down on the mat, staring up at the overhead, when there was a rap at his door.

"Enter," he said.

M'nondo, an enigmatic smile on his face, ducked to allow his head to clear the upper part of the hatch.

"Colin, Captain . . . Elizabeth has invited you to join us for supper in her cabin," he said.

He eyed the big, dark man suspiciously. "She wants me to join her for supper? You're not having me on, are you?"

"I do not understand this 'having you on,' but I assure you, the captain has issued an invitation, and it is not just with her. I will also be there."

Noticing how Elizabeth and M'nondo interacted, that didn't surprise Colin. He'd finally assumed that the big man was her lover. It bothered him, and he couldn't understand why, but M'nondo was also a good man to have on your side in a fight, and seemed to be favorably disposed toward him, so he decided that, since it was none of his business in the first place, he would forget it. Except, he couldn't forget it.

"Very well, when should I go?"

M'nondo looked at him with a disapproving, incredulous expression. "Why, now, of course. Did I not just issue the invitation?"

Of course. Colin shrugged, pushed himself up and followed the big man.

Elizabeth was waiting for them in her cabin, seated at a small square table in the center, upon which was a veritable feast, certainly more sumptuous than what they'd fed him on the voyage to Cat Island. There were three chairs and three place settings, two to either side of Elizabeth. She wore, instead of her trademark trousers and shirt, a simple one-piece blue dress that showed a disturbing amount of cleavage. She didn't seem to notice that he was straining not to stare at her breasts. She smiled up at him and pointed to the chair on her left.

"Thank you for the invitation, captain," he said, bowing at the waist. "To what do I owe the honor?"

She looked from him to M'nondo, an enigmatic expression on her face. M'nondo nodded almost imperceptibly, but Colin caught the movement. *Who the hell is really in charge here?*

"I wanted to formally thank you for stepping in the way you did today," she said. "M'nondo suggested that supper with the two of us in the captain's cabin would be an appropriate gesture."

M'nondo made a grunting noise. "That was not exactly what I suggested," he said.

"It was close enough." She frowned at him.

"But, he should—"

"Enough," Elizabeth said. "We will discuss this no further."

Colin had followed their back and forth with no small amount of curiosity. Finally, he could take it no longer.

"If I am intruding upon an intimate moment," he said. "I can eat with the crew, or if they do not wish to associate with me, I can eat alone in my . . . quarters."

They both looked at him, wide-eyed with shock.

"What do you mean, intimate moment?" Elizabeth asked.

"Well, it's apparent that the two of you are disagreeing about something. I do not wish to involve myself in a lovers' quarrel."

Their mouths gaped open. They looked at each other, and then started laughing.

"You thought we were—" Elizabeth could not finish the sentence.

"We are not lovers," M'nondo said, finishing it for her.

"But, I thought—"

"M'nondo is like my big brother," Elizabeth said. "He and I have been companions since we were both young, even though he is a few years older than me."

"When Elizabeth was brought aboard, not many months after Captain Cleague rescued me, I was ordered to be her servant," he said. "After a time, we became like brother and sister."

"Oh," was all Colin could say. He could not look either of them in the eye, and he knew that his cheeks were red.

"I don't know how you could even think such a thing," Elizabeth said. "On a ship this size, it would lead to nothing but strife, and no good captain would allow it."

"Well, of course," Colin said. "On a navy ship, such a thing would never be allowed. I guess I just thought things worked differently on a pirate ship."

M'nondo chuckled. "Colin, my friend, a ship is a ship, regardless of its mission or origins. In order to operate safely and effectively, there must be discipline. I would imagine that the discipline on a pirate ship is even harsher than it is on your navy ships, but that there is an even greater sense of family."

"From what I've seen on this ship, I cannot disagree with you."

"Now, let me explain what Elizabeth and I were arguing about. I suggested that she have supper with you, just the two of you, because I sense that there is much you need to tell each other. She insisted that I join you, for reasons I do not understand, but she is the captain, so when she ordered me to join you, I had no choice."

It was the most Colin had heard the man utter without stopping since he'd met him, but it explained so much. While he would have liked nothing more than to spend time alone with her, he had a feeling that it would do him no good, and he did like M'nondo's company.

"Well, I think it's a good idea," he said. "I have not really had a very interesting life, so having your story to add to the evening should keep things from becoming boring."

"So, now that we've settled that," Elizabeth said, pouring rum into Colin's glass. "Shall we toast our newfound understanding?"

With the ice broken, and misunderstandings cleared away, the evening proceeded without further incident. The food was delicious, and the rum much easier to take now that his palate was accustomed to it.

When supper was finished except for the dessert, fresh fruit that had been sliced and marinated in white wine for several hours, M'nondo cleared his throat.

"It is time to talk about what is really on your minds," he said. "Elizabeth, you are the host, so it is only proper that you go first."

She looked hesitant, but M'nondo's expression was stern.

"Oh, very well." She turned to Colin. "Let me tell you why I'm so interested in your *Intrepid*." She then proceeded to relate the story of *The Vixen's* first encounter with *Intrepid*, the capture of Captain Cleague, her mentor, and his murder by the *Intrepid's* captain without benefit of a trial. "I promised that day that I would hunt that man down and make him pay for what he did."

"Captain Dangerfield killed your captain? Are you sure?"

"Is your Captain Dangerfield a short, slightly pudgy man with the look of a mad man in his eyes, and scant regard for any other human?"

Colin had to admit that, while her description was brief, it captured Dangerfield perfectly. He nodded.

"Then," she said. "It is him. Now I have a name to add to the face."

M'nondo leaned across the table and looked directly into Colin's eyes. "Now, my friend," he said. "It's your turn."

"Uh, what do you mean?"

Dark brown eyes bored into Colin. He felt as if the man was able to peer into his mind, his very soul. For a long moment, M'nondo simply sat and looked intently at him across the table. Then, he reached across and placed his large, dark hand on Colin's.

"You have something inside you that troubles you, Colin," he said. "Like, Elizabeth, it is a burden that you do not wish to share, but believe me, sharing it will make it easier to bear."

While Colin had no idea what the man's words meant, sometimes, M'nondo's ways were as mysterious as the weather, and about as unpredictable. But, he seemed to be saying that Colin should confide something in Elizabeth, and there was one thing that had preyed on his mind for several days, something that didn't, he felt, affect his oath as a naval officer, but that he'd been reluctant to even think about. He took a deep, calming breath, and looked deep into Elizabeth's eyes.

"Very well," he said. "There is one thing I haven't told you. I think my captain, Captain Dangerfield, wanted me dead. His intent when he had me put in that boat, was for me to die."

Elizabeth and M'nondo looked back at him. Neither said anything for a long time, but there was a half-smile on M'nondo's face. Finally, Elizabeth broke the silence.

"That is your big secret? It was clear to me when we found you that whoever put you in that boat intended for you to die. Why would you be reluctant to tell me that?"

Colin's face felt hot. Why indeed?

"I . . . don't know. Mayhap it's because I didn't want to think that a fellow naval officer could do such a thing, but now that I've had a chance to think about it, I realize that Dangerfield is insane. I thought . . . I must have done something to trigger such madness in him."

"Dangerfield's madness is not your fault, Colin." Elizabeth placed a hand on his arm, sending a warm jolt through his hand and up his arm. "There is no need to blame yourself. But, he must be stopped."

Colin stopped breathing. He held his breath until his chest felt heavy. Slowly, he exhaled, and looked around the table. She was right, of course. Dangerfield was not just a danger to pirates, and one navy lieutenant for whom he'd apparently taken an intense dislike. He was a danger to the whole crew of *Intrepid*, and because he was sailing around the Atlantic on some personal quest rather than carrying out the mission expected of him, a danger to his country as well.

"You are right, of course," he said. "But, he has to be stopped in a way that does not endanger the innocent men aboard that ship."

Elizabeth's eyes blazed. "Those men knew the dangers they faced when they decided to go to sea. For the greater good, Dangerfield *must* be stopped. If it means a few innocents are hurt in the process . . . it is regrettable, but—"

"No!" Colin glared at her. "I am willing to help stop Dangerfield, but only if we do it without unnecessarily harming the crew of *Intrepid*."

Elizabeth matched him, glare for glare. "And, just how would you propose we do that?"

His brow wrinkled in concentration. "I need some time to think about it," he said. "Could I sleep on it, and we can talk of it on the morrow?"

"Until tomorrow, then," she said. Her voice was icy cold and her expression was as rigid as a marble statue. "And, if you have not come up with a plan, we do it my way. One way or another, Dangerfield will be destroyed."

Chapter Seventeen

July 1811, aboard *U.S.S. Intrepid*, Atlantic Ocean, south of Cat Island

Before sailing southeast to search for Lost Island, Dangerfield allowed his executive officer, Comstock, to convince him to sail to the island of Hispaniola, specifically to Haiti and the office of the American minister to the Haitian republic, to let that worthy know that *Intrepid* would be in his area.

In a private conversation with the minister, an avuncular business type who, in his white suit and panama hat, looked like some southern plantation owner rather than a diplomat. Under his ineffective looking exterior, though, he had a sharp mind, and he'd insisted on the *tete a tete*. It was when they were in the privacy of his office that Dangerfield understood why.

"Captain," he said. "I received a dispatch from

Washington earlier this week that pertained to you."

"To me?" Dangerfield kept his expression impassive. "Why would the Department of State be interested in *Intrepid*?"

"The State Department was merely passing along the concerns of the Department of the Navy," the minister said. "They ask that all of our missions in the area report if you are seen, and if you are encountered to inform you that you should return to Boston immediately."

"Did your instructions say why?"

The man smiled. "No, but I assume it to be important. In the same vein, I sense that you have no wish to see those instructions complied with."

"Let us say that this was the way of it," Dangerfield said. "What would one do to achieve that?"

The minister smiled, a look on his face that Dangerfield recognized. "Oh, I think we can come to some satisfactory arrangement," he said.

Four hours later, Dangerfield stood on the quarterdeck of *Intrepid* as its bow rose and fell to the rhythm of the waves, heading east by northeast. Now several gold pieces lighter, thanks to the 'arrangement' he'd made with the minister, he was more than ever determined to find and destroy *The Vixen* and all who sailed aboard her—including one Lieutenant Colin Worth.

He couldn't help but wonder, though, why fleet headquarters wanted his return, and wanted it badly enough to send dispatches to diplomatic posts to be on the lookout for him. The thought didn't stay with him long, though. His mind was consumed with the desire, a compulsion that even he knew bordered on madness, to find and destroy *The Vixen*. It occupied his every waking thought, and haunted his dreams, the only bright spot being when he'd swung his cutlass and that bastard pirate's head had tumbled to the deck.

Soon, he would know that feeling again. He would capture them all, Worth included, and would personally execute the bitch captain and Worth, while leaving the rest to his men to dispatch. Then, he would pile their worthless carcasses in the hold of that black ship and set it aflame, and watch it burn until nothing was left but gray ashes.

The arrival of Comstock, another worthless piece of shit in his estimation, but one who didn't have the guts to argue or disagree with him, broke his reverie. The expression on the man's round, pink face told Dangerfield that he had something urgent on his mind.

"What do you want?" he snapped before Comstock could speak.

"Permission to speak freely, captain?"

Dangerfield held the little man with a steely glare for several heartbeats, enjoying the sight of him squirming and shifting from foot to foot as if his bladder was about to burst—which, he thought wryly, it just might be. When he tired of the game, he smiled.

"What is it you wish to speak about, Mister Comstock?"

"Uh, well, sir . . . when we were in dock at Haiti, I overheard some of the dock workers talking . . . they said there'd been messages about us received there."

Shit, I should have known that if that damn toady of a minister knew about Boston's communique, word would be all over the town. "And, just what was the nature of these mysterious messages?"

"The things overheard, some of the men overheard stuff, too, were confusing, captain. Some people say we were damaged and probably sunk or captured by pirates, but there were some saying that we'd gone rogue . . . that we'd deserted the fleet and were out privateering."

Dangerfield wasn't surprised that the story about the ship was out, nor was he surprised that several versions were circulating. Sailors, he knew, were a garrulous lot, given to embellishing tales in the retelling. He wouldn't have been surprised to hear a version that had them deserting to the English side in their current disagreement.

"Well, Mister Comstock, as you are well aware that we've neither been captured by pirates not deserted our duty, I should think as an officer you'd be able to ignore such fanciful tales as sailors tell."

"B-but, captain, every story had other ships of our navy out looking for us."

Dangerfield's patience was wearing thin. He could only take so much of the man's timidity. Of course, they would. Sailors might make up tales, but they always add a bit of realism, you know this."

Comstock looked somewhat mollified, but not completely.

"Shouldn't we make for one of the Florida or South Carolina ports to let the fleet know we're okay, sir? What if these stories have made their way to the mainland."

Enough! "No, Mister Comstock, we will not allow our mission to be sidetracked by idle gossip. You've been given your directions. I expect this vessel to stay on the course laid out until we find this Lost Island."

"Ab-bout that, sir," he said. "I can't find a Lost Island on any of our navigation charts. Are you sure that it even exists?"

He had noticed that himself, but inside, Dangerfield was certain that the old man had told the truth. There *was* a Lost Island, and there he would find and finish *The Vixen.*

"I'm sure, lieutenant. This island, you must remember is a pirate lair, and it's small, or so I'm told, so it's hardly surprising it wouldn't appear on any of our charts. Many of the smaller islands in the Caribbean, some no more than a few hundred yards long, and merely strips of sand that are above water except during gales, don't appear on our maps." His voice began to rise, and spittle bubbled from the sides of his mouth. "We will not alter our course, and we are not returning to the mainland until our mission is completed. Do. I. Make. Myself. Clear?"

Comstock had gone pale and was trembling. He took two steps back. "Aye, sir, clear, sir. We stay on our course."

He turned and fled toward the helm as if he was being pursued by the devil.

Charles Ray

Chapter Eighteen

July 1811, *The Vixen* at Lost Island

It was near on to sunset when *The Vixen* came within sight of Lost Island. Elizabeth had had them sail in a loop north of the island, and they now approached it from the east. From five miles away, with the sun behind it, it was little more than a vague smudge on the horizon, a dark shape that might have been ignored by the unwary as a trick of the fading light. At dusk, with the last of the light when the sun goes down, it would have been missed entirely. It didn't take on the appearance of an island until they were a mile offshore, and then only because of the distinct shapes of palm trees silhouetted by the setting sun.

Kidney-shaped, Lost Island was a mile long along the north-south axis, and a quarter mile wide at its widest. At its highest point, near the center, it was about eight feet above sea level, and was ringed by a twenty-foot deep beach of pure white sand. At the southeast end, which just happened to be the widest point of the island, there was a concavity that was wide enough at the mouth for a vessel the size of *The Vixen* to enter, which widened out into a one-hundred-meter wide anchorage, which was ringed by fifty-foot-tall palm trees that effectively concealed any ship anchored there.

The helmsman, under Garcia's experienced guidance, steered the ship through the opening, bringing her to a smooth stop at the far end of the concave harbor where the anchor was dropped. At this end, a long jetty, constructed from palm logs, jutted out into the water. It was next to this structure that they dropped anchor and came to rest.

Getting down to the jetty involved dropping rope ladders over the side and climbing down ten feet. The ladders were left in place to enable them to reboard, and two of the crew were left to stand watch and sound the alarm if any other vessel should enter their hidden harbor.

Elizabeth, followed by Colin, M'nondo, Garcia, and the rest of the crew, set out for a break in the line of palm trees, and turned north on a well-worn trail. They walked, Colin estimated, for about half a mile through the thick jungle, surrounded by dark shapes and strange sounds, before coming to a large clearing that contained several large buildings with roofs of palm thatching. The buildings were in a rough circle like an Iroquois village, with the largest in the center. What surprised Colin as they approached was the flickering spots of illumination he could see on several of the farther buildings and through the windows of the nearest.

Fires were burning. He was instantly on alert, but his companions walked casually along as if nothing was amiss. Just ahead of him, he noted that Elizabeth had a swing in her step, which made her hips sway provocatively, and when she half turned, in the fading light, he could see that she was smiling.

When they passed between two of the buildings and entered the central area, he saw that he'd indeed been right. There were several fires burning, and all were being attended by the strangest assemblage of humanity he'd ever seen.

There were men, women, and children. The children were of all ages, the women ranged from just entering childbearing age to some who looked like grandmothers, while most of the men were old, except for a few younger looking men who were missing an arm or leg, and one who appeared to be blind, as he was being led around by a small child.

The children, except for the child guiding the blind man, were playing, as children are wont to do. The men were cutting wood or sitting around in small conversation groups. The women, just like the women Colin had seen in some of the villages near Tripoli during his brief time there, were all at work; doing laundry, tending the fire, fetching water from a well near the center of the buildings, cooking, or seeing to the children who were too young to play on their own.

He stopped as they entered the central area, his mouth agape.

"Welcome to the village of the lost," Elizabeth said.

"Who are these people?" Colin asked.

Hands on her hips, Elizabeth surveyed the busy

scene. A few people nearest them briefly paused in what they were doing to wave or nod, but most of the villagers continued with whatever they were doing as if an armed group entering their midst at dusk was a common occurrence.

"These," she said. "Are the families of my crew, as well as former crew members who were too severely injured to continue going to sea. This is our home."

"What do you call this place?"

She squinted at him. "The island is called Lost Island, mainly because it's not on any maps. We just call it home."

From where he stood, Colin could now see that the northern arc of the circle of houses was quite a bit thicker than its southern counterpart. While that line of huts was only one building thick, to the north, he could see paths radiating northward, with modest huts lining them. A quick mental calculation told him the population of this little settlement was about two hundred people.

"How do you survive here? How long has this place been here?" He had so many questions.

Elizabeth held a hand up to stop the flow of words. "You ask many questions, Colin. Many, most will be answered in time. For now, we've had a long and arduous voyage. I don't know about you, but I'm tired and need rest."

"Where will I, your prisoner, be staying?"

She smiled at him, that smile that caused warm feelings in his chest.

"I think, in order to keep an eye on you, I'll have you stay with me." She pointed to the large house in the center. "I have more than enough room. Right now, only M'nondo and I occupy that rambling structure."

Diego Garcia, who had been trailing behind them, keeping an eye on Colin, stepped forward, his face contorted in an angry frown.

"Captain, I do not think it is a good idea for you to keep the prisoner in your house. You should let me lock him on one of the empty buildings near the stock pens and post guards. You might be in danger having him so near."

"Your concern for my welfare, is touching, Diego," she said. "But, I believe I'm quite capable of taking care of myself. Besides, I have M'nondo with me." She turned and smiled at Colin. "And, our . . . prisoner has promised not to try anything, so I will take his word as the word of an officer and a gentleman." He returned her smile and bowed. "So, you see, Diego, you worry for naught. As for putting him under guard, for what reason. He doesn't even know where he is, and should he try to escape, there are miles of shark-infested water between here and the nearest land."

"I still think you should—"

"Enough, Diego," she said. "I've made my decision, so go on to your house and kiss your wife and children."

Garcia glared at her, his chest puffed out. His lips moved as if he wanted to say something. Elizabeth stood in a relaxed pose, her hand resting lightly on her sword. Finally, he snorted air through his nostrils like an angry bull and stormed past them.

"I get the distinct impression that Mr. Garcia does not like me," Colin said.

"Diego doesn't like many people, including me," she said.

"But, I thought everyone liked you. I sense that your crew respects you highly."

"Diego's the exception. When John . . . Captain Cleague, died, Diego, who had finagled his way up to the first officer position, assumed that he would take over as captain. When M'nondo and the other men proposed that I do it instead, he was devastated. He has never forgiven me for *stealing* the position from him."

"That's insane. If he was captain material, the men would have chosen him. Instead, they chose you, so the way I see it the job was never his, so how could you steal from him something he never possessed?"

"You sound like M'nondo," she said. "That, of course, makes no difference to Diego. I always watch my back when he's around, and I'd advise you to do the same."

'What do you advise him?" M'nondo asked. The man had approached them so silently, Colin felt like jumping out of his skin. *I so would hate to have him decide that I was his enemy.*

"We were just talking about Diego's desire to replace me as captain," Elizabeth said.

"That will never happen as long as I draw breath," M'nondo said.

"Garcia doesn't strike me as qualified to be captain," Colin offered.

M'nondo nodded. "You are right. The men barely tolerate him as first officer, and then only because they always have the captain to turn to. If he became captain, there would soon be a mutiny."

That reminded Colin so much of his former commander. And he smiled as he realized that he was not thinking of Dangerfield as his *former* commander, while he had no problems thinking of Elizabeth as his current captain—and, if fate continued to smile upon him, maybe even something more.

"Well," he said. "We'll just have to make sure he never becomes captain. Can't have mutiny, now can we."

M'nondo eyed him strangely, and when he seemed to decide that Colin was joking, or at least partly joking, he smiled that enigmatic, half smile that was a mere upward twitching of the ends of his lips.

"Just so. Now, though, I think we should move on to the house and get some food and rest."

The house proved to be as spacious as Elizabeth had indicated. A palm-frond-covered verandah ran completely around the building. The floors of the verandah were raised off the ground, as was the rest of the house, allowing air currents to flow beneath it. Inside the main entrance it had a large parlor with a mishmash of furniture, including pieces that had obviously taken from ships the pirates had raided, and local furniture carved from the woods of the surrounding jungle, and mats woven from the grasses that grew in profusion around the huts. Despite its haphazard appearance, it had a warm and inviting ambience. Beyond the parlor was a dining room with a wooden table that looked like it had been carved from a single piece of wood. It was long and wide enough to seat twelve people comfortably, and there were twelve chairs, carved from the same wood, arranged around it. To the left of the dining room was the kitchen and larder, which was presided over by a matronly, nut brown woman with a gap-toothed smile, who hugged

Elizabeth like a returning prodigal child, and smiled and bobbed her head at Colin and M'nondo as she babbled about her Lizzie finally come home. Elizabeth introduced her to Colin as Estrella, the cook. Another woman who, except for her pale skin looked like Estrella's sister, was introduced as Maria, the maid. She said nothing, just smiled, and hugged Elizabeth. When Colin smiled and bowed at her, her pale face turned red and she fled into the pantry. Estrella shooed them from the kitchen with the promise that she would prepare a special welcome feast. Elizabeth asked M'nondo to show Colin the rest of the house and his room, while she went and got herself cleaned up for supper.

The rest of the house consisted of four bedrooms, two on each side of a wide hallway, each with its own bath chamber with a white porcelain claw foot tub. Pumps had been constructed in each, allowing the occupant to pump water from an underground source directly into a large tub that sat on a brick platform, that M'nondo informed him was an oven for heating bath water. Colin had never conceived of such a thing—water pumped inside the house—how convenient it would be during Boston's frigid winters not to have to go outside to fetch water.

Elizabeth's chambers were on the left at the end of the hallway containing the bedrooms, and M'nondo had his own quarters directly across from her. He assigned Colin the chamber adjacent to Elizabeth's.

"You will find clothing inside that will probably fit you," he said. "You should clean for dinner."

"Would there perhaps be a razor, so that I can shave," Colin said, fingering the dark growth that now covered the lower part of his face.

"I would let it grow if it was me," M'nondo said. "Having a beard might come in handy in the days to come."

Again, with the cryptic conversation, Colin thought. But, on the other hand, it would be nice not having to hack at his face every day.

"Very well, I'll just wash the stink off and leave the beard."

An hour later, with the scum and stink of many days aboard ship scrubbed from every crevice of his body, his hair and beard lathered and squeezed until he was sure they were free of any lice or other vermin that might have taken up residence, and dressed in a pair of brown cotton breeches and an ivory colored silk shirt with a ruffled collar that, as M'nondo had said, fit him as if they'd been tailored especially for him, Colin pulled on his boots, which had been magically polished after he left them outside his bedchamber door while he bathed. *I could truly become accustomed to living like this.*

Tantalizing aromas coming from the vicinity of the dining room drew his attention in that direction until he heard Elizabeth's door open behind him. When he turned, his mouth dropped open and his eyes went round like saucers. He stood there, gaping at her, hearing only the thud of his heart beating against his chest.

She wore a pale lemon colored dress, off the shoulders, with ruffles all around, that only accented the perfect roundness of her ivory breasts peeking over the edge of the fabric. As she moved toward him, the silk fabric made a rustling sound as it brushed against her body, whose outline he could clearly see.

"Careful, Colin," she said in a throaty voice. If you close your mouth too fast right now, you'll bite your tongue off."

"Uh, er, I'm sorry. It's just that you are . . . the most beautiful woman I've ever seen."

She curtsied. "Why, think you, kind sir."

He wanted to say more, but was afraid that if he tried to speak he would make a fool of himself. He was saved by M'nondo exiting his room across from Elizabeth's. The big African was dressed in dark brown pants that hugged his muscular legs and backside, and a white shirt, open at the throat, displaying his muscular chest, which gleamed under the candles set in sconces high up on the walls.

"You two look almost presentable," he said. "Shall we go eat. I'm starved."

"So am I," Elizabeth said.

Nodding, Colin silently agreed. Elizabeth maneuvered herself between the two men and linked her arms through theirs.

Estrella, with Maria peeking from behind her, met them at the entrance to the dining room. She ushered Elizabeth to the head of the long table. Three places had been set, one at the head, and one to either side. Estrella left Colin and M'nondo to sort their own seating out as she held the chair for Elizabeth. M'nondo motioned at the chair to Elizabeth's right, indicating that Colin should sit there. Colin had a feeling that this was his usual place, but for some reason he was ceding it on this evening. He shrugged and, as soon as Elizabeth was seated, took his chair.

Only then did he look at the table, and he gaped in

awe. Estrella had promised a special feast, and she had been true to her word.

The table, laden with a large ham festooned with slices of some yellow fruit Colin didn't recognize, several bowls of colorful vegetables, and platters of fruits and nuts. Brown loaves of bread and rolls were stacked in a platter in front of Elizabeth's place, and to her right was a silver bucket in which rested a large bottle of white wine. On the table, next to the white wine was also a carafe of red wine. It looked like the table the sheik who joined the Americans in their mission to overthrow the Bey of Tripoli had set for the banquet he hosted on the eve of their departure. The only thing missing was the half-naked, but veiled, dancing girls and the whole roast lamb that occupied the center of the sheik's table. The other difference was there were dark wood, high backed chairs at this table, while at the sheik's palace, they'd reclined on cushions a few inches off the floor and eaten with their hands.

The various aromas coming from the food made Colin's mouth water, and his stomach growled loud enough to startle Elizabeth. M'nondo laughed, and rubbed his own stomach.

"I know how you feel, my friend," he said. "It is only years of discipline that keeps my belly from doing the same thing."

"Well, don't stand on ceremony, dig in," Elizabeth said, and with an unladylike maneuver, she picked up her knife and speared a piece of meat.

They ate with gusto, but in relative silence, until Estrella and Maria had cleared the table and brought out the dessert, a concoction of fresh pineapple, sprigs of mint, and thick cream that melted on Colin's tongue.

Elizabeth ate two spoons full of the *crema del fruta*, as Estrella called it, and then put her spoon down beside the bowl and leaned forward, fixing Colin with an intent gaze.

"Have you thought how we're going to get this Captain Dangerfield?" she asked.

Colin ate another spoonful of the creamed fruit, and then put his own spoon down.

"I said I would think on it and tell you tomorrow," he said. "But, as it happens, I have thought of a way to get him."

"Well, I'm listening."

Colin stabbed at the linen table covering with his finger. "The first thing I want you to understand, though, is that I will *not* do anything to bring harm to the rest of the *Intrepid's* crew. The target is Captain Dangerfield and *only* Captain Dangerfield."

She frowned, but nodded. "As long as you can assure me that Dangerfield will pay for his sins, I suppose I can accept that."

M'nondo nodded approvingly at Colin.

He then proceeded to outline the plan that had begun forming in his mind during the voyage, and had developed while he was luxuriating in the warm, soapy water of his bath. If it worked, Beauregard Dangerfield would get what his misdeeds had earned him, Colin's former shipmates would come to no real harm, and . . . well, he hadn't thought much beyond getting revenge on Dangerfield without hurting innocent people.

When he'd finished outlining his plan, Elizabeth stared at him for a long time, her expression unreadable. Then, suddenly, she began laughing.

Colin looked puzzled.

When she'd recovered, she patted his hand. "You know, Colin Worth, you have the soul of a pirate. I have never before heard such an audacious plan, but I do think that it might work. I would love to see Dangerfield's head on a platter, but given the nature of the man, your plan delivers worse punishment. What do you think, elder brother?"

M'nondo nodded and smiled. There was a twinkle in his dark eyes.

"I think it might work," he said.

"That settles it." Elizabeth slapped the table. "If this works as you say, Colin, I will drop you at a friendly port so that you can make your way back to America. Does that sound fair?"

"More than fair, captain," Colin replied.

He should felt happy at the outcome and the prospect of eventual freedom. Why, then, he wondered, did he feel sad?

Charles Ray

Chapter Nineteen

The three of them sat up very late, sipping wine and refining Colin's plan. Colin had no idea what time it was when he finally stumbled into bed.

The next morning, he was awakened by the sound of a cock crowing. Rubbing his eyes, he took a moment to realize where he was. The smooth sheet beneath his body and the silky covering he had pulled up to his chin felt better than any bedclothes in any bed in which he'd ever slept. He had to blink to remind himself that he was in a pirate's lair, a long way from home, and his eventual return to the life he knew depended upon the success of a hair-rained scheme, that in the light of morning, he was beginning to have doubts about.

After washing his face and dressing, he ventured out into the hallway. The house was ghostly silent, with only the sound of his boots on the wooden floor to keep him company as he made his way toward the dining room.

The dining room was empty, but he heard the muted sounds of conversation coming from the kitchen. In the kitchen, he saw Elizabeth sitting at the work table with a large mug of coffee cupped in her hands, Estrella was at the stove stirring something in a large pot with a big wooden spoon, and Maria was at the sink washing dishes. All heads turned as he entered.

"Welcome back to the land of the living," Elizabeth said.

"Coffee's in the pot on the counter," Estrella said, pointing to a long wooden counter with her free hand. "Maria, why don't you pour Mr. Colin a cup of coffee."

The shy little woman took her soapy hands from the water and dried them on her skirt. She scuttled across the room and took a mug similar to the one Elizabeth was holding from a shelf over the counter and filled it with the dark brew. She brought it to the table, put it across from Elizabeth and, with her head bowed and her gaze averted, returned to the sink.

Colin sank into the chair and picked up the mug. The woody aroma hit his nose, instantly wiping the last remnants of sleepiness from his head. He took a tentative sip and sighed.

"Ah, I needed that."

"You don't take honey in your coffee?" Elizabeth stared at him over the rim of her mug.

"Sometimes, but after the amount we drank last night, I find it best to take my coffee straight in the morning. It helps to get my mind working and my body moving."

"Well, you'd better have a second cup," she said.

"You'll need to be alert this morning."

"Oh? Why?"

"The people understand why we ignored them last night, arriving so late after such a long and arduous voyage. But, they're insisting on having a welcome ceremony this morning."

Colin snatched his mug up and took a much longer swallow, even though it scorched his lips and tongue. "Dare I ask why I need to be alert?"

As Elizabeth was giving him a look that made him rub at his beard to make sure he hadn't left soap in it, M'nondo entered the kitchen.

"You need to be alert and in good spirits, my friend," he said as he poured himself a mug of coffee, ignoring the scowl Maria gave him. "Because, you are the guest of honor. We have not had a new arrival on Lost Island for . . . well, a long time, and every woman will want to dance with you."

Elizabeth laughed at Colin's look of shock.

"Do you not have such customs in Boston?" she asked.

Colin took another gulp of coffee, and a deep breath. "I wouldn't know," he said. "I wasn't exactly in that strata of society in Boston. My father was a merchant, and in our neighborhood, we didn't have formal ceremonies, other than weddings and funerals. I left home before I was old enough to dance at weddings, and there was no dancing at funerals."

Elizabeth put her mug down, and stared at him. Even though she smiled, her eyes were wide with shock.

"Don't tell me that a naval officer and gentleman has never danced."

"Very well, I won't tell you." He returned her smile. "I *will* tell you that I do not know how to dance."

M'nondo sat at the table with Elizabeth between him and Colin. He took a sip of coffee and smacked his lips.

"It will not matter," he said. "Before an hour has passed everyone will be drunk and when drunk everyone can dance."

"I seriously doubt that I would ever be able to get that drunk. Mayhap it would be best if I did not go."

Maria dropped the dish she was washing. Estrella banged the wooden spoon into the pot and turned, glaring at him. Elizabeth and M'nondo only smiled.

"As the guest of honor," Elizabeth said. "Your presence is not optional." Even though she was smiling, Colin heard the note of command in her voice. "So, finish your coffee, the people await us in the square."

After finishing his coffee, taking as much time as he could, which elicited frowns from Elizabeth and a sly grin from M'nondo, he took a deep breath and put his empty mug on the table.

"Very well, the condemned man has finished his last meal," he said. "Let the execution begin."

And, in truth, as he marched through the house and out onto the verandah between M'nondo on his left and Elizabeth on his right, he felt like a man on the way to the gallows.

When they emerged into the blazing sunlight reflecting off the light earth, he was momentarily blinded. When his vision cleared, and he saw what awaited, he wished that he'd gone blind.

It looked as if every person on the island had

crowded into the open space in front of the house. A large wooden table laden with all manner of food, including a whole roast pig, had been set up about twenty feet from the edge of the verandah, and a large fire, over which another pig roasted, sat off to the left. On a smaller table on the right were row upon row of bottles of vari-colored liquids, ranging from deep brown to red to green to clear. He'd never seen so much liquor even in some of the bigger taverns he'd frequented with his shipmates. The population of Lost Island was lined up in deep rows to either side of the tables, all looking up at the verandah. When he walked down the steps, loud cheering erupted. The sound set Colin's ears to ringing, and seemed to go on forever until Elizabeth raised her right hand. Then, there was a silence so abrupt that, until he heard the raucous call of a bird in the nearby jungle, Colin thought he'd been struck deaf.

"Friends," Elizabeth said in a voice that carried across the crowd. "Thank you for such a warm welcome. Allow me to present our guest of honor, Colin Worth, late of Boston."

More cheers as the front rows pushed forward, men offering to shake his hand, and women hugging and kissing him—some even thrusting their pelvises at him. Even those children who could walk unaided came up to bid him welcome.

A wizened old man, the oldest man Colin had ever seen, with a completely bald, liver-spotted skull and sunken chest, stepped up and shooed the last of the well-wishers away.

In a voice that was surprisingly resonant and strong in one looking so infirm, he said, "Colin Worth of Boston, welcome to Lost Island. What's ours is yours." He clapped his gnarled hands. "Let the feast begin."

And, begin it did. Colin had food, drink, and offers to warm his bed thrust at him from all sides. The first two he readily accepted, and found all to his liking, although some of the liquor burned like blazes at the first swallow, the third, he diplomatically avoided by claiming to be still fatigued from the long sea voyage. Out of the corner of his eye he could see both Elizabeth and M'nondo enjoying his discomfort.

Just when he thought he could not eat another bite, or drink another drop, a group of men began setting up off to the side. One man carried a scratched violin, so even though he didn't recognize the other instruments, one of which looked like a corrugated board that women used to scrub clothes, he assumed them to be the music for the dancing. And, he was right.

Despite the condition of the violin and the strange combination of other instruments, the music was harmonious, and everyone began dancing. A woman about Colin's age, with breasts that threatened to burst from the blouse she wore, grabbed his hand and dragged him to the middle of the gyrating mob. She began twirling him around as she wiggled her hips and breasts, and urging him to copy her motions. A bit tipsy from the liquor, and unsure of the consequences of refusing, he tried his best, which delighted the crowd. During the next hour, he thought he must have danced with every woman there except Elizabeth. He was near the point of exhaustion, but, to his surprise, he was enjoying every minute of it.

He didn't notice Diego Garcia, standing at the edge of the crowd, not participating in the merrymaking. He merely glared at Colin.

When the musicians began to show signs of fatigue, the old man stood and bowed to Elizabeth.

"Cap'n Parker," he said. "With your permission, I will call a halt to the festivities. I be thinking you have business to attend to."

Elizabeth bowed. "Thank you, Jack. We have been most honored by all you and your people have done, but you're correct. There is business that must be attended to."

She turned and started back into the house. M'nondo stood and motioned for Colin to follow, which he was most happy to do. Extricating himself from the grasp of a sinuous blonde who had been refusing to believe that he didn't want her, he mumbled an apology, "Business first, fun later," and nearly ran for the verandah.

He followed M'nondo through the living room to the dining room, where they found Elizabeth seated at the head of the table. To her right, an angry scowl on his face, sat Diego Garcia.

"Why is he here?" he asked. "This business does not concern him."

"On the contrary, Diego," Elizabeth said. "It very much does concern him. In fact, he will be the one who plans our next operation."

Garcia's face went completely red. He stood and slammed his hands on the table.

"I cannot agree with that, captain." Spittle flew from his mouth. "This man is an outsider, and a naval officer at that. He does not belong here."

Elizabeth calmly returned his gaze. To her right, a sandy-haired man stiffened in his chair. Colin noticed that M'nondo's hand had shifted to his sword, and he wished that they'd returned his weapons.

"Sit down, Diego," Elizabeth said quietly.

"I'm sorry, captain," he said, his cheeks puffing in and out. "But, I think you are making a terrible mistake. You should not involve this man . . . I cannot agree with this. He must leave, immediately."

Her expression turned icy, except for the fire in her eyes. Colin almost felt sorry for Garcia, who apparently didn't realize that he'd crossed a line with her, a line that he might not be able to back away from.

"And, just when did you become the master of my house, the master of *The Vixen*." Her words were slow and measured like the ticking of a clock, and every word dripped with menace.

"I know that *you* are the captain," he said. "But, as your first officer, it is my duty to inform you when you are making a mistake."

"Your concern is noted. Now, sit down so that we can continue with this discussion."

Garcia looked as if he would refuse. But, Elizabeth's unblinking look must have gotten past the barriers in his anger-infected brain. He took a deep breath and sat, but he folded his arms across his chest and glared at Colin as he and M'nondo took seats at the end of the table, with Colin facing Elizabeth.

"Now, Lieutenant Worth," she said. "Tell us your plan to defeat *Intrepid*."

Perhaps the dancing had shaken up his brain and shaken loose the cobwebs that had impeded his thinking, but during the welcome celebration, as Colin saw the flickering torches set in large wooden urns around the square as he danced, an idea had come to him, a revolutionary idea that he wasn't sure was completely sane. But, the look from Elizabeth, an encouraging nod from M'nondo, and most importantly, the disdainful stare from Garcia, made him speak.

"You are aware, I'm sure, that fighting at night is not something most ships are good at," he said. "In fact, most captains go out of their way to avoid it if at all possible."

"For good reason," the sandy haired man said. "You can't see shit at night, so, unless you are right on top of your target, you waste shot."

"Right, and I imagine that your ship runs dark at night . . . for security reasons?"

Everyone but Garcia laughed. He merely snorted.

Colin continued, "What if there was a way to light up the ship you wish to target?"

"Oh sure," the man said. "You just light enough lanterns, but they mostly just light you up and make it easier for your enemy's cannons to blast you."

"Ah, but there is a way to avoid that," Colin said. "Many years ago, in Philadelphia, Mr. Ben Franklin experimented with glass when he was trying to build lenses to aid his vision, and a few years ago, in Europe, this Frenchman, Count Alessandro Volta invented something he called a voltaic pile." At the confused looks around the table, he hastily explained. "This voltaic pile is a kind of device that creates power, power that can create light. If we can get some of these, and the proper materials, I believe I can construct a device that will cast light over an area upon command."

Mouths dropped open and eyes grew round, except for Elizabeth, who eyed him through narrow slits.

"It would take months, if not years, to construct such a device," she said.

"Captain, you are not taking his ravings seriously, are you?" Garcia said.

"I happen to know that there is a man in the capital of the Bahamas who can construct a voltaic pile for us," Colin said. "I heard people speak of him in Boston. He is a friend of Count Volta who fell out of favor with Napoleon, and fled to the islands to avoid prison."

Her head tilted to the side, and she tapped a cheekbone with her finger.

"What else will you need?"

"I need a lens, as large as possible, wood, metal and fittings. If I could go to the capital, I should be able to purchase what I need in a day, and have the device ready in . . . a week?"

"Captain, Elizabeth," Garcia roared. "I will not allow you to do this."

She rounded on him, her eyes blazing with fury. "You will not allow *me*? Since when did *you* have the authority to allow or deny me anything? I have decided. You are either with us in this, or you're not. It's your decision, but, Diego, think carefully before you speak."

The man gulped, and his Adam's apple bobbed up and down. Colin had no problem figuring out his alternative to joining the mission.

Finally, Garcia nodded submissively. "Very well, captain," he said. "I will obey your orders. But I just want it known by all here, that I think this is unwise."

Colin watched the man's eyes as he spoke, and didn't believe a word he'd said.

Charles Ray

Chapter Twenty

July 1811, Nassau, New Providence Island, Bahamas

After approving Colin's plan, in principle, Elizabeth had ordered the crew to prepare immediately to set sail for Nassau. Although something of a colonial backwater for the British Empire, the town was a trading center for all manner of goods from Europe as well as the American mainland. It was rumored that with the appropriate amount of gold, one could buy just about anything there, including slaves, despite the English ban on the slave trade. The English colonial authorities, usually officials in bad favor with the ministry in London and thus posted to a second-rate colonial posting as punishment, had a tendency to look the other way and bide their time until there was a change in ministers, or their sins were forgiven.

The *laissez faire* attitude notwithstanding, she took

no chances, Colin notices. Instead of sailing on a direct northwest route, she took an extra day and sailed east first, and then north, coming in from the northwest, on the off chance that *Intrepid's* captain was foolhardy enough to be lying in wait for them in waters controlled by the English fleet. For that matter, it was to avoid that same fleet as well.

As an added precaution, rather than sail into the main harbor, she dropped anchor in a protected cove on the north side of the island and went ashore, where they paid locals to convey Elizabeth, Colin, M'nondo, Garcia, Rodriguez, and Devereux by donkey cart into the city itself. Once there, she sent Garcia, Rodriquez, and Devereux on an errand to purchase gunpowder and extra fuses for the cannons; Colin and M'nondo to procure the items and equipment Colin needed to build his magic lantern, and excused herself to 'take care of some personal business.'

Colin and M'nondo found a shop in a back alley off a back street in the meanest part of the city. A sunbaked adobe building with a faded green clay tile roof, it was piled high with the oddest assortment of merchandise Colin had ever seen. The proprietor, a rail-thin Chinese of indeterminant age, with a hunch back and a wandering left eye, welcomed them in British-accented English when they entered the dimly lit establishment.

"Welcome gentle sirs," he said, bowing low. "How may I be of service to you today?"

Colin described what he wanted, expecting the old man to say he either didn't have them, or didn't know what they were, and was pleasantly surprised when the man asked him to wait a moment, and disappeared into a room at the rear of the store. He was back in about five minutes, his arms full of a mass of boxes, wires and tubes, which he placed carefully on the dust-laden counter.

Colin inspected the merchandise, taking special care when handling the carbon rods, small cylinders slightly smaller around than a cigar, and a bit longer. He then counted to make sure there were enough zinc and copper cylinders and felt cloth. Next, he checked the two lenses he'd asked for, each about eighteen inches in diameter. He would have preferred something larger, but considering that the devices he planned to build existed only in his mind, he'd decided to stick with the smaller size. He finally nodded when he noticed that there appeared to be enough copper wire and small iron plates. The wood he would need he could get from the jungle.

M'nondo, he noticed, looked at him in puzzled silence.

"What's the matter, my friend?" he asked the dark man. "You seem troubled."

"I know you said you were going to build a lantern that we could use to illuminate a ship at night," he said. "But, I don't understand how any of these things can be used to do it. I see no wicks, nor a container for the oil."

Colin smiled and patted the man's shoulder. He chose his words carefully, because he knew that what he was about to say would sound strange indeed.

"These are the lantern's wicks," he said, pointing at the carbon rods. "as for the fuel, remember I told you about Count Volta's voltaic pile?"

"Oh yes, you said it created . . . electric power, like

lightning, but what does that have to do with making a lantern?"

"I'm going to send the power from the pile through the carbon rods," Colin said. "It will heat them and cause them to glow."

The Chinese merchant, standing silently by until then, chuckled. "Ah so, I see you have heard about Sir Humphrey Davis's experiments in generating light from the count's little invention."

Surprised, Colin turned to stare at the little man. "You know about Davis's electric lamp?"

The man bowed his head slightly. "Indeed. A man recently arrived from London told me about it. I do hope he perfects it. It would be so much better to light my home with such a device than with smelly, dangerous candles or torches. So, you plan to build two lanterns, do you? What will you do with the lenses?"

Colin thought it best that his true plan be restricted to as few people as possible. Not that he didn't trust the old man, but people talk.

"Oh, I want to try and construct a large spyglass, for use on board my ship."

The way the old man's brow wrinkled, Colin knew he hadn't believed that explanation, but he didn't pursue it further. Thankful that it probably wasn't all that unusual for buyers to have hidden motives for their purchases, he paid the rather exorbitant amount of gold the merchant quoted, took his purchases and he and M'nondo departed.

They met up with Garcia, Devereux and Rodrigues at a tavern called *Cock's Nest*, a rowdy, noisy place filled with rough looking men and overly-painted local women, that smelled like a combination of the bottom of an empty ale barrel left in the sun too long, and a chamber pot that hasn't been emptied in days. They found their three shipmates seated at a rough-hewn wooden table in the back corner of the place, that had just enough space for Colin, M'nondo and Colin's purchases.

A serving girl, her breasts spilled partially from the front of her ale-stained blouse, came to the table immediately.

"Whot'll it be, gents?" She swayed her shoulders, causing her breasts to spill further, as if to remind them that ale wasn't the only thing on offer.

Colin looked at M'nondo, who was studiously avoiding staring at the woman's assets.

"If we do not order a drink, they will not be happy," M'nondo said. "The captain should be along shortly, so I think one drink would be in order."

"Two ales," Colin said to the woman.

"Comin' right up, sweets," she said, and with another swing of her large breasts, she turned and walked away, swinging her hips in an exaggerated motion.

"Now, that is one tail I like to pluck," Rodriguez said.

"I am in total *accord*," Devereux said. "But, I don't think we have enough gold to afford that."

Everyone but Garcia laughed, although M'nondo's laugh seemed forced. Garcia just sat there scowling at Colin.

Uncomfortable with his scrutiny, but now wanting to start trouble, Colin ignored him. When the ale came, he focused his attention to the cloudy liquid in a mug that looked as if it could have used a good washing. But, when he took a sip, he found it not unpleasant.

"So, Lieutenant Worth," Garcia said. "What do you have in your parcel there? Did you find enough toys to waste the captain's gold on?"

M'nondo looked up, frowning. "Diego," he said in a harsh whisper. "We should not be using names or ranks here. Who knows who might overhear."

Garcia leaned forward, a malicious smile on his face. When he spoke, his voice was low, but laden with menace.

"Ah yes, the English might not be too happy if they knew an American naval officer was in their midst."

"That will be enough, Diego," M'nondo said. "You know the captain's orders. Now, drink your ale and stop being an ass."

Colin hoped the sting in M'nondo's rebuke would be enough, but the glint in Garcia's eyes told him otherwise.

"I'll wager they'd pay a fancy price for him, d'ya think?" he said.

M'nondo started to rise, his hands clenched into fists, but Colin put a hand on his shoulder.

"Now, look here, Garcia," he said. "I know you don't like me. If you must know, I'm not too fond of you either. But, you're putting your shipmates in danger with such talk, and your captain as well. So, why don't you hold your grudge until we're back on Lost Island."

"Are you challenging me, fancy boy?"

Colin laughed. "If you mean to a duel, no. You're not worthy of such. If you want to fight, though, back on Lost Island, I'll be glad to oblige you."

"So, you're a coward, are you?"

"Just what's that supposed to mean?"

"If you were a man, you'd fight me now."

"Dammit, man," Colin said. "I just told you, you'd be endangering the mission. Now, let it drop."

Garcia's face was red, and his eyes were wild. Colin wondered if he'd been ingesting something stronger than ale, like opium, perhaps. He knew that there were some who brought the drug from Cathay, as China was known to many, and he'd heard tales of it making men do incredibly stupid things. Until now, though, he'd not seen any of Elizabeth's crew take anything stronger than rum, and he seriously doubted that she'd countenance them addling their brains with anything else. Whatever the cause, the man was clearly spoiling for a fight.

"If you had any *cojones*, you *puta*, you would fight me here and now."

Colin didn't understand the Spanish words, but Rodriguez clearly did. He whirled on Garcia, his face angry. "Diego, there is no call for this. *El capitan* trusts Colin, and so should you. Do not forget, he fought with us."

The two men were sitting almost nose to nose, red-faced and glaring.

"So, you take the side of this *perro* over me, your shipmate?"

"No, Diego, I do not take sides, but Colin is right, you are acting *stupido*."

"You call me stupid." Spittle flew from Garcia's mouth. "When I finish with him, I will gut you like the pig you are." Shoving Devereux aside, he stepped over his legs and stood next to the table. "I will be outside, Worth. If you are a man, you will meet me there. We settle this once and for all."

He spun on his heels and headed to the rear of the establishment, disappearing through a door next to the bar.

"What the hell is that all about?" Colin asked.

"I think Diego fears that you are winning more than the captain's confidence," M'nondo said. He had a sad look on his face. "For a long time, even though he lusts for the captain's job, he lusts even more for her, but she does not return his feelings."

"B-but, I don't want to fight him. I'm not that kind of fighter. What do I do?"

"I am afraid, Colin, that you have no choice," Rodriguez said. "If you do not fight him, he will make a big thing of it with the rest of the crew. Most will not pay attention, but some will, and that will make it difficult for you to do what you must do for the captain. On the other hand, knowing Diego, if you do not fight him, he might just wait until you are not looking and stick a knife in your back."

Colin looked to M'nondo for help.

"I fear he is right. You must fight him."

"B-but, I don't have a knife, or any other weapon," Colin said.

"That is not a problem," Devereux said. He pulled a knife with a nine-inch blade from his belt and slid it across the table.

Sighing, he picked the knife up, then picked up his package and stood. The others followed.

"Well," he said. "Let's get this over with."

No one paid them any attention as they made their way to the back of the room. No one tried to stop them when they exited through the back door.

Garcia was waiting, standing near a pile of fetid, foul-smelling garbage, picking his fingernails with the tip of his knife.

"Well, well," he said. "So, you have some *cajones* after all. I will cut them off after you are dead, and have them mounted on my wall."

Colin handed his package to M'nondo, and turned to Garcia. "Why am I not surprised that you would be interested in such things."

Garcia, swaying and unsteady on his feet, looked confused.

"You trying to insult me, *carbon*?" he asked.

Colin just looked at him and laughed. That tipped him over the edge. He roared and rushed across the ground, thrusting the knife before him, aiming at Colin's chest.

That's when Colin knew the man was under the influence of something a lot more potent than rum. While he was not a knife fighter himself, he'd seen enough men settle their differences with the blade to know the basics, and one of the main things he knew was that you never thrust your knife far out in front of your body the way Garcia was doing.

He waited until the tip of the blade was a foot from his chest. Pivoting to his left, he watched the razor-sharp blade flash past, missing him by a mere fraction of an inch.

He slammed his free hand down on Garcia's wrist, hearing an eerie cracking sound, and the knife he was thrusting dropped from his now limp fingers. Reversing the knife in his other hand, he hit his left temple. For a second, Garcia stopped in his tracks, leaning forward with his arm stretched out and his left foot off the ground like a dancer posing for an artist. He made a 'hmph' sound, his mouth opened, round and wide as if to shout, but his eyes rolled back in their sockets, and his momentum carried him forward. He fell, face down in the foul-smelling dirt.

"Is he dead?" Rodriguez asked.

Colin knelt and held the blade of the knife to Garcia's nose. Two faint circles of mist appeared on the shiny metal.

"No, he's still breathing."

Rodriguez looked disappointed.

"You two hoist him," M'nondo said, stepping forward and pointing to Rodriguez and Devereux. "We must go and meet the captain."

The two pirates grabbed Garcia between them, draped his limp arms over their shoulders, and followed Colin and M'nondo back into the tavern . . . where they found an angry Elizabeth standing just inside the door with her hands on her hips, her eyes blazing, and her nostrils flaring. She looked momentarily taken aback when she saw the unconscious Garcia between Rodriguez and Devereux, then looked through eyes turned to narrowed slits at Colin and M'nondo.

"I don't suppose I should ask what this is all about," she said.

"Uh, we should get back to the ship," Colin said hastily. He held up his package. "Once we're at sea, I'll explain it . . . I think."

She looked at M'nondo who merely shrugged and settled his dark brown face in its normal impassive expression.

Chapter Twenty-one

Once they were back aboard *The Vixen*, and heading for Lost Island by as circuitous a route as they'd come, Colin, with M'nondo standing passively at his side in Elizabeth's cabin, did the best he could to explain the situation with Garcia, who was still unconscious and lying in the same space below deck that had served as Colin's prison when he first came aboard.

When Rodriguez and Devereux were called in and they confirmed Colin's story, Elizabeth was livid. After she'd dismissed the two pirates, she sat behind her desk, staring at Colin and M'nondo and fuming.

"I don't understand," she said. "I know he wants my job, in fact, I kind of respect that. But, to deliberately try and sabotage the mission, and go against my orders . . ."

"I'm not sure he was himself," Colin said.

She looked up at him, a question in her eyes.

"What is that supposed to mean?"

"I don't know, but watching the way he acted, it was as if he was mesmerized. I know he hasn't liked me since I came aboard this ship, but this was different."

"I noticed that, too," M'nondo said.

"That's even worse," she said. "He knows better than to allow himself to be put in a compromising position when we're in an unfriendly port."

Colin could tell from the way her brow wrinkled that she was pondering what to do. He didn't like Garcia, the man hadn't been anything but unfriendly from their first meeting, but, at the same time, he didn't want to be the cause of dissension within Elizabeth's crew.

"What if someone gave it to him without his knowledge?" he asked.

Her lifted brows told him that she hadn't considered that. "But, why would anyone do that?" she asked.

"That city struck me as a place where a man's smart to keep one eye on his purse and the other on a means of quick escape. Mayhap someone was planning to rob him. At any rate, it might be a good idea to find out everywhere he went while we were there."

She wasn't buying what he was selling, not completely, but there was a hint of doubt in her eyes.

"I agree with Colin," M'nondo said.

Thank you, my friend. "When he wakes, we should ask," Colin said.

Her eyes blazed again. "To hell with waiting.

M'nondo, go and fetch him. Drop him over the side with a rope attached to his waist if you must, but I want him in my cabin within the next ten minutes."

Bowing slightly, M'nondo slipped out. Colin wisely remained silent while Elizabeth sat with her elbows on the desk and her chin propped on her clinched fists, stewing.

She still looked unhappy five minutes later, when M'nondo returned, shoving a disheveled Garcia before him.

Garcia looked humbled, he stumbled when he crossed the threshold, and then looked surprised when he saw Colin sitting beside the captain's desk.

Elizabeth, her lips compressed in a tight line and her eyes focused sharply on Garcia, said nothing.

Finally, he shook himself like a wet dog and drew himself up to his full height, which left his head barely reaching M'nondo's massive shoulders.

"What is the meaning of this? Why was I put in the prisoner's space below decks?"

Elizabeth tapped a fingernail on her desk, and took a deep breath.

"Perhaps," she said. "It would be better if you explained why you did what you did." Her voice was cold and without inflection, and her gaze never left him.

"Me? What did I do?" He pointed at Colin. "That . . . Worth here, attacked me."

Beside him, M'nondo stiffened, but said nothing. Elizabeth turned to Colin, her gaze still cold.

"Is that true, Colin?"

Colin stiffened. He was conflicted. Here, he had the opportunity to rid himself of a potentially dangerous enemy, for he knew that if Elizabeth heard what had actually happened, the good captain that she was, she would get rid of Garcia. On the other hand, something deep inside his gut made him reluctant. He didn't like Garcia, but he feared *how* she might rid herself of the man.

He took a deep breath. "Not exactly true," he said. "But, not totally untrue."

Elizabeth's brows twitched. Garcia's mouth dropped open.

"He lies," Garcia said. "He attacked me for no reason."

Elizabeth shifted her head, looking from Colin to Garcia. She said nothing, but her expression clearly said that she was waiting for an answer from someone about what had happened.

Colin thought hard for a moment, and then made his decision. "I didn't *attack* him. At least, not physically. But, I fear that I might have provoked him. I recognized that he was drunk, and should have taken that into account. I did not, and for that I must shoulder at least part of the blame for what happened."

Elizabeth looked at M'nondo. "Is this true, M'nondo?"

Colin and M'nondo shared a look. The man's dark face was unreadable. Colin held his breath.

"Yes, captain," he said finally. "Diego was drunk and running his mouth. Colin, instead of ignoring his drunken rantings, did indeed bait him." He paused, and looked at Colin, understanding in his dark brown eyes. "I must also accept part of the blame. I should have put a stop to it, before it blew up into a fight."

Elizabeth slowly nodded her head. She looked at Colin, giving him a strange and appraising look. *Damn, she knows we're lying.* Colin braced himself for the outburst that he knew was coming. When she spoke, though, he nearly fell from his chair.

"Very well, then," she said. "We will put this down to the inability of both of you to control your emotions." She turned to Garcia. "I expected better of you, Diego. You know my rules about drinking too much when you visit ports that we do not control. You both will have to be punished, of course. Let me think, what would be appropriate?"

The cabin was as silent as a tomb, with no sound but the creaking of the planks in the ship's hull, as she sat with her hands steepled and her chin resting on the points of her fingers. Then, she smiled and sat back in her chair.

"I have it. You two are important to my plan to rid the seas of that damned Dangerfield, and it is critical that you learn to get along." She paused and let her words sink in. "Therefore, Diego, you are hereby assigned to help Colin build this strange device of his. As my first mate, you'll need to know how it works anyway, so what better way than to help construct it."

Both Colin and Garcia opened their mouths to protest, but a glance from M'nondo quieted Colin. Garcia, on the other hand, had no such reins on his temper.

"B-but, captain, you can't make me work with this . . . man. He is our enemy, why can't you see that?"

She slapped the desk, causing Colin to flinch, and Garcia to shrink backwards.

"I've made my decision," she said. "For the time

being, M'nondo will replace you as first mate. Colin, how long do you think it will take you to finish this contraption?"

"Uh, well, I was planning to build two," he said. "I had thought it would take ten days to two weeks, but since I now have help, I think I can do it in one week."

"Very well then." She clapped her hands. "You two get right to work. We will take the ship out to see if there are any fat merchantmen in the seas near Florida, and to scout for *Intrepid*. We will be back one week from today." She fixed a steely gaze on Colin. "Do not disappoint me."

Even though Colin felt small under that gaze, he realized that disappointing her was the last thing he wanted to do. And, it wasn't from any sense of fear.

Chapter Twenty-two

July 1811, aboard *Intrepid*, 50 miles east of the Bahamas main island

"Captain, I think we should change course and move closer to Florida," Comstock said. He'd been scanning the horizon, and was getting an itchy feeling at the base of his skull. They'd been sailing in and out, around the Bahamas Island chain for a week, and except for a few merchant ships, had seen no other vessels.

Dangerfield, standing near the helm, his feet planted wide apart and his hands behind his back, didn't answer his executive officer at first. Finally, he turned and fixed him with a gaze that felt like ice daggers piercing his chest.

"No, Mister Comstock. I know *The Vixen* is

somewhere in these waters. We are not leaving until we find her, and destroy her. Is that clear?"

"Yes, captain, but we're in waters that are controlled by the English, and we have no support. There could be trouble should we encounter the English fleet."

Dangerfield turned his attention back to the western horizon, on which the dark outlines of several islands could be seen, as if he hadn't heard Comstock talking.

"If the damned English were here, I believe we would have seen them by now, lieutenant," he said finally. "Helm, change course to the west. I want to check out those islands. Pirates could be hiding in some of the coves and bays. Maybe we can flush them out."

"Aye, sir," the sailor at the helm replied. "West it is, sir."

Comstock's face went white.

"S-sir, English warships could also be concealed in such places."

"*Mister* Comstock, am I going to have to assign a new executive officer?"

"N-no, sir. Helm, send the signal for full sails. We don't want to keep the captain waiting."

Dangerfield smiled. "That's more like it." He turned his attention back to the islands. The distance to them was rapidly diminishing as *Intrepid* sliced through the water.

They were within two hundred yards of the first island, a long stretch of white beach backed by towering palms, and a cone-shaped mountain thrust up on the north side, when the first sign of trouble appeared.

A British frigate seemed to emerge from a stand of trees on an outcropping at the right side of the island they were approaching, and then turned on an intercept course. Before the lookout could shout a warning, another frigate came around the left side of the island.

"Ships approaching from port and starboard," the lookout, a young sailor who looked to be in his teens, shouted.

Dangerfield rushed to the quarterdeck rail and craned for a look to the starboard, then ran to the port rail and peered ahead. He whirled and pointed at the helmsman.

"The ship to port's farther away," he said. "Hard aport, and get us headed east as quickly as you can." His voice, though raised to be heard, was unnaturally calm. Comstock, on the other hand, looked as if he was about to foul his pants. He stood at the starboard rail, grasping it so tightly, his knuckles were white.

Sluggish at first, *Intrepid* finally answered the rudder and began her turn. It seemed to take forever, but the bow was finally pointed east. Comstock ran to the main deck and began shouting orders to unfurl all sails and prepare for a full-speed run to get them out of the range of the 44 cannons each of the English ships carried, out of waters England claimed control over.

They seemed to be making headway. The two English ships were still pursuing, but not closing the gap between them. Dangerfield smiled, but as he looked out across the bow of the ship, the smile froze on his face.

Bearing down on them were two more English frigates, one coming from the northeast, and the other from the southeast, and on headings that would intercept them before they were well away from the islands.

Comstock, too, had seen the two new ships. White-faced, he stood beside Dangerfield.

"W-what do we d-do now, captain?"

For a brief moment, Dangerfield looked puzzled. Then, his face settled into a vulpine grin.

"It looks as if our English friends have us boxed in. I guess we have no option. If they want a fight, a fight they'll have."

Comstock gasped. "But, captain, each of those ships has 44 cannons with a longer range than our cannons. We might be able to prevail over one, even two, but we don't stand a chance against four of them."

Dangerfield knew, even though the man was a craven coward, he was right. To initiate battle with four English frigates would be suicide. He would have to use guile rather than guts in this situation.

"You're correct, Mister Comstock." Oh, how he hated to say those words. "Give the order to stand to. Bring the ship to a halt."

"Sir?"

"The English are nothing if not chivalrous. They wouldn't fire on a vessel that was showing no signs of hostility. We'll just say we lost our bearings, apologize for intruding in their waters, and I'm sure they'll let us be on our way. After all, even though we're not exactly friends at the moment, we are also not officially at war."

Comstock hesitated, his eyes blinking rapidly. Then, he shrugged and ran back to the main deck to relay the captain's orders.

Because of the speed at which they'd been running, it took almost half a mile to bring the ship to a halt, but halt they did, the main sails furled, and the smaller square sails set not to catch the wind.

It took another two hours for the four British ships to arrive. They took up stations in a loose circle around *intrepid* so that each had 22 cannons trained upon her. One of the ships that had come from the east, *H.M.S Exeter,* they could see from the fancy lettering just below the bow rail, moved to within hailing distance.

Two English officers, one youngish looking wearing blue coat, white trousers and black bicorne hat, the other older, with a portly build, wore a fancier version of the younger man's uniform, with gold epaulets and flashes of medals on his chest. The younger officer held a brass hailing horn to his lips.

"This is His Majesty's Ship Exeter of the Royal Navy, flagship of the Caribbean Fleet," his voice was tinny, but clear. "You have entered the sovereign territory of Britain. Prepare to receive a boarding party."

"S-sir, are we going to allow them to come aboard?" Comstock asked, looking goggle-eyed across the narrow space between the two ships.

"Look around you, lad," Dangerfield said in a mild tone. "We were outmaneuvered and we're outgunned, and we are in English waters. We have no choice."

The young officer looked skeptical, but Dangerfield continued to gaze placidly at the *Exeter,* as the young officer and ten blue-coated royal marine infantrymen got into a boat and were lowered over the side. In a matter of minutes, they were at midship of *Intrepid*, and the officer, whose natural voice wasn't quite as tinny as it sounded through the hailer, was demanding the ladders be lowered. Dangerfield turned and nodded at the four marine infantry standing at the rail. With the help of two sailors, they dropped two ladders over the side.

Two of the royal marines came over the rail first and posted themselves to the side of the ladders with their muskets held across their chests. The young officer and an older marine came next, and were quickly followed by the rest of the contingent.

"Comstock, go down and welcome our guests aboard."

After saluting, Comstock trotted down to the main deck, where the English officer waited, his hands clasped behind his back and a look of superiority on his face. From where he stood, Dangerfield couldn't hear what passed between his executive officer and the English officer, but from the way Comstock's back stiffened, he figured the pompous Englishman had said something insulting.

Comstock wheeled and headed back to the quarter deck with the Englishman in tow. He approached Dangerfield. His face was red, and he was almost in tears.

"Sir, this is Lieutenant Alistair Wellingham. He is in command of the boarding party," he said.

Dangerfield looked over Comstock's shoulder. The man was slender, with a narrow, straight nose and what he could see under the bicorne he wore had straight blond hair. His eyes were the coldest blue Dangerfield had ever seen, and as soulless as a block of winter ice. He was half an inch shorter than Dangerfield, but by damn, he thought, if the bugger isn't looking down his nose at me.

"Lieutenant Wellingham," he said. "Welcome aboard *U.S.S. Intrepid*. What can I do for you?"

He remained where he was just in front of the helmsman, rather than walking across the quarterdeck and greeting Wellingham, forcing the Englishman to come to him. The way his cheeks tightened it was clear that he knew he was being insulted. He stepped around Comstock and stopped three feet from Dangerfield. He touched an index finger to his hat.

"I bring compliments of Admiral Thomas Treworthy, in command of his majesty's fleet in the Caribbean," he said in a plummy English accent that grated on Dangerfield's ears. "To whom do I have the honor of addressing?"

"I am *Captain* Beauregard Dangerfield of the United States Navy. May I ask why your ships threaten us?"

A slight reddening of cheeks and a twitch of the muscles under his right eye were the only signs of Wellingham's anger. Dangerfield admired his self-control.

"My dear Captain Dangerfield," he said. "I assure you that we have not threatened you. But, I must point out that your ship *is* in our waters. Would you care to explain your presence here?"

Dangerfield's eyes went wide. "These are English waters? My word, my navigator must have plotted our course incorrectly. We *are* in the Atlantic Ocean, are we not?"

Wellingham's expression sent a clear message to Dangerfield that he knew he was being lied to, but he continued to maintain his poise. "I regret to inform you, sir, that you are at least fifty miles into the Caribbean."

"My apologies, lieutenant. I will discipline my navigator for making such a mistake. So, if you have nothing else, we'll be on our way."

"Ah, yes, just so, captain, but first, I'm afraid I must inspect your vessel to ensure you are not smuggling contraband."

"Sirrah, how dare you! I am an officer of the navy of the United States of America, not a common thief or pirate."

Dangerfield had to clench his teeth to keep from laughing. His show of indignation was, he knew, useless, but expected. To do otherwise would've looked suspicious.

"I am merely following my orders, sir. We are required to search all vessels for contraband . . . and English citizens." His words were polite, but his tone was backed by over one hundred cannons and probably twice that many muskets in the hands of royal marine sharpshooters. Dangerfield knew that he had at least four sailors who had recently come from either England or Scotland, and they were likely to be 'impressed' into the English navy, which was a smarmy term for being dragooned into service, like the blackamoors were used on the southern plantations. It would sting, but he had a mission, and the mission was more important than anything else.

"Very well, lieutenant, conduct your inspection. I

can assure you that we have no contraband. As for English citizens, I cannot say."

Wellingham bowed slightly at the waist.

"Your cooperation is appreciated, captain. My men and I will try to complete our task as quickly as possible, and you may be on your way."

Dangerfield returned the bow with a slight incline of his head.

"Carry on, lieutenant," he said, and turned his back on the man.

Charles Ray

Chapter Twenty-three

"Captain, we *have* to put in at the nearest American port, or at least the nearest non-English controlled port and report this," Comstock said.

"No, lieutenant, we're continuing our mission."

"Sir, I must protest. The fucking English took five of our crew, kidnapped them right off the damn ship." Comstock looked like his head would explode. His face was red, and tears of anger and frustration flowed over his chubby cheeks. That he stood, arms on his hips, arguing with his captain, and that he used profanity, something he never did, showed how angry he was. "They've been doing this all up and down the coast for months now, and we don't do shit about it. But, taking men off a U.S. navy vessel, well, that's an act of war, and headquarters needs to be told."

Dangerfield was amused to see that Comstock *did* have a little fire in his belly after all. Now, if he could just keep that fire stoked until *The Vixen* was dealt with.

"I'll make a log entry, lieutenant," he said. "And, once we've completed our mission, we will sail to Charleston and report this . . . unfortunate incident."

"Unfortunate incident?" Comstock waved his arms. Spittle spray shot from his mouth. "You call what happened an *unfortunate incident*? We were boarded by a fucking English naval officer and a detachment of marine infantry, and they kidnapped five of our crew. Captain, with all due respect, I call that something a bit more than just an unfortunate incident."

"Watch your tone, lieutenant." Dangerfield's voice was cold. "I could have you thrown in chains for insubordination."

Comstock wiped at his face, trying to wipe away the tears, but failed, only smearing them across his cheeks.

"Sir, I'm just doing my duty as a naval officer. I would be derelict if I didn't point out that we have a requirement to report any incidents involving the English navy."

"You're absolutely correct, lieutenant, we do have a duty to report," Dangerfield said. "And, we will report it." For some strange reason, Dangerfield found himself wanting to keep this young man on his side. "I know that many in the crew are upset right now, and I understand and share that anger. But, as much as the English are a threat, the pirates represent an equal if not greater threat." He paced back and forth, one hand behind his back, the other waving in the air as he made his points. "It is commerce that drives our nation, and an important component of that commerce is overseas trade, the purchase of raw materials and the shipping of finished manufacture. The pirates represent a direct threat to that commerce."

Comstock blinked. "I know this, sir, but . . . well, the men are really upset. Two of the men the English took were quite popular among the crew."

"You seem to know a lot about what goes on with the common seamen, lieutenant."

"Yes sir, I spend a lot of time among them. I learned that from . . . Lieutenant Worth. He said it was the best way to lead them, from among them, rather than staying separated from them. They trust me to do what's right for them, and they tell me what's going on all over the ship."

Damn, Dangerfield thought, I can't seem to get away from that damned Worth. I hope he's aboard that ship when we find her. Then, I'll have two nuisances out of my life. "That's very good, lieutenant," he said. "And, you're right. It's always a good idea to have a finger on the pulse of the crew. Tell you what, Comstock, I want you to give the men a message from me."

"Message, sir? What message?"

"Give me another week for our search for *The Vixen* and, if we don't find it, we make straightaway for Charleston. However, I'm pretty sure we'll be running across her soon, and when we do, the men can take out some of their anger on the pirates."

He watched closely the war of emotions that crossed the young man's face. Dangerfield knew that he was treading shaky ground at this point. He'd never in all the time he'd been master of *Intrepid* shown the slightest bit of concern about the welfare of his crew beyond that which was absolutely necessary to keeping the vessel shipshape, so he couldn't help but be concerned that Comstock might see his insincerity. At any other time, he wouldn't have given a fig, but in light of the man's newfound courage, and his own sense that they were close to their prize, there was no room for error.

"Don't you feel the desire to strike out at something, Comstock, to relieve some of that anger that's bubbling inside you," he said in his most calming tone. "We can't do anything about the English . . . right now, but, we can make the pirates pay."

He saw a glimmer of anger in Comstock's eyes. There, he thought, almost there, just a little further. Comstock's jaw muscles quivered.

"Aye, sir," he said. "I am angry, angry and . . . I don't know . . . maybe a bit ashamed. We meekly allowed the damned English to board our ship and take our men, and we . . . stood by, doing nothing. It's just not right."

"Yes, lieutenant, it's not right. Someone has to pay. The day will come when we make the English pay, but for now, we have a pirate ship out there, a ship that has preyed on our merchants for too long. Shall we make them pay?"

Something snapped in Comstock. Dangerfield could see it in his eyes. "Aye, sir," the young lieutenant said. "Let's find the bastards, and kill them all."

Chapter Twenty-four

July 1811, Lost Island

"You know I do not want to be working with you," Garcia said. "I want nothing to do with you."

Colin and Garcia stood in the thatched shed Elizabeth had given Colin as a workshop. Elizabeth and the rest of the crew of *The Vixen* had set sail an hour earlier for parts unknown, and Colin and Garcia had returned to the workshop to work on his 'secret' weapon that he'd assured Elizabeth would tip the scales in *Vixen*'s favor when they encountered *Intrepid*, or any other warship for that matter.

Garcia had been looking strangely at him since their encounter in Elizabeth's cabin aboard *The Vixen*, as if he wanted to say something but couldn't find the words. Now, they stood face to face over the work bench upon which Colin had arranged the items he'd purchased.

"I'm sure of that, Diego," Colin said. "I'm not all that fond of you, either. But, we both have the captain's orders, so I suggest that we put aside our differences and make the most of it."

"You have a point, but before we start working on this devil's contraption of yours, I am curious about something."

"And, that is?"

"Aboard ship, when the captain asked about our little encounter, you could have said that I attacked you. Instead, you accepted part of the blame. Why?"

Why, indeed, Colin thought wryly. It had been a sudden impulse, something that felt right at the time. He wondered if he'd come to regret it. Now, though, he had to try and explain it so this thickheaded pirate would understand.

"If I had put all the blame on you," he said. "I imagine it would have simplified my life, but it would have driven a wedge between you and your crewmates. It would also have put Elizabeth, the captain, in the position of having to take disciplinary action against you, which could have had a negative effect on her relations with the crew. I didn't want to do that."

Garcia seemed lost in thought. Then, a half smile appeared, only briefly.

"Okay, I can understand that. Thank you for what you did. But, do not think that this makes us friends or anything."

"I would never do that," Colin said.

"Good, see that you do not. Now, what do you want me to do?"

Colin turned to the workbench and began pointing out and explaining the function of the items arranged there. He put like items together, explaining what things were when Garcia asked, starting with the carbon rods, which would be the source of light; the zinc and copper disks, for conducting the power; and the felt, which would be cut into circles, soaked with salt water and placed between the metal disks as a source of the power. None of it made any sense to Garcia, who continued to look at the stack of items as implements for some experiment in alchemy, and, in truth, Colin had no idea how or why they worked, but he'd read the news articles that assured him they would work.

He set Garcia to work cutting the felt into circles, the same size of the metal disks, standing behind him and watching him do the first few. He was surprised, and somewhat pleased to notice that the pirate had nimble fingers, and was a conscientious worker, carefully cutting near-perfect circles using one of the metal disks as a guide. Next to him was a wooden bowl filled with sea water which he instructed Garcia to put each finished circle in and cautioned him to make sure they were fully submersed so they would soak up as much of the water as possible.

Satisfied that Garcia knew what he was doing, even if he didn't know why, Colin set himself to creating what would be the centerpiece of his devices; boxes to hold the carbon rods and lenses, his lanterns.

After measuring the diameter of the lenses, he took two panels of thin wood and, using a knife he'd been given by M'nondo just before the ship's departure, he cut holes in them which would allow the lenses to fit snugly. He then constructed two boxes of flexible ten, with front and back open. To the front of each, using copper wire and his knife to punch holes, he affixed the lens panels. He then cut tin panels for the back, and attached them by lacing copper wire through holes he'd punched, so that both easily swung open. He then punched a hole in the left side of each, and matching holes in the boxes. Through these holes he threaded a long copper wire, which he would use to secure the 'doors.' In the bottom of each door, he cut out a small rectangle. His lanterns were ready for the critical components, which would be both inside and outside the boxes.

The first components were the carbon rods. His plan was to set two rods in blocks of wood; a few inches apart, or so he'd read, when power from his voltaic pile, which he would construct last, passed through the rods, it would generate heat which would cause the ends of the rods to glow and begin to vaporize. The vapor that collected between the tips of the rods, heated by the power from the pile, would glow. The light from that glow, with the lens as it only means of escaping the box, would, should, emit a bright beam of light. Or, so he hoped.

Before installing the rods, though, he would have to construct the voltaic pile and experiment to determine the correct placement of the rods. Too far apart and the power wouldn't flow, too close, and it would simply vaporize both rods.

Satisfied that he'd done all he could, he turned to help Garcia, surprised to find the man standing with his hips pressed against the table, staring at the two boxes with a look of fascination, and not a little fear.

Behind him, Colin saw four neat stacks of felt circles resting in a wooden bowl filled with sea water as he'd instructed Garcia to do. He smiled in satisfaction.

"What the hell are those things?" Garcia asked.

Beaming proudly, Colin patted the strange looking contraptions. "These are lanterns," he said. "But, more powerful than any lantern ever known."

Garcia walked over and examined them. He tried to peer through the lenses, he opened the back and looked in. Then, he turned to Colin.

"I know what these pieces of glass can do. They focus the light. So, I suppose a few candles inside the box would shine a bit brighter, but I don't see how you'll make it shine more than a few feet." He pointed to the other items. "And, what in the name of all that's holy is all this junk for?"

"For a start," Colin said. "This lantern will not use candles. In fact, there will be no fire at all, at least, no fire of the type you think."

Garcia's eyes narrowed to slits. "I knew it! You are some kind of alchemist, or worse, a witch. How the devil do you think you can make light without fire?"

Colin put his right hand behind his back and crossed his fingers. "I am unable to explain it to you, because, to tell the truth, I don't fully understand the principle. But, with your help, I can demonstrate." He clapped his hands. "Now, let's get to work. Come here and hand me the items I ask for."

Still looking skeptical, and a bit wary, Garcia moved and stood across the table from Colin.

"Is this dangerous?"

Again, Colin slipped his hand behind his back and crossed his fingers. "Of course not," he said, hoping he was telling the truth.

For the next four hours, they worked without talking, except for Colin asking for something, and then having to point it out, or explain what it was.

He started with a wooden base, a square of wood about an inch thick, in the center of which he inserted a three-foot-long wooden peg which tapered at the top. Once the rod was securely in place, he placed a copper disk over it and slid it to rest on the wood block. He then put another copper disk on top of that one, followed by one of the wet felt circles. Atop that he put a zinc disk, another felt circle, and another copper disk, repeating the process until he had five alternating zinc-copper pairs sitting on the bottom copper disk. He then put a zinc disk on top of the pile. The next step was to affix a copper wire to the second copper disk on the bottom and the next to last zinc disk on top. Each wire had a flat copper semi-circle attached to the free end. He stepped back when he'd finished, looking with pride at his handiwork.

"What is that for?"

"This," Colin said. "Is a voltaic pile. The two metals, copper and zinc, react with the salt in the felt, and generate energy, which flows through the wires."

"This is that . . . voltaic pile you keep talking about?"

"It is, and now let's test it."

A flicker of fear crossed Garcia's face.

"Test it? How?"

Colin picked up two carbon rods and affixed copper wire to the bottom of each. He then set them upright in a crevice in the table, about six inches apart. Picking up the wires running from the pile, he gingerly placed them on the ends of the two wires coming from the rods. Nothing happened.

"Uh, I think they're too far apart," he said.

He put the pile wires down, careful to keep them far apart, and adjusted the distance between the rods, this time, putting them three finger widths apart.

Again, he touched the pile wires to the rod wires. For a few seconds, nothing happened. Then, there was a sizzling sound, and a smell like the air after a thunderstorm. Sparks formed between the two carbon rods, getting brighter and brighter until, suddenly, there was a small sun between them. The light was so bright and came so suddenly, Colin was momentarily blinded, and so startled, he bumped the table, breaking the connection. The little sun disappeared.

"*Madre de Dios*, what the hell was that?" Garcia asked.

Colin had to wait a few seconds for his sight to return, and even when it did, he had spots before his eyes, but he was smiling broadly.

"That, my friend, is one hell of a lantern. One that doesn't need fire. Now, help me build the second one and get the rods emplaced."

Garcia crossed himself, but pitched in and followed Colin's instructions numbly, his eyes constantly straying to the two carbon rods sticking up out of the crack in the table.

"This is the work of the devil," he mumbled.

"No, Diego. This is science. This is a look at the future. Imagine being able to light a ship below decks without fear of accidently starting a fire, or being able to light it up instantly without having to run around with lit tapers. This thing will even work in the rain."

"Okay, so maybe it is not magic." Garcia crossed himself again. "But, how is this thing going to help us defeat an armed frigate?"

"I've been thinking about that, and I think I have an idea."

Chapter Twenty-five

Colin and Garcia had both lanterns constructed and successfully tested the day before Elizabeth and the rest of her pirate crew returned to Lost Island. Although, he wasn't totally convinced that Colin was in league with the Devil, he was impressed with their invention. He was less sure, though, that Colin would be able to come up with a plan to defeat *Intrepid.*

Elizabeth walked into the hut just as they were lifting the two devices from the work table.

"What have we here?" she asked, looking curiously at the devices. "Is this all I get for all the gold you spent, Colin?"

"It works, captain," Garcia said. "I did not believe it would, but Colin made it work, and it is . . . *magnifico.*"

She gave her first mate an appraising look. "So, it looks like the two of you have declared a truce in my absence. Are you ready to return to your duties,

Diego?"

"*Si, capitan,* and I apologize for my behavior. It was wrong, and I deserved the punishment you gave me. How was your voyage?"

"Yes, captain," Colin said. "Did you accomplish what you set out to accomplish?"

She smiled. A smile that warmed Colin's heart and sent a shiver of fear through his body at the same time. Her smile was the smile of a hungry wolf who has just cornered a rabbit.

"Yes, I believe I did. We'll discuss it at my house, but first, show me your little toys."

After the demonstration, which caused even M'nondo to jump back in fright, she apologized for calling them toys. "After we discuss what I learned, Colin, you can tell me how we'll use these lanterns of yours."

"Should we take them with us to your house?"

"No, it's best we leave them here. M'nondo, put two of our most trusted men here to guard them, and tell them, under no circumstances is anyone other than me, you, Diego, or Colin to be allowed inside." M'nondo nodded, and after casting one last frightened glance at the lanterns, left to comply with her orders. "Now, you two, come with me. We have a lot to discuss."

Thirty minutes later, the four of them sat in her dining room, with her at her usual place at the head of the table, Colin facing her from the other end, and M'nondo and Garcia respectively at her right and left side. For once, when Garcia looked at Colin, it was with respect rather than anger, which Elizabeth didn't fail to notice.

"Before I share my news," she said. "I'd like to

compliment you and Diego, Colin. You did a very good job on your lanterns."

They both nodded, and it didn't escape her notice that they shared a look.

"Captain," Garcia said. "Did you learn anything useful?"

"Most useful, I think." She leaned forward with her hands in a prayer position. "*Intrepid* has been seen many times around the islands. Though, it seems that they've received information that puts us in the northern part of the chain, so they've not ventured this far south . . . yet."

"Given that it's plain to see that you sail south when you leave ports," Colin said. "I wonder why Dangerfield would think you're in the north."

She smiled that wolfish smile again. "Well, let us just say that the people of the islands are not the type to talk out of turn to strangers."

The look in his eyes told her that he understood. He nodded.

"That's good for us," he said. "It means that he will be looking in the wrong direction when we find him."

"Just so. There's more, though," she said. "It seems that Captain Dangerfield had a bit of an encounter with a flotilla of English warships recently."

Colin's eyes widened, and worry creased his features. "Were there casualties?"

"Oh, it wasn't that kind of encounter. He was surrounded by four ships, and boarded. Some of his men were impressed into the English navy, and he was allowed to go on his way with a warning to stay out of English-controlled waters."

"Then, he must have made for the nearest

American port to report it."

"One would think so," she said. "But, one would be wrong. The word I received is that he sailed east into the Atlantic, and then doubled back and is now playing cat and mouse with the English. He is still out there, and according to my informants, he is looking for us."

Colin looked puzzled. "B-but, our orders are to immediately report any encounter with the British, especially if they've taken men. I can't believe his executive officer didn't push him to make for the nearest American port."

"Again, this is not confirmed, but it appears that his executive officer has no sway with him, and his crew is . . . shall we say, very upset with him."

"That," Colin said. "Is probably putting it mildly. He's putting the ship and every man aboard her at grave risk, not to mention, if fleet headquarters learns that he's failed to report as required, he will be in big trouble."

"That doesn't seem to affect him. The few people who have seen him say he has the demeanor of a mad man."

"The man is a disaster." Colin made a growling sound deep in his throat. "If he's not stopped, he's likely to get his entire crew killed, or taken prisoner by the British."

Elizabeth laughed. "That, though, should make our job easier. A mad man is dangerous, but not thinking clearly. How do you propose we deal with him?"

This was what Colin had been waiting for. The night before, he'd reviewed his plan just before falling asleep. It had its drawbacks and dangers, but, if

Dangerfield was losing it, it might, just might, work. He leaned forward, and fixed Elizabeth with a serious stare.

"Before I tell you what I propose, I ask only one thing . . . we will do all that we can to avoid harming any of the crew on *Intrepid,* they are not responsible for Dangerfield's misdeeds."

"I've given you my word. We will do no more harm than necessary to protect ourselves. If your former crewmates resist, though, I can make no promises. You understand that, right?"

"Yes, I suppose that's the best I can hope for. If my plan works, we might not have to worry about it.

She leaned back in her chair, her hands steepled in front of her lips. "Ah yes, your plan. Why don't you tell us about it?"

There it was. She looked at Colin to see if there was any hesitation on his face, or in his manner. He seemed calm as he leaned forward and raised a finger as if to make a point.

"I gave it a lot of thought," he said. "First of all, I realized that we have no chance in a head-to-head encounter with *Intrepid*. But, I believe we're faster and more maneuverable. The other factor in our favor; I know the captain, and how he thinks . . . or rather, doesn't think. He's a man of moods, and has a tendency to overextend himself. He also has an inflated sense of his own capability."

Elizabeth leaned back and regarded him carefully. "Tell us something we do not already know."

Colin's cheeks reddened.

"Sorry, I don't mean to sound like a prissy schoolteacher. It's just the way I think. I need to align everything in order so that I make sense, even to myself." He cleared his throat. "Okay, Captain Dangerfield's weakness is that he thinks he *has* no weakness. He assumes that everyone fights a ship the way he fights a ship, and he considers himself superior in that regard." At the impatient looks around the table, he tapped the table with his finger. "And, that is how we beat him. We don't fight his fight. We fight *our* fight. We steal a page from the Continental Army's rule book, and make our own rules."

"But, Colin, my friend," M'nondo said. "We are pirates. We already make our own rules."

Colin smiled.

"Yes, you fight like pirates, and Dangerfield knows that. So, in confronting him, we don't fight his way, but we also don't do what pirates normally do."

"But, if we don't fight like pirates, and we don't fight like the navy, how *do* we fight?" Garcia asked. He looked completely confused.

"Let me ask you a question. Do you ever attack a ship at night?" Colin asked with an innocent look on his face.

"Unless it is an unarmed merchant, of course not." Diego looked offended. "We need to be able to see in order to board if there is the possibility of armed resistance."

"Right. So, you attack at first light, or early dusk, so you can see what you're fighting against. That's what we change."

"What! You're suggesting we attack an armed frigate in the dark. The marine infantry sharpshooters will cut us to pieces, or the ship's cannons will."

"Yes, if they can see us, and if it was our plan to

board or engage in a battle. That's not what I propose."

M'nondo looked interested, and Elizabeth was wondering what the handsome young American was leading up to.

"If we are not boarding, or giving battle, what are we doing?" she asked.

"For want of a better term, I call it hit and run," Colin said. "We're faster and more maneuverable than *Intrepid*, and our hull is black. If we're running without lights, with just enough sail to get quick speed, we can be on top of them before they know it. We pull alongside, within our cannons' range; they will have minimum lights on deck to enable the crew and marines to navigate, so we'll be able to see them clearly, or clearly enough."

"We can do that, of course," she said, beginning to see the rough outlines of his plan. "But, once we fire our cannons, we will be like ducks sitting fat and happy in the water. Their cannons will cut us to pieces once they see us."

Colin smiled. Elizabeth recognized it. John Cleague had the same smile just before boarding a fat merchantman that lay dead in the water after being holed by *The Vixen's* cannons. She felt a twinge of sadness, thinking about the old man, and looking at Colin, with that wolfish smile on his now sun-tanned face, with a full beard framing his chin, she felt another twinge, one she hadn't felt in too long.

"They would do just that . . . *if* they could see us. Tell me, captain, what happens when you look at the sun, I mean, directly at the sun?"

"Why, you're blinded. Every child in the islands knows that it is dangerous to look at the sun."

"And that, my dear captain, is where my lanterns come in. Once we've fired a broadside, we turn them on, aimed directly at *Intrepid's* main deck, while we raise sail and get away as quickly as your crew can manage. By the time they regain their sight, we should be well out of range."

This, she thought, was an interesting plan—if it could be made to work. He seemed so confident, though.

"Will your lanterns work well enough, I know they seemed to work in the hut, but we'll be on the open sea."

"They should work even better. The water will act as a reflector, a mirror if you will, adding to the glare. They won't see a ship, just two small suns blasting light into their eyes; until, that is, they go blind."

"I have seen them many times, captain," Garcia said. "I am confident they will work."

Now, there was something, Elizabeth thought. Diego Garcia coming to Colin's rescue. Her plan to force them to work together to get past their differences had worked far better than she had hoped it would. Even M'nondo was nodding appreciatively. Hell, she thought. It just might work. She slapped her hand on the table.

"Very well then. We have a battle plan, so let's get to work. Diego, you have your job back as my first mate. M'nondo, you're in charge of the gun crews."

"What about me?" Colin asked.

"You will be my navigator and battle tactician when we have *Intrepid* in sight. Diego will be in charge of getting us alongside the target, and M'nondo will be positioned to see your signals. He will fire on your command. You have two of the lanterns. You will need someone to light them. Pick two men and teach them how to do it. Does that meet with your approval?"

"Yes, it does, except, I would request that our cannons be depressed to hit the target right at the water line."

"Why," M'nondo said. "We usually aim for the gun ports, to try and disable the cannons."

"A number of reasons. First, if you aim at the gun ports, you will kill many innocent sailors, and that's not our aim. Secondly, if you hole the ship at the waterline, she won't be able to maneuver well or chase us. Besides, my lanterns will make sure the cannons don't fire. By the time they can see well enough to aim, we won't be there."

M'nondo nodded, smiling. "I see. If the captain approves, I will do that."

"It sounds reasonable to me," Elizabeth said. "So, that is what we'll do. Now, before we get to work, how about a drink to celebrate our upcoming victory?"

Charles Ray

Chapter Twenty-six

August 1811, aboard *The Vixen*, 50 miles southeast of Great Abaco Island

It had taken them over a week to prepare, most of the time for Colin to explain the working of his lanterns to Rodriguez and Devereux, the two men he'd selected to operate them, and to discuss with M'nondo and Garcia his concept of the maneuvers needed by the ship for his plan to work. He'd also talked extensively with Elizabeth about what she'd learned during her last voyage, in an effort to estimate where *Intrepid* would be, and to plot a course that would allow them to intercept her at the appropriate time of day. His plan was to wait until full dark to avoid a sharp-eyed lookout spotting them, figuring that, after the encounter with the four English ships, those on board *Intrepid* would be sensitive to such. Elizabeth had learned that one of the ships of that flotilla, *H.M.S. Valiant*, had shadowed *Intrepid* for several days before the encounter, sailing at a distance just over the horizon, and coming in closer for brief periods from time to time to keep track of the ship's course, and no one aboard *Intrepid* had been aware of the presence of a stalker until the trap was sprung.

No matter, thought Elizabeth, as the bow of *The Vixen* plunged briefly beneath the top of a giant wave that washed over the main deck. The ship nosed forward briefly until it reached the bottom of the swell, and then began a graceful rise as it met the leading edge of the next.

She had sat with Colin for hours, going over her conversations in dozens of taverns and markets on several islands, big and small, and poring over charts of the area, as they traced *Intrepid's* movements since the ship entered the Caribbean area after chasing *The Vixen* from the north Atlantic.

If the accounts were correct, Beauregard Dangerfield had been sailing a serpentine course in and among the Bahamas Island chain, stopping occasionally at some of the smaller islands to question locals, but because of the information he'd received, had concentrated his search to the northern end of the chain.

On the second day of their voyage, they'd received an update on *Intrepid's* position from a fisherman who had spotted her the day before sailing northward to the west of Abaco Island. After some debate, as to whether this meant that Dangerfield had given up the hunt for them and was heading back to his home port of Boston, she finally agreed with Colin that

Dangerfield would probably sail around the northern of Abaco and head south, and that he'd probably stay close in to shore to enable *Intrepid* to duck into one of the coves that dotted the island, in the event an English ship was spotted. Garcia pointed out that this was a stupid strategy, because if the English flanked Dangerfield to the east, his ship would be trapped. Colin agreed with him, if they'd been talking about a sane skipper, but reminded him they were talking about a man who would put his executive officer in a boat without oars and limited food and water, and leave him in the ocean to die—not a rational man. No one argued the point with him, and as mad as the scheme sounded, it struck Elizabeth as *exactly* what Dangerfield would do.

Based on the fisherman's estimate of *Intrepid's* speed and position the day before, Colin estimated that it would reach a position just southeast of Abaco well after dark, probably around 10:00 or so. He'd convinced Elizabeth that an area of the ocean that was relatively shallow and dotted with several small islands, too small to support inhabitants, but that were occasional stopping points for fishermen and pirates, would be a good place to intercept Dangerfield.

Fortunately, by the time they reached the designated location, the seas had calmed, and it was still light enough to navigate among the small islands without running aground. Colin, Garcia, and M'nondo paid careful attention to the location of each island as they sailed in, mentally plotting their escape route.

The sun was low in the western sky when Elizabeth finally picked a location to stop, using adjustments to the rudder and the slack sails to maintain position rather than dropping anchor. The ship's bow pointed roughly north, the direction from which *Intrepid* would come. The plan was to wait until the ship was almost abreast of them, then sail out and match course and speed until they were abreast and just within cannon range. At that time, Colin would give the signal to fire, at the same time ordering the lanterns to be turned on. As soon as the cannons fired, Garcia's job was to get *The Vixen* as far away from the area as possible in the shortest time possible.

Simple, Elizabeth thought, as long as everyone executes his part of the plan without a hitch, and assuming the gods are smiling down upon us. It grated on her. As captain, it was to her to approve the plan, but as soon as that was done, she was useless. Her only role in the encounter itself was to stand near the helm, her fists clinched, praying to whatever god who might be listening that all would go well.

It was not, she knew, that either of the three men felt that as a woman she wasn't qualified to participate. As Colin had said when she raised an objection to the fact that his plan didn't include a role for her, "Captain, it's your job to tell us where you want us to go. It's our job to execute those orders faithfully. As we do that, you should stand off and above in order to intervene wherever and whenever something goes wrong, all the while praying that you will never have to intervene. If you had any other task, you wouldn't be able to fulfill your role as captain."

She ground her teeth together in frustration. She hated it when someone else had to point out the obvious to her. She'd been a ship's captain long enough to have remembered that basic truth. The captain who became too involved in the petty details, rather than empowering a ship's officer, or even a common sailor, to take care of them, very soon became a captain with no real control of the ship.

Now, she stood on the quarterdeck, staring morosely toward the bow which rose and fell with the rhythmic motion of the sea. Garcia was standing near the helm, focused on the ocean beyond the bow, and ready to maneuver the ship at a moment's notice. M'nondo was on the gun deck, preparing the cannon crews, and down below, on the main deck, she saw Colin instructing Rodriguez and Devereux on the operation of his lanterns, which he'd had mounted on small two-wheeled carts to enable them to be moved from one side of the ship to another with ease, although, if things this night went to plan, they would be at the port side, which is where the big lenses, like the dead eyes of a cyclops, pointed.

After patting each man on the shoulder, Colin turned and saw her on the quarterdeck. He waved, and then bound across the deck and up to where she stood.

"Well, all is ready," he said. "Everyone knows what they are to do, and I'm confident they will do it well."

She folder her arms under her breasts. "I guess all we can do now is wait."

"That's always the part I hate," he said. "Waiting is worse than the battle itself."

But, wait they did, with Elizabeth standing as still as a statue, despite the swaying of the boat, and Colin pacing from one side of the quarterdeck to the other as the night sky grew darker and darker, until it was impossible to see someone standing over ten feet away.

"You had better get to the main deck," Elizabeth said. "If your calculations are correct, they should be here soon."

Shaking his shoulders, Colin nodded and loped down to the main deck, where he positioned himself where he could see both M'nondo at the center of the cannons, and the two men with the lanterns, perched atop the hatch in the center of the deck.

"Remember," he said to M'nondo in a voice just above a whisper. "When I say 'lights', make sure you and your men are facing outward. Wouldn't want to blind my own gunners."

M'nondo grunted and nodded, and turned back to whisper to the gun crew nearest him. Colin could just make out heads turning and hear unintelligible whispers. He turned and looked at the main mast. A pirate stood at its base, craning his neck to look upwards. Between him and Colin stood another pirate, his eyes on the man at the base of the mast. This was a last-minute arrangement Colin had put in place. The lookout atop the main mast, when he spotted lights coming from the north, would tell the man at the base of the mast in a normal voice rather than shouting as was the norm. The word would then be relayed to Colin by the two men on the deck. The way sounds carried over the water at night, even this was dangerous, but it was the best he could come up with, hoping that a normal conversational level wouldn't be heard over the sounds of the sea and wind-filled sails.

He kept his eyes on the man standing loosely about eight feet away, and tried to will himself to relax.

Even with his anticipation of the event, the near-whispered words, "A ship's lights, two points off the starboard bow," caught him by surprise. He froze for a heartbeat, and then, his experience in combat, honed in the battles against the Barbary pirates, galvanized him into action. Spinning around in a smooth movement, he pointed at M'nondo to get his attention.

When the big man nodded to indicate that he saw, he said, in a low voice, "Ship off the starboard bow. It has to be her. Get your men ready."

He looked up toward the quarterdeck, but the shifting movement of the deck under his feet told him that Garcia had also received the lookout's report and had sprung into action. The ship was already beginning its swing to starboard. He moved closer to the port rail and looked out into the darkness, so deep that it was impossible to tell where sea ended and sky began. But, by straining, he could just make out the faint twinkle of lanterns swinging from hooks about the decks, and he recognized the pattern. It was *Intrepid*, and she was sailing south. About a quarter mile off and that east of them, which would give them sufficient room to turn and slip in behind and beside to execute his plan.

As the ship made its turn, the lights seemed to be drawing closer. On the quarterdeck, Elizabeth peered intently into the darkness. She worried that *Intrepid* might be too close to the islands, cutting off their turn, but as she looked longer, she could see that the impression that it was closing on them was just a trick of the darkness. The ship was on a slightly slanted course, which would enable her ship to make a complete turn just as it passed, putting them behind about one hundred yards and off about half that.

Using runners, Garcia was navigating the ship

silently, or at least not with the shouting that was normal during such a maneuver. The only sounds were his whispered commands to the runners, and the slap of their bare feet on the deck as they ran to relay them to the men working feverishly at manipulating the sails. There was a flapping sound as the main sail filled with air, which she hoped wouldn't carry to *Intrepid* over the sound of her own sails.

The turn, which seemed to her to take forever, but in fact, was just a matter of minutes, was completed without an alarm being sounded, and she saw as she stared ahead that they were just where Colin had said they would be, slightly behind *Intrepid* and off her starboard side, well within the range of the cannons *The Vixen* carried. She tried to suppress the thought that this meant they were also within range of *Intrepid's* larger and more numerous cannons. This plan, Colin's plan, is going to work.

She maintained her pose, standing with her legs spread at the front of the quarterdeck, in plain view of the helmsman, and where the men on the main deck could've seen her if there'd been enough light—but, she was sure they knew she was there—silently watching as her crew did what they did best, moved *The Vixen* through the water with the speed and deadly precision of a great white shark.

From the rear, she could only see two lanterns, on port and starboard sides, marking the target, but they told her that they were rapidly closing the distance. The next few minutes were crucial.

There were so many things that could go wrong, and they were all crowding her mind. A sharp-eyed lookout aboard *Intrepid* could spot the dark and menacing shape coming up behind them, one of her men could knock against something and make a noise that alerted their prey, and on, and on. Though her mind was in turmoil, years at sea under the tutelage of John Cleague had taught her to keep her feelings hidden. He outward expression was calm

Their bow was now even with the aft lights, and the shape of *Intrepid* was becoming apparent, a bit darker than the sky and water, as she unknowingly plowed ahead.

Closer . . . closer, and then they were alongside. The damn ship looked close enough to touch, and she could make out flickering shadows as men on her decks went about their business, apparently unaware of the danger keeping pace with them.

She was beginning to wonder when Colin would give the word to fire when her ears were assaulted by a might boom as every cannon on the port side belched flame and smoke, and then the night lit up. Two circles of light, so bright, they hurt her eyes, causing her to quickly look away before they blinded her, suddenly appeared in the middle of her main deck, and a wide and expanding beam of light stretched across the deck and across the water, illuminating *Intrepid* from bow to stern as clear as if had been the middle of a clear and sunny day.

Once the spots cleared from in front of her eyes, she could make out men at or near the rail of *Intrepid*, shielding their eyes from the light, while others stumbled about blindly. She could hear the shouts and cries of surprise and anger clearly across the gap between the two ships. But, what brought a smile to her face, as the gap between them began to widen, as

Garcia gave orders to make the turn to starboard, were the gaping holes in the hull, at the waterline as Colin had requested, and some extending below the water. There weren't enough, and they weren't large enough, to sink her, but she wouldn't be giving chase for a good long while. With the amount of water the ship had to be taking, she would have to limp along at a snail's pace to the nearest port or island and be repaired, which she knew could take a week or two, if not longer. With luck, she would be found by an English warship and taken prisoner. That would, indeed, destroy Dangerfield.

Actually, she smiled at the thought, being bested by a smaller ship, a pirate ship at that, and taking damage without even being able to return one shot, if word got out, would destroy his reputation. She had wanted him dead, but as she considered what life would be like for him with this night's events hanging over his head, she realized that Colin was right. It wasn't necessary to kill him. She'd just consigned him to a living hell. Now, she hoped he would live a long, long life.

They sailed in silence for a full two hours, keeping close to the smaller islands, but avoiding the more populated ones, until they were only a few hours from Lost Island. Only then, did she allow a few lanterns to be lit, which really weren't needed as dawn was fast approaching.

She stood at the quarterdeck's forward rail and looked down at the smiling faces of her crew. Standing in the middle of the quiet group, Colin and M'nondo stood shoulder to shoulder, looks of satisfaction on their faces. Garcia, also smiling, took up his position to her left.

"Men," she said, in a clear, strong voice. "My congratulations for a job well done. I don't think we'll see that ship in these waters again for a while, but, thanks to Colin Worth, and all our fine efforts, we now know how to fight it. When we get home, I think we'll stay for a while. Celebrate, spend time with your families. You've all earned it."

Her words were answered with a loud roar, and then, "Huzzah! To the best damned captain what ever sailed the sea," a voice said from the middle of the crowd.

She looked down at them, her men, her crew, but her gaze kept drifting to one man in particular. Taller than everyone else except M'nondo, Colin Worth stood, receiving claps on the back and shoulder and handshakes from men nearby, he was paying them no attention. He was looking up at her, a half smile, a look of expectancy on his face.

"You know, captain," Garcia said. "I think Colin likes you."

She turned on him, trying to frown and not quite making it.

"What do you know about it?" she snapped.

"I see the way he look at you. Yes, he likes you, likes you very much. And, I think you like him."

"Oh, shut up and get back to your post, Diego."

Charles Ray

Chapter Twenty-seven

August 1811, *U.S.S. Intrepid* at Little Abaco Island, Bahamas

Comstock's face was beet red, and he stood facing Dangerfield with his hands on his hips. The two marines standing behind him, both privates, looked nervously from him to the captain, who sat in the chair behind his ornate desk, staring out the porthole.

"Sir, we have no choice now," he said. "the ship is in need of repairs, and we have several injured men. We *have* to make for the nearest American port."

Dangerfield continued to sit and stare through the porthole.

"Sir, are you listening, we have to head for home, now!"

Slowly, Dangerfield turned in his chair and looked

at Comstock. What the young officer saw chilled him to his marrow. Dangerfield's eyes were the eyes of a madman.

"There are no English ships in this port, lieutenant, and the locals seem friendly enough. I think we can get the necessary repairs done here, and then resume our search for *The Vixen*."

Colin took a step forward. "Sir, we have two holes that are below the waterline. Those are being patched as we speak, and should be done within the next two hours. As for the rest, we can send men ashore to get whatever we don't have onboard, and work on the other holes while we're underway to an American port."

"No, we stay here and get the repairs done, so we can get back the hunt." Dangerfield was sounding like a petulant child.

"Captain Dangerfield," Comstock said, slowly and evenly. "Need I remind you that this is an English port, and the surrounding waters are controlled by a British flotilla. We've already lost men to them. I would not want to lose more."

Dangerfield's expression hardened. "They are not your men to worry about, lieutenant. They are mine, do you hear me, mine to do with as I please, and right now, I please to have them help me find and kill a pirate."

"That's not our main mission." Comstock's voice was harsh. "And, right now, we're not even capable of doing that. Captain, I must insist that you give the order to set sail and head for home."

Dangerfield stood, waving his fist. "You insist? You insist? Who the hell are you to insist? I am the captain of this vessel, do you hear that, I am, not you. You do not insist on anything."

"You're not leaving me much choice, captain. As a navy officer, I have a responsibility to my country, but more importantly, I have a responsibility to my ship and my shipmates, and, you sir, are putting both at risk, not to mention what might happen between us and England because of your actions. I am therefore, sir, relieving you of duty."

Dangerfield's fist stopped moving, still held in the air. He stared goggle-eyed at Comstock.

"You. Are. Doing. What?"

"Sir, it is my belief that you are currently not mentally competent to continue in command of this vessel. As executive officer, and second in command, it is my duty to take charge and see that the ship and men are returned safely to home port."

Dangerfield smiled, a dangerous, frightening smile.

"You little weasel. So, you think I'm crazy, do you? Do you actually think that you are capable of taking over from me?" He looked at the two nervous marines. "You men, take this man and put him in chains in the brig."

They didn't move.

"Did you hear me? I gave an order."

"S-sorry, sir," the older of the two said. "B-but, we think the lieutenant's right. You ain't yourself, sir. It be best if he takes over, 'till we get to Charleston or someplace where you can get some help."

"So, the two of you are siding with this, this traitor?"

"He ain't no traitor, sir," the other marine said. "He's just doin' what he think right."

Dangerfield rolled his eyes and looked at the overhead.

"What he thinks is right. Hah! Well, my good friends, you thought I was crazy, did you? Well, I was sane enough to figure someone would try something like this. Sergeant, you may come in now," he yelled at the door to his cabin.

The door burst open and the senior sergeant of the marine unit on board, accompanied by six marines armed with muskets, came rushing in. While the marines leveled their muskets at Comstock and the two confused looking marines, the sergeant faced Dangerfield and salute. "Aye, sir. What do you be wantin' me to do with 'em?"

"Sergeant, these three are guilty of mutiny. They could be hanged or shot, and if we had time, that's exactly what I would do." Dangerfield rubbed at the stubble on his chin. "Mister Comstock did have one good idea, though. We can't stay here in this port. We need to find a secluded island, preferably with lots of hidden coves, where we can hide until the ship's repaired. On the way there, we'll put them in a boat. Maybe, if they're lucky, the English will pick them up and impress them into service. If not . . . well, such is life, eh."

The sergeant saluted again. "Aye, sir." He turned to his men. "You heard the captain, get these vermin out of here and into a boat 'n over the side."

Chapter Twenty-eight

September 1811, In the port at Little Abaco, Bahamas

Three weeks after their encounter with *Intrepid*, and hearing no further word of her presence in the area, Elizabeth decided it was safe to venture out. *The Vixen* made port at Little Abaco Island at midday on a Saturday, a day when the markets were bustling, and the taverns near the port were filled to capacity with sailors looking for wine, women or gambling, not necessarily in that order.

As they made their way from the pier where they'd tied off the ship's boat used to ferry them ashore— Elizabeth still refused to allow the ship to be boxed in by being tied up to a pier, preferring to leave it at anchor in the harbor where it could make a quick getaway—Elizabeth, as befitting her position as captain, led the way. Behind her, Colin, M'nondo, and Garcia walked three abreast, with Garcia, as the smallest, in the middle. With M'nondo on the outside and Colin on the left, walking close behind Elizabeth and scowling, it had the effect of clearing the sidewalk ahead of her. Behind the four of them, the rest of the crew, minus a few men left on board to guard the ship, was stretched out over fifty yards in groups of two and three. Elizabeth insisted on at least two, preferably three or four in each group. Under no circumstances was anyone other than her to go anywhere alone.

As they came abreast of a tavern with a sign hanging over the door that said, *The Widow Maker*, Elizabeth stopped and turned.

"I suppose you three want to stop here to fill your guts with food and drink," she said, smiling.

"Well," Colin said. "Not to be insulting the cook, but shipboard rations aren't exactly what the French would call *haute cuisine*."

"If that means pig slop, it is actually," Garcia said.

"I'll be sure to tell cook what you three think of his food," she said.

"I said nothing," M'nondo said. "I think the cook's food is quite acceptable."

"Well, the two of you," she said, pointing at Colin and Garcia, who held their hands up in surrender.

"Please, captain, we were just joking," Colin said.

"Yes, whatever you do, don't tell cook I said anything," Garcia said.

She laughed. "Okay, but stay out of trouble. I will meet you back here in . . . three hours?"

"Aye, captain," they said in unison.

She made a sniffing noise, turned and walked off. They stood at the entrance to the tavern and watched her walk away. Dressed in a one-piece dress, light blue, that though modestly-cut, did brush against her figure as she walked, drawing appreciative stares from men and women alike. They watched to make sure no one molested her, although, with the dagger she had concealed in the large bag she carried would take care of any would-be assailants. Each of them, Colin was certain, had his own motives. M'nondo, he'd come to learn, considered himself her elder brother, and would break the neck of any man who so much as looked at her the wrong way. Garcia respected, admired, loved, and resented her in equal measure. Having worked his way up from a mere cabin boy to John Cleague's second in command, he saw himself as the rightful heir to his captaincy. He resented Elizabeth for taking that from him. He had to recognize, though, she was a better mariner, and had more of the respect of the men. At the same time, he'd been in love with her since her teens. As for Colin, he too had his reasons, and they were probably as confused and confusing as Garcia's. He admired her, of that there was no doubt. She was as capable a ship's master as any he'd ever known, and he'd known some great ones. Even though she could rule with an iron fist when the need arose, she had a gentle, non-abusive way of bending men to her will, without resorting to the teasing games some women feel they are forced to use when dealing with the male of the species. Then, there was that other thing. That which he'd forced as far to the back of his mind as he could, but that kept forcing its way back to the front. He could not take his mind off her. Even in battle, one part of his mind was concentrating on what to do, while another strayed to her, and worried about her safety. He silently cursed himself for a fool. His mind should be on getting back to America and his duties as a naval officer. He simply could not be falling in love with . . . a pirate.

As Elizabeth slipped out of sight around a corner, he shook himself like a dog coming out of a stream.

"Well, lads," he said. "What say we enter and see what this fine establishment has to offer?"

"I feared you would stand here and stare at the empty street all day," M'nondo said.

"What?"

"He means, you were staring at the space the captain had just vacated, like she was still there," Garcia said.

"I most certainly was not."

"Hah, your mouth says one thing, but your eyes, they say another, my friend."

"Would you two stop your constant bickering," M'nondo said. "By the gods, it was better when you hated each other. Now, let us go inside before they run out of food and drink."

As they pushed through the door, and entered a place of constant noise, and a combination of smells, some inviting, some not so much so, thoughts of Elizabeth temporarily were pushed aside by the wonder of his relationship with Diego Garcia. Just weeks earlier, the man had tried to kill Colin. But, after working with him on building the Volta lanterns and cooperating with him in the defeat of *Intrepid*, as Colin called them, his attitude had done a complete turn-around. Now, he was his almost constant companion. War does indeed make strange bedfellows, Colin thought.

They made their way through the crowded establishment, weaving to avoid tripping over drunken customers or smashing into one of the dozens of buxom serving girls whose every asset was on display through the scant and near-diaphanous costumes they wore. They were scurrying about the room, laden with trays heavy with mugs of ale or glasses of stronger stuff, wiggling their hips, not to entice, but to escape the grasp of customers who wished a free sample of what Colin was sure was available for the right number of gold coins.

They were lucky enough to find an empty table with four chairs near the back of the room, not far from the exit, something that had become a habit for Colin since 'joining' Elizabeth's band of pirates. They avoided being too near the front or main entrance, because ofttimes, trouble came from that direction. Likewise, they avoided the middle of the space, because you were then hemmed in in case of trouble. At the rear, though, near the exit to where trash and chamber pots were dumped, you had a spot that was usually relatively clear—thanks to the odor of the aforementioned chamber pots and other offal—and unimpeded access to a handy exit in the event things went awry.

As they seated themselves and waved at a buxom bronze-skinned serving girl with improbably bright yellow hair, Colin marveled at the fact that he'd even become accustomed to the smell of garbage. It no longer bothered him as he ate or drank.

The three of them watched with great appreciation

the way the woman's body moved beneath her clothing as the blonde wound her way between the close-packed tables to get to them.

"Whot kin oy git ye, gents?" she asked. Her accent another oddity, because up close, Colin could see that she was a mixture of the aboriginal inhabits of the islands, the Caribs, and African, probably the result of a union between an Indian and a runaway from one of the English plantations.

"What is best food you have?" Garcia asked.

"We got yer roast pig, mate, 'n wit it we got the froyed plantains."

"It sounds good to me. Colin, M'nondo, what about you?"

"I'll have the same," Colin said.

M'nondo nodded.

"Whot'll ye gents 'ave to drink wit yer food?"

"Rum," Garcia said.

"Ale," said Colin.

"I too will have ale," M'nondo said. "You should consider doing the same, Diego."

Garcia's face drooped in embarrassment. "You have no need to worry, my friend. I learned my lesson. Only one will I have, I promise."

M'nondo shrugged, and they turned their attention to watching the way the blonde's hips moved underneath the thin fabric of her dress as she walked away.

"I wonder how much that dish costs," Garcia said.

No one responded. There was no need, Colin knew. Garcia, when it came to the local ladies of leisure, was all talk and no action. In fact, Colin was beginning to suspect that the man was a virgin. M'nondo, on the other hand, with his smoldering, dark looks and muscular physique, he drew the attention of women everywhere they went, but never seemed to notice. About him, Colin worried that he was one of those men who . . . he shuddered at the thought . . . liked other men.

As if reading his thoughts, M'nondo pointed a finger at Garcia. "As for the woman, I would not advise availing yourself of the services of any here. Just around the corner is Madame Toussad's. The women are much better."

Colin gaped at him. "M'nondo, do you mean that you've been in a house of ill repute."

The dark man smiled. "Do I look like a statue? A man has needs, especially after a long voyage. I have . . . someone on Lost Island, but when I am not there, well . . ."

"You sly fox," Colin said. "I would never have guessed."

M'nondo shrugged. "A man should not advertise his activities. It gives others too much to use against you."

"And, a gentleman does not kiss and tell," Colin added, looking pointedly at Garcia, whose cheeks reddened.

"I told nothing," he said.

They were laughing at his discomfort when the serving girl returned, carrying two large flagons of ale and a slightly smaller glass of rum, which she set on the table, kicking up little puffs of dust from its surface.

"Oy'll be right back wit' yer food," she said, and flounced away.

Colin lifted his ale. "Here's to gentlemen," he said.

"And, may we always be thought of as such."

They clinked containers and took sips. The ale, frothy and heady tasting to Colin, left a small white mustache on M'nondo's upper lip, which the man licked away with a quick swipe of his tongue.

"Ah, the first ale of the day; always the best," he said, belching to punctuate his assessment.

The serving girl came back, carrying a large metal tray on her shoulder. On the tray were three large plates upon which were two large pieces of golden-brown pork glistening with juices, a pile of sickly-green plantain leaves also swimming in grease, a large chunk of bread, and a potato partially wrapped in a banana leaf. She set a plate in front of each, and from a pocket in her dress, withdrew three forks and three knives, which she placed beside the plates.

"Enjoy yer food, gents," she said, as she turned and flounced away.

The food looked greasy, but the aroma made Colin's mouth water. Without further conversation, they picked up their utensils and attacked it like starving men, the only sounds they made the clink of fork and knife on plate, and the smacking of their lips.

When all was gone except for a piece of bread, Colin used it to sop up the last of the meat gravy from his plate. After chewing it a few times, and swallowing, he sat back in his chair and loosened the waist of his trousers.

"Now, that was a meal worth waiting for," he said.

"You have pieces of bread in your beard," Garcia said, pointing at Colin.

Colin picked at his lush beard, removing a piece of bread the size of the end of his thumb, which he popped into his mouth.

"Well, so I did," he said, after chewing and swallowing it. "Thanks. Hate to let food go to waste."

Leaning back again in his chair, Colin looked around the room. As his gaze swept past the entrance, three men walked in. All wore the unkempt and ragged garments of common laborers and had several days' growth of beard on their faces, but the smaller of the three walked with a familiar gait.

As the three men approached a serving girl, and the two larger stepped back to allow the small man to talk, the way he waved his arms as he spoke awakened a memory in Colin. *My God, that's Albert Comstock!* As Colin stared, Comstock glanced his way and for a moment his eyes widened, then he squinted as he looked at Colin, who quickly turned his head away.

"Finish your drinks, gentlemen," he said quietly. "We need to go find the captain."

Charles Ray

Chapter Twenty-nine

As they exited the tavern, Elizabeth came around the corner about a building away. She carried a large cloth bag in her left hand and held an unopened umbrella across her shoulder in her left. She smiled when she saw them.

"Did you three get your fill?" she asked as she came abreast of them, noting a worried look in Colin's eyes.

"Yes, captain," M'nondo said. "But, Colin here was suddenly in a rush to depart."

"Yes, and I was just getting ready for my second rum," said Garcia.

She looked at Colin. He was shifting slightly from one foot to the other, and glancing back over his shoulder at the closed door.

"What is it, Colin? You look as if perhaps you've seen a ghost."

He turned and caught her eye, a deep frown creating a crease between his brown brows.

"Uh, captain, we have to talk, but not here. Could we go back to the ship?"

His worry was infectious. Now, she felt a twinge.

"Is it that important?" she asked.

"If my eyes didn't deceive me, it's extremely important."

"Then, by all means, let us go to the ship." She handed him her bag, which he accepted without comment.

As they walked along, she shifted the umbrella until she was using it almost as a cane, tapping the end on the uneven boards of the sidewalk. She noticed that he kept looking down at it curiously, but he said nothing.

In fact, not another word was spoken until they were back on the ship and in her cabin with the door shut.

She placed the umbrella on her desk and took her seat behind it, folding her hands in her lap. "Okay, Colin, now can you tell me what has you so fidgety?"

He placed her bag down next to the desk and sat in the chair at its side. M'nondo and Garcia took chairs in front of the desk, and like her, fixed their gaze on him.

For a moment, he just sat there, tugging at the luxurious growth of beard that covered the lower half of his face.

"Captain, Elizabeth, if I'm not mistaken, and I am almost certain that I am not, I saw three crewmen from *Intrepid* in that tavern."

Everyone leaned forward.

"What would your former crewmates be doing on Little Abaco? I didn't see their ship in the harbor."

"Nor did I," he said. "And, that worries me. Furthermore, they were dressed in rags and had grown facial hair. For one of them, Lieutenant Albert Comstock, who was the quartermaster officer who Dangerfield put in my job when he put me overboard, that is completely out of character."

Elizabeth frowned. "I would have thought, after the damage we did to his ship, your former captain would have made straight for an American port for repairs."

"That's what any sane captain would do, but we both know that Dangerfield is not completely sane. I wonder if he is lurking about among the islands, still looking for us."

Elizabeth tapped her fingers on the umbrella and studied him. He was clearly worried. And, he was right, Dangerfield was demented. He seemed obsessed with her and her ship. Would he risk a confrontation with the English in order to get at her?

"Do you think these men could be spies, sent to gather information about our whereabouts?"

He seemed to think about that for too long before responding. Then, he shook his head.

"Not Comstock," he said. "He's a good lad, but not the most energetic or brightest officer in our navy. He doesn't have the gumption to be an effective spy."

"Then, why are they there? And, why are they dressing like common laborers?"

He fingered his beard again. She caught herself staring at it and at his face, and having thoughts that were, under the current circumstances, quite inappropriate.

"This is just a thought," he said. "And, I might be mistaken, although, I think not." He hesitated, as if unsure of himself. "I think that Dangerfield has done to them the same thing he did to me. He abandoned them for some reason. And, now, I think he's holed up somewhere making repairs to *Intrepid*."

"Why would he do that . . . not the part about making repairs here, that I can believe, but why would he jettison three men? It makes no sense."

"I was his second in command, and he put me off the ship just because I disagreed with his plan to go chasing after your vessel. After the shellacking we gave him, I imagine Comstock must have suggested going back to America. That would have gotten him kicked off the ship. I have no idea about the other two, who I think I recognized as two of the marine infantry we had on board."

"An officer and two marines," she said. "That sounds like a spy mission to me."

"Anyone but Comstock, and I would agree with you. But, the man is not spy material."

"So, what would you have us do?"

"I would like your permission to approach them, discretely of course, and see if I can find out what happened."

"That is not a good idea," Garcia said. "If they are spies, you might give us away."

Colin looked offended.

"I give you my solemn word that I would not do that. Diego, you have worked with me, Elizabeth and M'nondo, you have as well. You know me as a man of my word."

"Uh, sorry, Colin, I did not mean to imply that you

would deliberately expose us. But, if they are spies—remember, they saw you with us—they might put two and three together and figure it out."

Colin smiled. "You mean, put two and two together." When Garcia looked confused. "Never mind. I think I can do it in a way that wouldn't risk exposing any of you. After all, Comstock saw me being put off the ship. I'm sure I could come up with a story to explain my presence here."

"Over a thousand miles from where you went into the ocean?" Elizabeth looked at him with an expression of incredulity. "*I* would like to hear that explanation."

"As I said, though, Albert, while a competent enough officer, does not have the quickest mind. I'm sure I can come up with a story he would believe. He just might have the information we need to avoid Dangerfield, or if unable to do that, discover his location, and be prepared for him."

She continued to play with the umbrella. Finally, Garcia asked her why she had bought such an impractical item.

She lifted it, holding the curved handle in her right hand, with her left hand curled around the folded cloth. Then, in one swift motion, she pulled at the handle, and in her right hand was a wicked looking blade, about three feet long and half an inch in width. A rapier with a curved hilt. The blade glinted in the light from the lantern on the wall behind her desk.

"*Madre de Dios*," he said. "Where did you get that?"

She held it up, admiring the workmanship of the blade. "I had it made to my specifications at a shop in Little Abaco. I ordered it the last time we were here."

"But, why do you need such a thing, *Esi*? You have a perfectly good sword." M'nondo looked puzzled.

"Sure, my sword is fine when I'm properly dressed," she said. "But, when I have to put on this damnable dress for our trips to places like Abaco, all I have for protection is a tiny dagger. There is no place to conceal a proper blade in a lady's dress. This, however, is perfect. And, when I don't need it for protection, it shades me from the sun and rain."

"But, you have us to protect you." M'nondo looked as if she'd just kicked him in the crotch.

"And, you, *Kofi*, know that I am perfectly capable of protecting myself." She smiled demurely at him. "I can hold my own against *any* man."

"That is true, M'nondo," Garcia said. "Remember when she was sixteen, she wrestled both of us, and pinned both of us."

"At the same time?" Colin asked.

"Oh, no," Garcia said. "One at a time, but she defeated us, right M'nondo."

Looking as if this was a memory he would rather forget, M'nondo glared at the smaller man. Finally, he grudgingly nodded. "But, I think perhaps she cheated," he said.

"I did not," Elizabeth said in protest.

"Yes, you did. You grabbed my . . . you know—"

"It's not my fault that you men have certain parts of your anatomy that are very sensitive."

Colin laughed, he laughed until tears flowed from his eyes.

"What is so funny?" M'nondo asked.

"Oh, I was just picturing you, bent over and yowling in pain. I would pay to see that."

M'nondo winced, and looked down at the table. Wisely, Colin pursued the matter no further.

"Look, Colin," Elizabeth said. "I'll give some thought to your proposal to try and talk to these men, careful thought. I'll give you my decision after supper tonight."

"We are eating aboard ship, I assume," M'nondo said.

"I think we can let a few of the men go ashore," she said. "But, the three of us should remain close . . . just in case."

Charles Ray

Chapter Thirty

Albert Comstock itched. He itched all over, from his torso to his face. His clothing, he was convinced, was infested with tiny, invisible lice that crawled over his body, invading every crevice each time he dressed, and the hair on his face, its growth patchy and uneven, all contributed to his miserable feeling. That, and the smell—his smell. The horrible hovel they'd been able to procure with what little gold he'd been able to get from his cabin just before the sergeant of marines escorted him and the two marines to a boat and hoisted them over the side, had to be husbanded carefully. The fee for the three of them in what was little more than a stable without water nearby, and nothing to keep flies and other pests out, still made a significant dent in his coin. For a hot bath and a shave, though, he was tempted to spend more. But, he wouldn't be able to afford such amenities for all three, so, since his men, which was how he thought of the two unfortunate marines, since his men suffered, it was only right that he suffered, too.

It was Joseph, the older of the two marines, who had suggested they ditch their uniforms and let their beards grow. The English navy and colonial officials here in the Bahamas wouldn't take kindly to American military in their midst, and there was always the danger of being impressed into the English navy. The clothing, which was too small for the two marines and two big for him, had been stolen from a clothesline outside a humble dwelling half a mile in from the beach where they'd managed to bring the big boat ashore. He considered himself lucky that the sergeant had allowed them to keep the boat's oars, and that he hadn't been cast off alone, for he would never have been able to row it himself. The two young marines, though, fell to, and managed to get their bearings, heading west, or as near west as they could estimate. When night fell, they made sure to keep the North Star to their left, and rowed and rowed until Comstock thought they would drop from exhaustion.

They were, in fact, almost too tired to row any further when they heard the unmistakable sound of waves breaking on a shore. And then, they saw the darker shape against the night sky, an island, a secluded beach.

After coming ashore, it was Joseph again, who suggested holing the boat and sinking it out just beyond the breakers. No sense leaving it for the English to find, he said, which would provoke a search, since it was obvious where it had come from. Leaving Comstock waiting on the beach, the two young men rowed out, sank the boat at the point where the slope into deeper water began and swam back.

They lay on the beach until sunrise, just glad to be alive.

Now, they were working as casual laborers at the docks, spending up to twelve hours per day, heaving barrels and boxes from warehouse to ship or from ship to warehouse. No one questioned their obvious American accents. Their clothing marked them as vagrants, possible criminals come to the Bahamas a step ahead of lawmen from wherever they had come.

They worked the long shifts Monday through Friday, and only a half day on Saturday. Sunday, there would only be work if an important cargo arrived and had to be unloaded immediately. Fortunately, in the three weeks they'd been on Little Abaco, there had been no Sunday emergencies.

Comstock looked forward to the day and a half away from the back-breaking labor, the sweat, the stink, and the constant cursing. They had made *The Widow Maker* their home away from home, because the prices were reasonable, the food was good, the ale passable, and the serving wenches among the most beautiful, desirable women Comstock had ever seen in his short life. Not that he'd availed himself of their services. At twenty-three, he was, despite being a naval officer, still a virgin. He didn't know about the two marines, and was too shy to ask. The more he went into *The Widow Maker*, though, and the more the pittance they were paid to work the docks piled up, the more he was tempted to end his celibate status. He'd had his eye on a particularly tempting serving wench, a petite woman with large breasts, raven hair, and eyes so blue he thought when she looked at him he would jump in and drown in their depths. He would not, though, purchase such entertainment until he was sure his companions—his men—had enough to do so as well, unless they wished not to.

They walked into the tavern just after noon. The place, as was usual on Saturday, crowded, noisy, and smelly. But, the sight of Felicia, *his* girl, caused Comstock not to notice any of this.

What he noticed, the only thing he wanted to notice, was the bronze skin that glowed under the flickering light of the lanterns, the hair so black its highlights seemed blue, and lips that looked as ripe and delicious as freshly picked strawberries.

When he caught her eye across the crowded space, he smiled. She smiled shyly back. He began to make his way across the room to her, stumbling over clumsily placed feet and apologizing the entire way, until he stood before her, finally, close enough to touch, but without the courage to do so.

"Good day, Andrew," she said, using the name Joseph had suggested he use if he had to introduce himself to anyone. "You are late today. I was beginning to think that you did not wish to see me." She fluttered long eyelashes at him. He could feel the pulse in his neck, beating like an Iroquois war drum.

"We had t-to unload a barge full of palm fruit before the boss would let us leave," he said. "But, I came as soon as I could."

She was carrying a tray loaded with flagons of ale, but held it effortlessly in one hand. Such strength, he thought, in such a fragile looking body. With her free hand, she reached up and stroked his patchy beard.

"Okay, I will forgive you, this time. You and your

friends, find yourselves a table, and if another girl comes to serve you, you tell her that you belong to Felicia, no?"

"Yes, er, no, I mean, I'll do that." Just as he turned to search for a table, movement to the left caught his eye. He stopped and blinked. *No, that's impossible. It can't be him. But, it looks so much like him, except for the beard.* He shook his head and turned to his companions. "Joseph, William, see the man over in the corner near the back, the large one with the beard?"

The two men craned to see.

"No sir, all I see is an empty table," Joseph said.

Comstock whirled around, and stared. Sure enough, the table at which three men, two white men and an African, had sat was now vacant. Where had they gone? Had he only thought he'd seen . . . no, it had to be him, but it couldn't possibly be him. He was dead. He had to be dead.

"What did you see, Mr. Com-, Andrew?" William asked.

Comstock blinked and shook himself.

"Nothing, I thought I saw someone I knew," he said. "Must be from too much work in the hot sun and not enough to eat or drink. Never mind."

But, as they made their way to the just-vacated table, Comstock was almost certain that he'd seen Colin Worth, even though he knew it was impossible that he could have made a journey of over a thousand miles, alone in a ship's boat without a sail or even an oar for propulsion. The two marines with him had explained that Colin had been put in the boat with only enough food and water for two to three days, a week at most. Even with the currents, he would have been dead from thirst before the boat drifted this far. The man he'd seen, that he thought he'd seen, showed no signs of deprivation that a man who spent that many days in a boat, exposed to the elements . . . his mind was racing with the possibilities and impossibilities, the improbabilities.

Yes, he thought, I just thought I saw what I saw.

"Let's eat, drink, and be merry, gentlemen," he said. "For, we know not what the morrow brings."

Chapter Thirty-one

Colin ate his evening meal with the rest of the crew. The men accepted him, but he noticed that old Peg Leg Pete, the ship's cook, kept giving him the evil eye throughout the meal, and looked surprised when Colin cleaned his plate and asked for seconds. Someone had told. Either M'nondo or Garcia had, he was sure. It could've been Elizabeth, for she had a wicked sense of humor he'd learned, but he preferred not to believe she would do that to him. No, it had to be M'nondo or Garcia, and his money was on the smaller man. M'nondo hadn't shown any signs of having that kind of sense of humor, and Garcia, fearing someone might tell the cook that he too had insulted his cooking, might have done it in a preemptive move to deflect attention from himself. Pete was still looking askance at him, even after he'd polished off the second helping of the unidentified mashed concoction, which actually didn't taste half bad, so Colin was happy when one of the men from deck watch came and informed him that the captain wanted to see him immediately in her cabin.

He made it a point to compliment Peter on the food before leaving, causing the old man to squint at him with his one good eye as if that would help him tell if Colin was shining him on. Then, he made his way to the captain's cabin, just below the quarterdeck.

"Come in, it's not locked," her husky voice responded to his knock on the door.

He stepped inside and was greeted by the soft, orange glow of several candles placed around the room. But, what caused the breath to catch in his throat was Elizabeth, sitting on the small settee along the bulkhead near her bed, wearing a light blue, diaphanous gown that hugged every curve of her body. Worse, it had slipped off one shoulder and in addition to showing off the delightful curve of her décolletage, displayed the succulent-looking roundness of the breast on that side. She had an ornate crystal bottle filled with a dark amber liquid on the table at her knees. Beside it were two exquisitely-shaped crystal glasses unlike anything he'd ever seen before, not even when he and his men had raided the castle of one of the lesser princes during the war against the pirates in Tripoli.

She was gazing dreamily at a spot on the bulkhead to Colin's right, and didn't seem to notice that he'd entered. He cleared his throat.

"You wanted to speak to me, captain?"

"Yes, Colin. Please sit here by me." There was a husky throatiness in her voice that made his heart race, and created ungentlemanly thoughts in his mind.

He walked across and sat on the settee, about six inches from her, but he could still feel the heat from her body.

"Would you care for a drink? We took this off a French ship bound for Haiti last year. I've been saving it for a special occasion."

As he walked forward, Colin felt as if he was pushing through a thicket of gauze hanging from the overhead. He could feel his pulse pounding in his throat.

"Uh, well, yes, if you're having one." His tongue felt thick in his dry mouth.

As she leaned forward to pour, more of her breast was exposed. He felt himself respond and quickly half turned to his right to try and conceal the growing response to her. She glanced up briefly from filling the two glasses. A slight widening of her eyes and the appearance of spots of red on her cheeks informed him that he'd not been successful. His cheeks burned. He crossed his legs, and even though it hurt to do so, he was at least satisfied to note that she could no longer see how excited he'd become. *Dammit, not is not the time. I have to convince her to let me go to Comstock.*

She lifted the two glasses from the table and passed one to him. As he took it, their fingers briefly brushed, and he felt a tingle from the tips of his fingers to his shoulder. Her cheeks became darker.

She lifted her glass and cleared her throat.

"Here's to . . . happiness, success, and riches," she said.

"Sure, why not," he said, tapping the rim of his glass against hers.

He took a sip. The liquid felt hot on his tongue and

going down his throat, but the taste was not unpleasant. *Say what you will about the bloody frogs, they do know how to make good liquor.* He took another sip, looking at her over the rim of his glass, which made sitting cross-legged even more uncomfortable. *Why does she have to be so damned beautiful? Keep your mind on business, Colin.* His mind, though, had a will of its own. It was imagining the feel of his lips on hers, the taste of her skin, what it would be like to rip the rest of her dress away and gaze upon . . . *Oh Lord, this is madness.* As he looked into her eyes, he saw a flicker of nervousness there, and wondered if, could it even be possible, he thought, she was feeling anything.

She put her glass down and turned slightly on the settee to face him.

"You are no doubt wondering why I summoned you."

He put his glass down. "I, uh, I assume it's to talk about my proposal to contact Albert Comstock."

A half smile formed on her face. He felt as if his heart was flipping around in his chest, and found it hard to concentrate on the business he knew they should be discussing.

"No," she said. "I did not."

"Huh?"

She placed a hand on his knee. It felt as hot as a poker just drawn from the fireplace. What is going on here, he thought, as she gently massaged his knee.

"Colin, you must know by now that I fancy you," she said. "And, from the way you look at me sometimes." She looked down at his crotch. "And, the way you are . . . right now, I know that you also fancy me."

Colin felt like crawling under the settee. This was not going the way it should be going. They should be discussing business, or if not, it should be him doing the seducing, not the other way around. But, when he looked into her eyes, he felt his resistance to the turn-about in their situations beginning to melt.

"W-well, of course I . . . think that you're one of the most beautiful women I've ever seen in my life. I . . . yes, I fancy you."

The pressure of her hand on his leg increased, and he could feel it moving slowly up his thigh.

"Then, you fool, why are you not kissing me?" She leaned forward. He could smell the scent of fresh flowers in her scarlet hair and from the translucent skin where her neck met her shoulder. Her right breast was now almost totally exposed.

As their lips met, more of the sparks he'd felt when their fingers touched, flew between them. He felt a rushing noise in his ears.

Her tongue, moist and oh, so tasty, flicked between his lips and began darting around in his mouth. And her hand, her hand was . . . grasping him, his . . . oh, my goodness, he thought as he felt her other hand snake around his neck and pull his head forward, where did her dress go.

Later, when Colin was capable of conscious thought, he noticed that they were lying on her bed. Him on his back, with her nuzzled in the crook of his arm. Both were as naked as newborn babes, and while he would have ordinarily been uncomfortable to be lying so exposed, he felt completely at ease.

She ran a hand through the matted tangle of hair

on his chest.

"Why did we wait so long?" she asked, her voice muffled as she was kissing his neck, and sending tingles throughout his body.

"I, uh, that is—" He found himself unable to continue. The words were in his heart, but he couldn't form them with his mouth.

"What, does the cat have your tongue? Such a brave man in battle, and here, you are like a—you were not a . . . virgin, were you?" Her eyes went wide.

He looked at her, his face red with a combination of chagrin and embarrassment. "No, I was not a v-virgin," he said. He took a deep breath. "It's just that I am not accustomed to the woman . . . taking the lead like you did."

She pushed away from him, causing her breasts to sway in a way that once again aroused him. He closed his eyes.

"What? Do you not find me pleasing to look at?" She slapped him lightly on the cheek.

His eyes snapped open. "You are extremely pleasing to look at. Too much so, in fact. Oh hell, Elizabeth, I've been lusting after you since I first laid eyes on you. I just never thought . . . and I still have to . . . I just wasn't sure how you felt."

She put a leg over his, rubbing it up and down.

"And, now that you know how I feel, what happens next?"

"That's just it," he said. "I don't know how you feel. Was this just to satisfy your . . . needs, or do you really care for me?"

He hated the way he sounded. It wasn't supposed to be like this. He waited expectantly for her answer, fearing what it might be.

"Do I care for you?" She laid a finger on her nose. "Well, let me think." She smiled as he frowned at her. "No, I don't *care* for you, Colin Worth, I am in love with you."

He opened his mouth to issue a stinging retort, when the meaning of her words hit him like a ten-pound cannon ball. He gasped.

"You . . . you love me? Really?"

"Really. Now, what do you plan to do about it?"

"Well, I suppose we should get married?"

She laughed.

"Are you sure that is such a good idea, my darling. The dashing American naval officer, married to a dastardly Caribbean pirate? What would your superiors think?"

"Oh. I hadn't thought about that."

"That's because you men are always thinking with the wrong head," she said, swatting playfully at his rapidly deflating manhood. "I suppose we could get married, but we would have to conceal it from the world, for both our sakes."

"How would you be—oh, I see. I guess it wouldn't do your reputation much good if your fellow pirates learned you were consorting with a navy officer."

"My, my, handsome and smart as well. Aren't I a lucky woman." Then she released him and swung her legs off the bed. She strode, naked, across to her desk and sat behind it, motioning toward the chair in front.

Colin grabbed a pillow to cover his exposed front and made his way to the chair to her silent amusement.

"Okay, let's get down to business," she said after

he'd adjusted his naked bottom to the cold wood of the chair. "You still want to make contact with this former shipmate of yours, Albert Comstock?"

"Yes, I'm convinced he's no spy, and I think he'll have information that could prove useful to us."

"Very well. Tomorrow, you'll go ashore and talk to this Comstock. We'll see where it leads from there. Now, that concludes business, shall we return to bed?"

Chapter Thirty-two

The next morning, at cock's crow, Colin roused Devereux and Rodriguez from their hammocks and had them help him put one of the small ship's boats over the side. They left the ship and rowed to the docks, where he left the two men to watch the boat. He made his way through the near-deserted docks to the crowded street where the tavern was located.

It was an early hour, but the place was already open, serving drinks to those who drank round the clock, and gruel to those who were suffering from too much drink the night before. At some tables, men slept, slumped over the tables with their heads on folded arms.

Colin had guessed from the state of their attire that Comstock and the two marines occupied mean lodgings, and since the tavern had a reputation for never closing, would likely to spend the night there.

He'd guessed right. At the table that he and his

friends had so hastily vacated, he found Comstock, head on folded arms, making little bubbling noises with his pursed lips as he slept. The two marines had apparently had more to drink. They were sprawled back in their chairs, heads thrown back, snoring as loudly as a saw ripping through a tree trunk.

Colin pulled a chair from a nearby table and straddled it next to the sleeping Comstock. He tapped him softly on the arm.

"Huh, wha-, who the hell are you?" the half-asleep Comstock said. He cocked his head and looked up at the intruder through bleary eyes. "Go away and leave me alone. I have no coins to give you. Let me sleep."

"Albert," Colin said quietly. "Wake up and listen to me."

Comstock's eyes snapped open, and he jerked upright, staring at the apparition sitting next to him. "God, it can't be! Colin, is it really you?"

"Yes, it is," Colin said in a harsh whisper. "But, lower your voice. I don't want the whole place to know who I am."

Comstock grasped his hand. Tears welled up in his eyes.

"W-we thought you were dead for sure. W-when I saw you yesterday, I thought I was hallucinating. How d-did you get all the way down here?" His voice was low, but filled with excitement.

"It's a long story, Albert. I'll tell you one day. But, now we have a more pressing matter to discuss, starting with why the three of you are here."

Comstock gave him a forlorn look. "It was my fault," he said. "All my fault."

"It weren't all your fault, sir," Joseph, the older of

the two young marines said. He stretched and yawned and poked his comrade to awaken him. Then, he looked across the table at Colin and smiled. "Good mornin' to you, Lieutenant Worth, didn't think I'd ever be seein' you again. Anyway, Lieutenant Comstock, the only one to blame's the captain. The man's as crazy as a loon, and he ain't got no business bein' a ship's captain."

William, the younger marine, responding to his friend's prodding, stretched, yawned, and gaped, goggle-eyed at Colin. "Mister Worth, sir, you be alive? Really. What you doin' all the way down here? What's goin' on?" All of this came out of him in a torrent, the volume of his voice rising on each sentence. Colin felt fortunate that his name had come out in the first sentence that was a croaked whisper.

"Shut your trap, William," Joseph said. "I got a feelin' the lieutenant ain't wantin' the whole place to know who he be."

Colin was impressed with the young man's perceptiveness, and nodded his thanks.

"That's correct, private, thank you," he said. "Right now, I'm think of how to get the three of you back to American soil." He turned back to Comstock. "But, first, you were telling me how your current situation came to pass."

Comstock gulped. "Like I said, it was my fault." He snuck a glance at the two marines. "Sort of. The captain was acting crazier than usual, and after we were boarded by an English warship and some of the men were taken away, I insisted that we follow orders and get to the nearest American port and report it. He refused, and when I tried relieving him of command as the regulations require, he put me and the marines I'd brought along to escort him to his cabin and guard him put off the ship."

Colin nodded. "Aye, it's the same thing he did to me, and all I did was express my opinion that we should focus on our main mission and not go chasing after a single pirate ship."

Joseph made a snorting noise. "Like Lieutenant Comstock said, the captain's got bats flyin' around in his belfry. If somebody don't stop him, he's either gonna get the whole crew kilt, or worse, taken by the damn English."

"Not if I can help it," Colin said. His anger at that moment was white hot.

"I don't know what you have in mind, sir," Joseph said. "But, me and Billy here, we'd like to help."

"I would like to as well," Comstock said.

"No, I have another mission for the three of you, and in order to carry it out, you have to get back home. I know some small cargo ships that can get you to Hispaniola. From Haiti, it should be easy for our minister or consul there to arrange your passage to Florida or South Carolina."

"B-but, Colin, how will you handle Dangerfield alone?" Comstock asked.

"I . . . I'm not alone. Don't worry about that. Now, before we get you on a boat and out of here, tell me as best you can where you were marooned, and which way *Intrepid* sailed after you were put overboard."

The two marines had a pretty good recall of the direction *Intrepid* had gone, as they were facing backwards rowing the boat—southeast—and, Comstock, a diligent executive officer with a good head for numbers, knew the ship's approximate location at the point where they left it. Colin, from his months with Elizabeth and her crew, knew most of the islands scattered about the eastern edge of the Caribbean, both those shown on sailing charts, and many that were not. The area the three men described, the ship's need for avoiding English warships while under repair, and the direction they'd last seen it sailing, gave him a good idea where to find it.

The area, south of Great Abaco, where the Bahamas chain points to the southeast like the long, slim blade of a knife, around Cat Island in particular, also has a number of small islands, some with a small population, some uninhabited, many with hidden coves in which a ship the size of *Intrepid* can be concealed. He also knew that the area was seldom patrolled by the English ships, their preference being the heavier traveled sea lanes.

As he mulled it in his mind, one name kept coming to the fore, the ideal place to hide a ship, get repairs, and be relatively sure you won't be pestered by local colonial authorities: Skull Island.

Charles Ray

Chapter Thirty-three

September 1811, Skull Island

After escorting the three men to the docks, and arranging passage to Haiti on a leaky old cargo ship run by a captain that Devereux knew, Colin went back to *The Vixen*, where he briefed Elizabeth, M'nondo and Garcia on what he'd learned from them.

They all agreed with his assessment that Dangerfield was probably on Skull Island.

"Damn the man's eyes," Elizabeth said, slamming the top of the table in her cabin with such force it rattled the cups of coffee on it. "He just will not go away and leave us alone." She looked at Colin, fire in her eyes. "Now, we do it my way. We swoop down on them while they're unable to sail, and we destroy them."

Colin returned her look, but kept his expression and voice neutral.

"I agree that we have to do something about him. But, I have a proposal that doesn't involve *swooping*, and might just be as effective in ridding us of him forever."

"I'm listening." Her expression, however, remained skeptical.

"If it is Skull Island," he said. "We can enlist the help of the islanders." He looked to M'nondo. "I remember hearing sailors talk about it during some of our forays ashore, its current population is mainly escaped former slaves, right?"

"That is correct." The big man nodded. "Before the English banned the slave trade, many on the islands here had slaves, mostly from the west coast of Africa. From time to time, some would escape. They made their way to Skull Island, where they hid in the jungle. Eventually, they built a settlement, and by the time the slaves here were finally freed, they had a small village of about two hundred people. They still live in the jungle, have little to do with people from other islands, and like people in Hispaniola, follow the old religions that the French call *vudu*. If the American captain is there, they will try to avoid him."

"With a madman like Dangerfield, that's easier said than done," Colin said. "But, we still might be able to enlist their help to rid us of him." He described what he had in mind, thinking as he spoke that it was the craziest thing he'd ever come up with, and being surprised at the end when M'nondo nodded and said it just might work.

They set sail for Skull Island at dusk, relying on the navigational skills of the Irishman, O'Reilly to find the small speck of jungle-covered sand and coral encrusted rock in the dark.

And, find it he did. Not only that, but he'd remembered the topography of the island well enough to find a cove in which they could conceal *The Vixen*, but still be positioned for a fast exit should the need arise.

"Mister O'Reilly, you are amazing," Colin said as the crew was dropping anchor. "I've been going to sea for many years, but would never have been able to find this place in darkness."

"Oy, mate, tis nothin'," the freckle-faced O'Reilly said. "Bludy English tink we bog Irish ain't fit for nuttin' boot emtyin' their chamber pots, boot, I done showed 'em, I has. I said rings 'round every feckin' Limey sailor wot's out 'ere. Every feckin' Yank, too, no offense intended."

Colin clapped the man's shoulder. "None taken, Michael, none taken at all."

The shore party consisted of Colin, Elizabeth, M'nondo, Rodriguez and Devereux. Garcia had wanted to come along, but Elizabeth had left him in command of the ship.

After grounding the small boat on the sand, Elizabeth left Rodriguez and Devereux to guard it, and with M'nondo leading the way, the three of them set out through the jungle.

"Are you sure it's safe for just the three of us to be

going in here?" Colin asked the big man's back as he hacked a trail for them through the thick vines with his saber.

Without looking back, M'nondo replied, "The people who live here are peaceful. They will not harm us if we do nothing to harm them. If they see a large group coming, though, and believe me, they would, they will melt into the jungle and we'll never see them."

"How do you know so much about them?"

M'nondo grunted and kept hacking at the vines. Colin decided to drop the subject.

The jungle ended suddenly. From the dappled light that filtered down through the interlacing tree branches, they stepped into blazing sunlight. The clearing was large, consisting of fields of maize and other plants in neat rows, and about a hundred mud and palm frond huts arranged in a rough circle in the center. The villagers were all African, their differing skin colors, from a light brown to almost inky black, and different facial structures marked them as coming from many different tribes, but they were all dressed similarly. The men wore simple loin cloths, secured with leather thongs, while the women, regardless of age, wore gaily-colored skirts, leaving their breasts bare. Smaller children wore nothing, playing naked in the dirt between the huts, or sitting with older women who tended the cooking fires.

In addition to tending the fires, the women worked the fields. The man, carrying large baskets woven from some kind of straw, short spears, and long-bladed knives, seemed to be engaged mainly in hunting and fishing.

The hum of conversations in the village, starting

with those in the outer fields who saw them first, stopped in waves collapsing into the center when they stepped out of the jungle.

The first to see them was a young woman carrying a woven basket filled with what looked like sweet potatoes to Colin. She dropped the basket, shrieked, and ran toward the huts, with her young breasts bouncing wildly. Others stopped what they were doing, and a group of men, brandishing spears, rushed toward them.

When the men were about twenty feet away, they stopped and stared. M'nondo motioned with his hand for Colin and Elizabeth to stop. He then turned back to the group of armed men and raised his right hand, clenched into a fist, and said something in a guttural language that Colin did not understand. A man almost as large and imposing as M'nondo, stepped from the group and advanced until he was a few feet from M'nondo, his spear held loosely at his side, and a wide smile on his nut-brown face.

"How you come, brudda? It dem long time no see."

"Know dem bin," M'nondo said. "How de body, brudda?"

The two men embraced, slapping each other on the back, then stepped back, smiling at each other.

M'nondo motioned Colin and Elizabeth to step forward.

The villager looked warily at them.

"Kojomo," M'nondo said. "This is Elizabeth, my *Esi*, and Colin, my friend. This is Kojomo, he is the war chief of this village."

Elizabeth inclined her head, while Colin stuck out his hand.

"Pleased to meet you, Mr. Kojomo," he said.

Kojomo stared at his hand for a few seconds, and then, switched his spear to his left hand and grasped it. To Colin, the man's grip was strong, and his palms were callused and dry.

"It is my pleasure, Colin," Kojomo said.

Colin looked surprised.

"Kojomo was foreman for a British plantation owner before slavery was abolished," M'nondo said, laughing. "He speaks better English than either of us."

M'nondo, my friend, you should not tell my secrets to every stranger who comes here," Kojomo said, but he laughed as well.

"Colin is no stranger. He is one of us."

"Well, then we must welcome you and your friends properly." Kojomo turned and signaled the other men that all was well. They trotted back toward the village, speaking to the women in the field as they ran. The war chief and his new guests followed at a more leisurely pace.

Colin gazed around in awe as they passed scenes that must have replicated their homes across the ocean. He saw that Elizabeth was doing the same.

While life for these people was no doubt difficult, but now that they had been deemed no threat, he could see no sign of unhappiness.

Kojomo led them to a cleared area in the center of the circle of huts, which contained a large square of logs around a pile of ashes. He motioned for them to be seated, and then sat across from them.

Very shortly, a couple of young women came out carrying four large gourds. They gave the first one to Kojomo, and then one to each guest.

"Welcome to Tswalu," Kojomo said. He put the opening of the guard to his lips and tilted his head back. Drops of an orangish liquid spilled over his cheeks.

Colin lifted the gourd and sniffed at it. Whatever the liquid was it had a pungent, sweet odor. He glanced at M'nondo and Elizabeth, who were both already taking large swallows, so he lifted the gourd and let the liquid pour into his mouth and down his throat, and almost gagged.

It had a slightly sweet taste, but burned like live coals. His eyes burned and watered, and his mouth felt on fire. He managed to swallow what was in his mouth, but began to cough violently. M'nondo laughed and slapped him on the back.

"Palm wine," he said. "It takes some getting used to. Much stronger than even rum."

When Colin could breathe normally again, he looked at his friend through teary eyes. "You could have warned me," he said.

"But, that would have been no fun."

Elizabeth laughed. Colin noticed that she'd taken smaller sips, but without any adverse effects. He glared at her.

"You've had this . . . palm wine before?"

She smiled and ducked her head. "M'nondo brought some back the last time he visited."

"Well then, thank *you* for warning me."

Kojomo watched it all with a knowing smile on his face. After a while, he raised his hand, and everyone fell silent.

"My brother, M'nondo," he said. "I am always happy to see you, but I have a feeling that your visit is not social."

"As always, my brother, you see inside my heart. We do need your help. There is a bad man that we seek, and we think he might have come here to your island."

Kojomo's face darkened. "Huh, you mean the mad man and his ship of fools? Yes, he is here. He has hidden his ship in Devil's Cove where they labor to repair it."

"You have had contact with them?"

"They met some of our hunters in the jungle, and tried to hire them to help with the work. When they refused, they were taken captive. Two managed to escape and came back to warn us. Fortunately, they do not wander far from the cove, so they have not found our village."

"And, you do nothing to free your people?" Colin asked.

Kojomo scowled. M'nondo held up a hand.

"It is not so simple, Colin," he said. "Kojomo's people are basically peaceful. They have men who are willing to make war."

"But," Kojomo said. "The crazy man has many muskets and cannons. We have spears and knives. How can we fight them?"

Colin smiled. "Like the horsefly attacks the largest horse," he said. "It is so small, the horse does not see it until it has stung."

"I do not understand." Kojomo frowned, his dark brow furrowed.

"When you face a stronger enemy, you do not attack from the front, you strike from the back, you wait until he looks away, and you hit and run." He then proceeded to explain what he had in mind to Kojomo, who smiled as understanding dawned.

"I see," he said. "We use speed and our knowledge of the jungle. It sounds like a good plan, friend Colin. I will go and select a few of my best warriors and we will leave right away."

"So, Colin, now you are an expert at jungle warfare, too?"

"Jungle or forest, British or American, when a small force has to fight a large force, the masters of war are the native tribes that inhabit the American frontier. They win when they fight their way, lose when they try to fight like the white man."

She looked confused. He laughed.

"What I mean is, Dangerfield is restricted to that cove because his ship is there. So, he must stand and fight. He has the muskets and cannons, so in a set piece battle, he has the advantage over a force armed with nothing but spears and knives. But, in order to use those muskets and cannons, he has to see something to shoot at."

The light of understanding came on in her eyes.

"Hit and run. Like we did with him on the ocean."

"Precisely."

"Colin Worth, you are a most devious person."

Colin bowed. "Why, thank you, captain."

Kojomo came back with twelve warriors, ranging in age from late teens to one man whose peppercorn hair was totally white, but all looking fit and ready for battle. Using Kojomo as an interpreter, Colin explained what he wanted them to do, and what equipment they would need. They were all quick studies, and soon were off to gather the necessary supplies.

Two hours later, Colin and M'nondo were following Kojomo's broad back as they made their way quietly through the jungle. Elizabeth had complained at being left behind in the village, but Kojomo had explained that his men would not allow a woman to go into battle, so she grudgingly agreed, but stomped feet on the hard-packed earth at the 'unfairness of it all.'

It took them four hours to make the trek from the village to Devil's Cove, and it was late dusk when they arrived at the edge of the sandy clearing.

Crouched in the dense undergrowth, they looked out over the mango-shaped cove. In the dying light of day, the water of the cove was a deep purple, with inky black reflections of the towering palm trees that encircled it. *Intrepid* was a large shadow at one side of the pool of water, the bow of the ship up on the sandy shore. The wood of the hull reflected the light from a dozen torches that ringed the bow in a semicircle. Sailors, stripped to the waist, hung in rope harnesses attached to the rails, patching the holes *The Vixen's* cannons had made in its starboard side, while musket-bearing marine infantry stood guard over a group of dark-skinned men wearing loin cloths, who were being used to cut trees from the forest at the side opposite where Colin and his party were concealed. They then, hauled the cut trees to a stretch of sand near the ship, where other Africans, also under guard, were cutting and shaping them into pieces that could be used to patch the holes.

Next to Colin, Kojomo made an angry growling sound deep in his throat.

Whatever Colin had doubt of his abilities as a fighter vanished. There was, he knew, no greater motivator in battle than anger, and right now the warrior beside him was livid with rage, a controlled rage—the perfect mood for battle. He would fight. Colin's only worry was whether or not he would stick to the plan he'd outlined.

Charles Ray

Chapter Thirty-four

Fuming, Dangerfield paced back and forth on the hard-packed earth at the edge of the sandy beach that led down to the lagoon in which his ship, his once beautiful ship, bobbed like a useless cork in the water.

Things were going slow, far too slow. Even with the extra labor, the blackamoors his men had captured, the pace of work did not increase. The damn blacks were sullen and he was convinced that they were deliberately slacking. His own men were affected as well, many of them disappearing into the nearby jungle from time to time, or going aboard the ship under some pretext of other and not reappearing for long periods of time. He also noted that some of the men gave him sullen, almost insubordinate looks when he passed them.

It was extremely frustrating.

He approached his new executive officer, William Pettigrew, a solid officer if a bit of a dullard, who stood over a seaman who was trying to instruct one of the blackamoors how to use an adz to plane a piece of wood into the proper shape and thickness.

Pettigrew stiffened to attention when he approached, his weak chin tucked into his chest.

"Mister Pettigrew," he said, hating the petulant tone he heard in his own voice. "We must get these people working faster. We've been here for two days and it hardly seems as if any progress has been made."

"Yes sir, well, sir," Pettigrew said, his eyes darting from side to side. "It bein' so late 'n all, n' the men, sir, they haven't had much sleep since we come here."

An unassuming person, with his rounded shoulders and youthful face, he seemed to shrink into himself under Dangerfield's withering glare.

"What does the lateness of the hour have to do with getting the work done, lieutenant?"

"W-well, sir, I was j-just thinking that mayhap we should allow the men to g-get some sleep?"

Dangerfield moved up and leaned over until his nose was almost touching the quivering officer.

"They can sleep when the repairs are completed. Do I make myself clear, Mister Pettigrew?"

"Y-yes sir, but they're all exhausted. They can't continue to work at the pace you desire."

"Mister Pettigrew, you are a Virginian, are you not?"

"Y-yes, sir."

"And, in Virginia, what do you do when your slaves begin to slacken in their labors, or even refuse to work?"

"S-sir, my family owned no slaves." Pettigrew cheeks turned dark.

"Well, what did those who *did* own slaves do?"

"Uh, sometimes they whipped them."

Dangerfield nodded, and smiled. "Just so, Mister Pettigrew, just so.," he said. "Sometimes a judicious use of the lash can have a stimulating effect, even on white men."

"S-sir, you can't be asking me to take the lash to our own men?"

"No, Mister Pettigrew, I can't, because I'm not *asking*."

Before the man could respond, Dangerfield turned to watch a group of the Africans enter the forest under the guard of one of the marines. He then turned back to Pettigrew, who stood there, mouth agape with a goggle-eyed look on his insipid face.

"What are you waiting for, lieutenant?" he asked sharply. "I expect to see the pace picked up here at once."

Just then, there was a shriek from the forest, from the general vicinity that Dangerfield had seen the work party just moments before. A few moments later, two round, flaming objects came arcing out of the forest, and landed in the iron pot of bubbling tar that was being used to caulk the hull. The tar instantly burst into flame, and all hell broke loose in the clearing.

Charles Ray

Chapter Thirty-five

Colin watched the activity in the clearing long enough to get a sense of the pattern of movement. He took note of Dangerfield, who paraded about, his head held high, looking down his nose like some ancient potentate.

When he noticed that groups of Kojomo's tribesmen were periodically taken into the forest, guarded by one, sometimes two, men from the ship, an idea formed in his mind.

He motioned to M'nondo and Kojomo and told him his plan. Both men agreed.

They continued to watch. They saw Dangerfield berating a young man that Colin recognized as William Pettigrew, who had been promoted to junior grade lieutenant just before their last voyage, and had been placed in charge of the gun crews aboard *Intrepid*. He couldn't hear clearly what Dangerfield was saying, but from the way Pettigrew cringed, it was apparent that he was receiving a tongue lashing.

Then, Colin saw an opportunity. A group of four Africans, guarded by one man, a marine whose name Colin couldn't recall, headed for the forest, not too far from where they were hiding.

"Okay, gentlemen," he said. "It is time to put our plan into action."

With Kojomo leading the way, M'nondo, Colin, and one of Kojomo's warriors moved silently through the thick bush in the direction of the work party. Colin walked close behind M'nondo, marveling at how the two big men in front of him managed to slide effortlessly and silently through the tangled vegetation, while he had to keep his hands in front of his face to keep from stumbling into a swinging branch and making noise. Behind him he could feel the heat from the body of the following warrior, but the man also made no sounds.

He bumped into M'nondo's rock-solid body and had to press his lips tightly to keep from gasping. Over his friend's shoulder he could see Kojomo crouching and pointing at an opening in the foliage. Beyond the opening he could see movement and heard the sound of a blade biting into wood.

Using hand signals, Kojomo motioned for Colin and the two warriors to wait. He and M'nondo then moved to the side and in a heartbeat, had disappeared into the dark bush.

A few minutes later, he heard a grunting sound, followed by a piercing shriek.

"Colin, you can come now," he heard M'nondo's deep basso voice say.

He pushed forward, the warriors pressing in behind

him, and found Kojomo, his spear pressed against a frightened marine's throat. M'nondo held the squirming man in a vice-like grip. At his feet, the man's musket lay on the ground. Beyond the three of them, the dark-skinned workers stood, smiling, their machetes held loosely in their hands.

The struggling man's eyes went wide when he saw Colin emerge from the bush. "What? Who are you?" he asked in a quivering voice. "Where the hell did you come from?"

Colin remained silent. He vaguely recognized the man, one of the marine infantry on *Intrepid*, but was sure that with the beard covering his face, the man probably didn't recognize him. He nodded at M'nondo, who tightened his grip on his prisoner.

"Be silent," M'nondo said in a harsh whisper. "If you wish to live, you will speak no more."

Kojomo lowered his spear and removed a cord of braided straw from around his waist. Using the cord, he bound the prisoner tightly. M'nondo took a dirty cloth from his pocket and used it to gag the man, then lay him down with his back against a tree.

"Kojomo, you can tell your people they are safe," he said. He motioned for the two warriors standing beside Colin. "Bring the bombs."

At the word 'bombs' the bound marine's eyes went wide and he mumbled something unintelligible under the gag. The two warriors, with Colin following, slipped past them and headed for the edge of the clearing.

As the edge, each took a small gourd that had been strapped to their waists and held them up to Colin. The gourds had been filled with gunpowder and had a makeshift fuse made of cloth strips stuffed into the opening. Colin took his flints from his pocket, and with a few strikes ignited the strips.

"You'll see a big iron pot near the front of the ship," he said. "Throw them as close to it as you can."

The two men smiled and crab-walked forward until they were just at the edge of the thick brush. Standing, they quickly cocked their hands and tossed the gourds that sailed in arcs, both landing in the middle of the cauldron of hot tar.

There was a flash, followed by a loud bang, and flames erupted from the mouth of the cauldron.

And, all hell broke loose in the clearing.

Colin clapped the two men on the shoulders and motioned with his head for them to follow him. Wheeling around, he ran back to join M'nondo and the others.

The shouts of confusion and anger in the clearing behind him made his heart soar.

The battle was on.

Chapter Thirty-six

"We're under attack," someone yelled.

Men were running to and fro, in confusion as they tried to figure out where the attack was coming from.

Dangerfield fumed and turned in a circle, peering at the thick foliage that encircled them. He then turned to see Pettigrew standing next to him looking bewildered.

"Rally the men," he shouted in the man's face. "And, get someone to put that fire out before it spreads to the ship."

The sergeant in charge of the marines ran over and pointed at the area of the jungle into which the work party had gone.

"Sir, those fire bombs came from there," he said, his voice barely under control. "Johnson just went that way with a work party. From the cry I heard, I think he's been taken."

"Well, take a few men and check it out," Dangerfield

said. "Have someone form the rest of the men into a defensive perimeter. We must protect the ship."

"Aye, sir." The sergeant saluted quickly and ran to rally the milling crowd of men.

Two of the ship's crewmen ran to the flaming cauldron and started throwing sand into it in an effort to quench the fire, while the sergeant corralled five armed marines and started trotting toward the jungle. At that moment, four more flaming orbs flew out of the jungle from the opposite side of the clearing. One landed in a pile of freshly sawn boards and exploded, while the other three hit in the sand, sending geysers of sand up into the air when they exploded. Confused, the sergeant and his men stopped, their heads swinging from their intended direction toward the new threat.

The sergeant pointed at two men and then toward the original path, and motioned the rest to follow him as he turned and ran toward the source of the new bombs.

Over the shouting of confused men, strange trilling sounds came out of the jungle. Everyone stopped in their tracks, looking around. The sounds seemed to come from everywhere.

Dangerfield stood near the burning cauldron, which was now all but extinguished, looking as confused as everyone else.

"Why are you just standing there, you fool?" he asked the sergeant, who was now standing near the edge of the clearing peering into the dark undergrowth.

The man turned around, his face ashen. "Captain, I think we're surrounded."

As if in answer to his remark, another fire bomb

was lofted from another point in the jungle. It bounced off the hull of *Intrepid,* and exploded in the sand close enough to Dangerfield to shower him with the gritty powder, and causing him to fall backwards.

"Captain," Pettigrew said. "We'd better be getting out of here. If we're surrounded, our only safe way out is the sea."

Dangerfield stared up at him, still shaken from the explosion.

"But, the repairs are not finished," he said.

"They're almost finished, enough that we can sail. We can do the rest underway."

Dangerfield nodded as he pushed himself up. Standing, he brushed sand from his clothing. "Yes, yes, you're right," he said. "Get those blackamoors to help push the bow off the sand. Sergeant, get your men back here and cover us while we board, then come aboard and we'll get underway. We've got a pirate to find."

"N-no, sir," Pettigrew said.

"What? What do you mean, no?"

Pettigrew drew himself up to his full height, still half a head shorter than Dangerfield.

"Sir, we are not going to go after that pirate ship. We are sailing immediately for the nearest American port."

Dangerfield's face darkened. "Are you trying to assume command, mister? Need I remind you of what happened to the last two officers who defied me?"

The marine sergeant came trotting over and stood behind and slightly off to the side of Dangerfield. He held his musket loosely at his side.

"No sir," Pettigrew said. "I know what happened to

them. I also know that you continue to put the ship and crew at risk for this foolish venture of yours, and that you are forsaking your duty as a naval officer." He looked at the marine. "I am, therefore, relieving you of command. Sergeant, please escort the captain to his quarters aboard ship."

"You can't do that," Dangerfield said. Spittle bubbled on his lips. "Sergeant, arrest this man for mutiny."

The sergeant stood rock steady, looking at Pettigrew.

"Sergeant, did you hear me?" Dangerfield asked, his voice rising.

Pettigrew stepped forward and pulled Dangerfield's sword from its scabbard.

"Sergeant, get the captain to his cabin. I will rally the men."

"Aye, sir." The sergeant grasped Dangerfield's arm. "Sir?"

"You can't do this, sergeant. I'll have all of you hung for this. Arrest Lieutenant Pettigrew, that's an order!"

"Sorry captain," the sergeant said. "But, the lieutenant is right. You ain't yourself, sir. Now, please don't make this any harder than it has to be."

The sergeant nodded his head, and two burly marines came up and, one on each side, pinioned Dangerfield's arms.

"You'll all regret this," Dangerfield said, as they half dragged, half carried him toward the gangplank.

The sergeant turned to help Pettigrew round up the rest of the crew, just as two marines burst through the bush, holding a still trussed up marine between them.

"We found Johnson, sergeant," one said. "He was

trussed like a pig and left in the jungle. Said a bunch of black savages led by a wild white man attacked him, and they're all over the jungle."

"Get him aboard quick," the sergeant shouted. "And, then help us push her into the water. We're gettin' the hell out of here. We're finally goin' home."

The remaining natives, who had stood by looking on with smiles as the strange white men milled about and scuttled around in panic, happily pitched in to help shove the ship off the sand.

They were still smiling as the ship's bow turned slowly toward the gap in the foliage that covered the exit to the ocean, and as the sails began to fill with air, propelling it out of the lagoon.

No one on *Intrepid* saw the group of men who came out of the jungle as the ship passed through the gap in the jungle, out into the ocean.

Charles Ray

Chapter Thirty-seven

They came out into the clearing just as *Intrepid's* stern slipped past the overhanging vines. Colin looked around at his makeshift army, M'nondo, and a group of fifteen smiling Africans, dressed in loin cloths and armed with spears, knives, and the remaining four gourd bombs. He shook his head. *We did it. With this rag tag group, I just defeated the pride of the American navy.*

"I hope that is the last we see of him," M'nondo said. "Although, I must admit, that was probably the most fun I have ever had in a battle."

Kojomo walked up to stand beside them. "I was always told that the white man was superior," he said. "Except for you, Colin Worth, I do not think they are so superior after all."

Colin smiled at him. "Well, Kojomo, I certainly have

an earful for the next person who tells me that black men don't make good soldiers. Shall we go home?"

It was a tired, but happy band that arrived back at Kojomo's village just as the sun was rising. The first person to see them, an old woman building a cookfire, alerted the village, and by the time they entered the central area, they were surrounded by a mob of happy, crying people.

Colin found himself pressed up against Elizabeth as people patted his back, pulled at his beard, and rubbed the skin of his arms.

"Another successful fight, I see," she said, gazing into his eyes.

"Very," he said, returning her gaze, and finding that he liked looking into her eyes. "Captain Dangerfield was relieved of his command, and the ship's on its way to America, and the end of his career."

"Can you be sure of that, Colin?"

He hesitated. There was one way to be sure, and he'd been working toward that end from the very first day he woke up in the hold of her ship, but now, he wasn't sure anymore. Part of him know where his duty lay, but part of him wanted to remain where he could put his arms around her and gaze into her eyes. He took a deep breath, cursing the part that won out.

"There is a way I can be sure," he said.

She looked at him and quickly looked away. *She knows. I can see it in her eyes.*

"Is there no other way?"

"I fear not," he said. "We both knew that one day it would come to this. I . . . there is nothing I would rather do than stay here with you forever, Elizabeth, I hope you know that. But, I think war is coming, and I have a duty to my country, to my shipmates."

"You mean the shipmates who stood by while you were tossed overboard like refuse?"

He bit back an angry retort. "You of all people should understand that," he said. "It takes a lot for the member of a ship's crew to stand up to the captain."

She pulled away and faced him, her hands on her hips. "You stood up to him."

"Yes, and look what it got me." Then, he smiled. "On the other hand, if I'd never stood up to him, I would never have met you."

"Or I, you. Colin, I know I promised that if you helped me rid these seas of Dangerfield, I would let you go, but now . . . oh, damn your eyes. I know you must. Just . . . do not forget . . ."

"Never, and that is my solemn promise."

"I don't believe you. You will fall into the arms of the first comely wench you encounter once you're back home."

He put a hand over his heart. "I will not, and you know by now that I am a man of my word."

Charles Ray

Chapter Thirty-eight

September 1811, Lost Island

On their way back to Lost Island, *The Vixen* had made a detour to Haiti, where a lone passenger disembarked. There were no long goodbyes. He had simply shaken hands with the crew, bowed to the captain, a slight figure who stayed on the quarterdeck, and walked off the ship.

Two days later, Elizabeth and M'nondo sat on the verandah of her house with a bottle of rum on the table between them.

She took a sip of the fiery liquor and sighed.

"Do you think he will tell his masters about us?" she asked.

M'nondo stared at her over the edge of his glass.

"He swore an oath that he would not. I believe him to be an honorable man."

She looked at him, a wistful expression on her face, for a long, long time. After another sip of rum, she smiled.

"Yes, you are right, *Kofi*, as you always are. Colin is indeed a man of his word." She sighed. "We need more like him here."

M'nondo laughed.

"Why do you laugh at me, elder brother?" She frowned.

"Oh, little sister, if you could only see yourself now. Your lips say one thing, but your eyes say another, and I can hear your heart, for it speaks loudest of all."

"You know, M'nondo, I've known you most of my life, but, sometimes you make no sense at all, do you know that?"

He reached across the table and patted her hand. "Oh, I think you understand me, Elizabeth. You just refuse to admit it to yourself."

"And, just what is it that I refuse to admit?" She cocked her head and looked at him.

"Ha, I remember when you were young, you did that whenever you were planning to play some trick on me. You know what I am talking about."

"Yes, elder brother, but I want to hear you say it."

"Ha, it is not for me to say. It is for you to admit."

She sat back and folded her arms under her breasts, a pensive look on her face.

"Oh, you're no fun at all, you know that." She pouted like a little girl, knowing full well that it would have no effect on him. "Very well, if you insist. I miss him, I miss him so much."

He cocked his head to one side, emulating her, which made her giggle. "And?" he asked.

"And . . . I . . . love him. There, I said it. Is that what you wanted to hear?"

Vixen

He patted her hand again.

"It is what you had to say, little sister."

Charles Ray

Chapter Thirty-nine

October 1811, Naval Headquarters, Charleston, South Carolina

The room had high vaulted ceilings and was paneled in oak. Large windows ran down each side from the large double doors at the entrance to the solid wood wall at back. Heavy purple drapes covered the windows. The only light was from twelve large lanterns, six mounted high on each wall. Wooden benches with straight backs were arranged in two perfectly straight columns, in twelve rows back to front, ending about six feet from two tables, with two plain wooden chairs behind each. At the very end of the room, facing the tables and benches was a long counter, that sat on a platform. The counter, or as it was called in this room, the bench, was also made of oak, the same color as the walls. A waist-high wall extended from the left of the bench, behind which was another hard-back chair, which was for witnesses.

Behind the bench, attired in full uniforms with the double gold shoulder insignia of navy captains, sat three serious looking men, men with more gray in their hair than the color they were born with, and with wrinkles that signaled many years at sea being buffeted by salt-laden wind and spray. They neither smiled nor frowned, but looked out over the room with serious expressions befitting their purpose.

Facing them, at the table to their right, sat Beauregard Dangerfield, also wearing the blue waistcoat with the double insignia of a captain, but his face bore a scowl as he looked up at them. Next to him sat a portly man, one Edgar Sutterwaite, attorney-at-law. At the adjoining table sat Captain Phillip Deering, who fiddled with his mustache as he looked at Dangerfield out of the corner of his eye.

Every bench was filled. The officers and men of *U.S.S. Intrepid*, with the officers occupying the first two rows on both sides, sat at attention, their eyes glued, not on the three senior navy officers facing them, but on the back of the man who, until the debacle at Skill Island, had been their captain.

Two marine infantrymen in blue ceremonial uniforms, their muskets at parade rest, stood to either side of the double entrance doors. Another two stood outside.

It was warm for October, and Charleston was, as usual, humid, so the air inside the closed room was stuffy. More than one dark blue uniform tunic bore the dark half-moon shape of perspiration from armpits.

The center captain at the bench, a broad-shouldered man with a prominent nose marked by red veins, bushy white brows over piercing blue eyes, and slightly fleshy lips that were so red they looked as if might perhaps have applied color to them, cleared his throat and looked out across the audience.

The room went quiet except for the buzzing of a fly in the back corner.

"This court martial is called to session," he said in a deep, booming voice. "The matter before us is Captain Beauregard Dangerfield, commanding officer of the *U.S.S. Intrepid*, assigned to North Atlantic Fleet in Boston. The charges are dereliction of duty, failure to obey a lawful order, and conduct prejudicial to good order and discipline. Is the defendant present in the court?"

Sutterwaite rose and adjusted his jacket. "The defendant is present, your honor," he said.

"I am the president of this tribunal, sir," the captain said. "You may address me as mister president."

Clearing his throat loudly, Sutterwaite covered his face with his hand. "My apologies, Mister President," he said. "I'm just an old country lawyer. I never had much contact with you military boys."

The captain's face turned red. "First of all, *sir*, we are navy. The term military applies to the land forces, and secondly, we have no *boys* in the navy. Now, if you will kindly identify yourself we can carry on with these proceedings."

Sutterwaite gulped. A member of Charleston's political elite, he had never been spoken to in such a manner. But, he swallowed the perceived slight for the sake of his client.

"Again, sir, my apologies. I, sir, am Edgar Montague Sutterwaite, Esquire, of the law firm Sutterwaite, Davis, and Calhoun."

"Thank you, Mr. Sutterwaite. How does your client plead?"

"Mister President, my client pleads not guilty."

The three captains at the bench shot hostile looks in his direction, and the president's left eyebrow wiggled. With a gloating smile on his face, Sutterwaite sat.

The president turned his attention to the captain sitting alone at the other table. "Who represents the navy?"

The captain stood. "Captain Llewelyn Morris, sir," he said.

"Captain Morris, are you prepared to present your case>"

"Yes, sir."

"Mr. Sutterwaite, is the defense prepared to proceed?"

Sutterwaite stood and bowed slightly at the waist, bunching up his jacket. "Yes, sir, your hon-, er, Mr. president."

"Very well, then, the prosecution may proceed with your opening remarks. Mr. Sutterwaite, you will have your chance when he concludes."

Morris stood. He put a leather attaché case on the table and opened it. He extracted a leather-bound log book and a thick sheaf of papers, and made a great show of arranging them on the table. Then he looked up at the bench.

"Mr. President, members of the tribunal," he said. "My duty here today is a sad one, one that I would rather have been assigned to someone else. But, it was not, it was assigned to me, and as an officer in the navy of the United States of America, I will carry out that duty to the best of my ability." He turned and looked at Dangerfield, who was staring at something on the wall behind the bench, ignoring him. "Captain Beauregard Dangerfield has been charged with offenses that, for an officer, are most serious, most serious. He is charged with failing to obey the orders given him regarding patrolling the North Atlantic off the coast of Maine and Massachusetts to watch for incursions by British warships. He is further charged with deserting said posting, and taking his ship to the Caribbean Sea in pursuit of a single pirate ship. A ship, we're told, that defeated his vessel in a surprise attack that, while it resulted in only minor injuries to the men aboard, but seriously damaged the ship. And, lest we forget, Captain Dangerfield allowed his ship to be boarded by officers of the English navy, and allowed them to remove four of his crewmen. He is accused of mistreating his officers and men, to wit, when one officer, Lieutenant Albert Comstock, objected to his irrational behavior, and when said behavior continued, followed proper naval protocol and attempted to remove him from command. Captain Dangerfield's response to that was to put Lieutenant Comstock and the two marines accompanying him, in a boat and maroon them in unknown waters somewhere in the Caribbean.

He cleared his throat and rubbed his brow. For the first time, Dangerfield looked at him, and he shuddered. In Dangerfield's eyes, he saw madness.

"After this, rather than returning to an American port and reporting all that happened, including the loss of his executive officer near Boston, Captain Dangerfield persisted in his pursuit of this pirate ship. It is our belief, therefore, not only is Captain Dangerfield guilty of failure to obey orders and dereliction of duty, but that he has exhibited his unfitness to command, or indeed, to be an officer in the navy. We will present evidence of Captain Dangerfield's actions, and in the end, we believe that this tribunal will decide that Captain Dangerfield should be relieved of his command, be discharged from the navy, and serve time in prison for his crimes. Thank you."

He took a deep breath and sat, looking exhausted.

Edgar Sutterwaite took his time standing. When he finally did, he stepped away from the table and turned in a full circle, making eye contact with every man in the room. He then turned and faced the three judges.

"Mister president, distinguished officers and gentlemen," he said in his genteel South Carolina accent, bowing slightly as he spoke. "What we have before us is not a simple case, not simple at all." He stopped and looked around. He cleared his throat. "Mister president, might I trouble the court for a glass of water. The heat and dust here has parched my throat, and I fear that without water, I will have difficulty speaking."

The tribunal president picked up a gavel and pounded the bench. "This court martial will be in recess for thirty minutes." He pointed the gavel at the marines in the back. "One of you men go get three pitchers of water and glasses; one for the bench, one for the defense, and one for the prosecution. You spectators, might want to avail yourselves of this opportunity to wet your throats as well. I will not abide any disruptions once the hearing resumes."

There was a general push toward the exit as everyone left to comply with the president's instructions. Since they were all required to be present for the proceedings, it seemed the prudent course.

Twenty-five minutes later, they were all back in their places. The president banged the gavel. "Mr. Sutterwaite, you may continue your opening statement."

Sutterwaite took another sip of water from the glass at his elbow, and stood.

"Thank you, sir," he said. "As I was saying, this is not a simple case. The prosecutor has accused my client of abandoning his duty, of being derelict. Yes, gentlemen, my client did leave the area he'd been assigned to patrol, but was that act an act of dereliction, or was he doing what his oath to defend this great nation of ours demand that he do?

He walked around behind Dangerfield and put his hands on his shoulders, unable to see the look of distaste on his client's features. After patting Dangerfield's shoulders, he returned to the front of the table, careful not to approach to close to the three stern-faced judges.

"Gentlemen, what is the biggest problem facing this nation at this very moment? I know, you'll probably say the British with their ships prowling the oceans so close to our shores, and their support of the Indians on the western frontier. And, don't mistake me gentlemen, I am not saying these are not grave threats. But the gravest threat of all is the threat to our commerce. Without active commerce with markets far beyond our shores, we would soon cease to exist as an independent nation. Pirates, gentlemen, are a clear and present threat to that essential commerce. I maintain, gentlemen, that what my client did was not a dereliction of his duty, but a wise interpretation of that duty as he saw it at the moment and in the place he found himself. Rather than charging my client with a crime, Mr. president, you should be giving him a medal. If you value your country, if you love it as much as my client loves it, you have no choice but to find him not guilty of all charges, and during the course of this hearing, we will demonstrate that beyond the shadow of any doubt. Thank you."

The introductory formalities were over. Each side had laid down its markers. Under the rules, the prosecution, which even in a military tribunal had the burden of proof, although a lighter burden than a civilian court would face, would present its case. The defense would, subject to the decision of the bench, be able to challenge prosecution evidence and witnesses. Sutterwaite, a veteran of dozens of trials in South Carolina, though inexperienced in dealing with the strictures of the uniformed services, was looking forward to it.

Morris, seated and looking relaxed now that the speechifying part of the trial was out of the way until it was time for them to present closing arguments, looked up at the bench.

"Mister president, I call to the stand Lieutenant William Pettigrew."

The rear doors opened and a nervous William Pettigrew, attired in a brand-new uniform, stepped through. He made the walk from the door to the witness chair, trudging with his head down, looking like a man on his way to the gallows. He sat in the chair, but immediately stood when Morris approached him.

Morris held out a large Bible. "Lieutenant, would you put your left hand on this book and raise your right hand, and repeat after me," he said. When Pettigrew had complied, he continued, "I, state your name, do swear that the testimony I am about to give is the truth, the whole truth, and nothing but the truth, so help me God."

Pettigrew mumbled, but managed to comply. Morris nodded for him to be seated.

"Now, lieutenant, would you state your name and your previous duties?"

"Lieutenant W-william P-pettigrew. I was originally in charge of the gun crews, but after Lieutenant Comstock left, I was p-promoted to executive officer of *U.S.S. Intrepid*."

Morris smiled. "Lieutenant Comstock was the previous executive officer?"

"Y-yes sir, he was promoted from quartermaster to executive officer when Lieutenant Worth was lost."

Morris went on to take Pettigrew through the incident when they first encountered *The Vixen*, and Lieutenant Colin Worth was, according to Dangerfield's log entry, 'lost during the encounter, presumed washed overboard.'

Dangerfield sat quietly throughout, not looking at Pettigrew, not looking at his lawyer, looking, in fact, at nothing in particular, as if the proceedings had nothing to do with him.

When Morris finished with the witness, Sutterwaite stood. He perched his fat butt on the corner of his table and fixed Pettigrew with a steely gaze.

Pettigrew became visibly nervous after a few moments of sitting there with the fat man staring at him and saying nothing. Even the judges started looking agitated.

"Any time, Mr. Sutterwaite," the president said. "Or do you not wish to cross examine this witness?"

Sutterwaite pushed off the table. "Oh, I do wish to question him, Mr. president, I surely do. I was just thinking on how to frame my first question." He walked across the room and positioned himself directly in front of the prosecutor's table, which put him in front of the witness as well. "Tell me, lieutenant, how many of these incidents you related in your testimony did you personally and directly observe?"

"Sir?" Pettigrew looked confused.

"Let me explain, then. You said, the captain had Lieutenant Comstock put off the ship. Did you personally hear the captain give that order?"

"Well, uh, no sir, I did not."

"Did you personally see Lieutenant Comstock and the other men put off the ship."

"N-no, sir."

"Were you on the quarterdeck when the captain made the decision to pursue the pirate ship?"

"No, sir, I was down with the cannon crews."

"So, except for the events you described on Skull Island, when you led a mutiny against the captain, you don't have personal knowledge of anything, do you?"

Morris shot to his feet. "Objection, Mr. president. Lieutenant Pettigrew is not on trial here."

"From what I've heard, perhaps he should be," Sutterwaite said.

"That will be enough of that, sir," the president said. "The objection is sustained. Sir, you will confine your questions to Captain Dangerfield's actions."

"Sir," Pettigrew said, his face red. "I did not mutiny."

"Yes, sorry, lieutenant. I have no further questions for you."

"You may call your next witness, Captain Morris," the president said.

"The prosecution calls Lieutenant Albert Comstock," Morris said.

For the first time, Dangerfield showed emotion. His head whipped around, and he stared at the big double doors which were beginning to swing inward.

Charles Ray

Chapter Forty

A rumble of low conversation started when Albert Comstock entered the courtroom.

"Order in this court," the president said, pounding on the bench. "There will be silence in this courtroom."

The room fell silent, but all eyes were on Comstock as he walked slowly toward the witness chair. He was still dressed in the clothing of a dock worker, complete with the scraggly beard.

As he approached the bench, the president looked down at him with a withering glare.

"Lieutenant, do you wish to explain why you are not in proper uniform?

Morris stood. "Sir, if the court would indulge me, I think the lieutenant's answers to my questions will explain his lack of military decorum."

"Very well, captain, but this had better be good."

Dangerfield continued to stare at Comstock with a disbelieving look on his face, while beside him, Sutterwaite looked like someone had just stepped on his foot.

After Comstock had been administered the oath

and seated in the witness chair, Morris stood and adjusted his uniform jacket.

When he'd had Comstock identify himself and his former duties as executive officer of *Intrepid*, he leaned forward, his fingers splayed on the table, and said, "Lieutenant, would you please tell the court why you appear here this morning in such a disheveled condition."

Comstock looked at the three judges. "Yes, sir," he said. "And, I beg the court's pardon for my appearance. My men and I just got off a cargo vessel, which our consul in Haiti arranged to bring us here. We came straight from the docks, so I've not had time to acquire a new uniform."

The room was unnaturally quiet. All eyes were on Comstock, who sat calmly in the witness chair, his back erect. He occasionally glanced at Dangerfield, and when he did, a flicker of anger flashed in his eyes.

"Why were you in Haiti, lieutenant?" Morris asked.

Comstock quietly, but in a strong voice, recounted the encounter with the British ships, his pleas to Dangerfield to make for an American port in order to report the incident, his decision to relieve him of command. "At that point," he said. "He had me and the two men with me, marooned. Fortunately, unlike what he did with Lieutenant Worth, he left the oars in the boat, so we were able to row to an island."

Over the next forty minutes, Morris took him over the events occurring on *Intrepid* before his 'departure,' returning several times to what he'd taken to calling the 'precipitating event,' Colin Worth's removal. As Comstock related the events in a strong, clear voice, Dangerfield and his lawyer leaned in toward each other until their heads touched, whispering. Sutterwaite looked skeptical, but an agitated Dangerfield kept nodding vigorously as he occasionally glared at Comstock.

Finally, Morris announced that he had no more questions of the witness. With a satisfied smirk on his face, he bowed toward Sutterwaite, "Your witness, sir," he said.

Sutterwaite took a look at Dangerfield, who nodded. He took a deep breath. He stood and adjusted his jacket, and then walked from behind the table and approached Comstock, coming much closer than was usually accepted in courtrooms. The three judges watched him, frowning, but said nothing about his breach of courtroom etiquette.

He stopped before Comstock, frowning severely at the young man, who returned it with a calm expression.

"So, Lieutenant Comstock," he said finally. "Because of what happened to your friend, Lieutenant Colin Worth, you hated Captain Dangerfield, is that correct?"

"No, sir, I did not hate the captain."

"Come now, lieutenant, the death of your friend had to affect you. Was that not the reason you conspired to remove Captain Dangerfield from command?"

"Colin's not—, uh, I mean, the reason I felt that the captain needed to be relieved was his . . . irrational behavior. From the moment that we spotted that pirate ship, he seemed obsessed. He was putting the ship and crew at risk for—"

"The *Intrepid* is a warship of the United States Navy, is it not?" Sutterwaite asked, interrupting

Comstock.

"And, as such, it is its mission to go into danger?"

Comstock looked frustrated and momentarily confused. His cheeks turned bright red.

"Uh, yes, but in pursuit of our mission—"

"Your mission is to protect the interests of the nation, is that not correct?"

Morris rose and pointed a finger at Sutterwaite. "*Mister president*, I must object. Counsel is badgering the witness."

"I am merely trying to ascertain the witness's understanding of his duties as a naval officer, Mr. president," Sutterwaite said with an innocent look on his face. "After all, he *is* accusing my client of dereliction of duty. Should I not be allowed to establish whether or not he correctly understands that duty?"

The president glared at him. "Objection overruled, but I warn you, Mr. Sutterwaite, this tribunal will only tolerate so much."

Sutterwaite bowed. "Of course, sir." Turning back to Comstock, he smiled a vulpine smile. "Lieutenant, you implied that my client acted I a cowardly manner during the engagement with four English vessels just before you were expelled from the ship. Please explain to me the contradiction here. You called him rash, and engaging in a dangerous activity for pursuing a single pirate ship, but a coward for not risking the destruction of ship and crew against a numerically superior enemy."

Comstock glared at him.

"He left our assigned area of patrol to chase the pirate ship," he said levelly. "When we encountered the English warships, we were well within the waters they control around the Bahamas, an area, I might point out, we were not supposed to be in. When we spotted the first two ships, rather than turning north and making a run for American waters, the captain had us turn toward the open ocean."

"That sounds like a prudent course of action to me." Sutterwaite shook his head. "On the open ocean, a fast ship could elude pursuers, just as the pirate ship eluded you, could it not?"

"Maybe, maybe not, but American waters were closer, and we might have found help from other American ships. Instead, he got us surrounded, and then surrendered without a fight. He allowed the English to board us and remove four crewmen without the slightest resistance."

"So, coming so soon as it did after the death of your friend, Lieutenant Worth, this tipped your anger against the captain to the point that you decided to mutiny?"

Comstock opened his mouth to speak.

"I am not dead," a clear voice said from the back of the room.

Sutterwaite turned and stared open-mouthed at the apparition appearing in the open doors. Dangerfield turned, and his face went white. All heads in the room turned in the direction of the door, mouths open in shock, eyes wide in disbelief, except for Comstock, who had a smile of relief on his face.

The president of the tribunal was the first to recover.

"By God, Lieutenant Worth," he said. "You were thought dead. Would you care to come forward and explain your presence here today?"

Colin strode forward. He was dressed in a new uniform and his facial hair was gone, giving his face, pale from the cheeks down, and sun-brown from there up. Men reached out to touch him as he passed. He nodded and smiled at them.

He stopped before the tribunal, his eyes fixed on the captain sitting at the center. He brought his hand stiffly to his brow in a crisp salute, "Lieutenant Colin Worth reporting for duty, sir," he said. He looked askance at Comstock and winked.

The president acknowledged his salute with a nod of his head.

"Very well, lieutenant. Now, explain yourself."

"Mr. president, I object," Sutterwaite said. "This individual has nothing to offer this tribunal regarding my client's actions."

The president fixed him with an icy glare.

"On the contrary, sir. As you yourself were just saying, it was Lieutenant Worth's departure from *Intrepid* that was at the root of all that followed. Lieutenant Comstock, you may step down, but hold yourself ready should you be required."

Comstock stood quickly and nodded at the tribunal. He paused briefly as he reached Colin. "I am so glad you made it," he said.

Colin smiled and patted his shoulder. He then took his place in front of the witness chair. The marine sergeant sitting at the side came before him with the Bible and administered the oath, and he sat and crossed his legs.

"Captain Morris, do you wish to question this witness?" the president asked.

"I hardly know where to start, Mr. president.

Lieutenant Worth, would you please tell us what you know of this affair, starting from the beginning, if you please." Morris sat back and folded his arms across his chest.

Colin nodded, and began speaking. He started, not with the encounter with the pirate ship, but with Dangerfield's abusive behavior towards the crew, his failure to listen to counsel from his executive officer, and then, after the encountered the ship—which he did not name—his change in demeanor, leading Colin to fear that he was becoming unbalanced.

When he got to the part about Dangerfield ordering him marooned in a ship's boat without oars simply because Colin had disagreed with his plan to leave their patrol area and chase the pirate ship, the three judges were all frowning and casting disapproving glances at Dangerfield, who, his face still ashen, had sunk down in his chair. Colin finished speaking and sat back.

"Lieutenant Worth," Morris said. "Was it Captain Dangerfield's order that you not be given oars?"

"Yes, sir."

"And, this happened just off the coast of Maine?"

"How, sir, did you survive?"

"A passing ship spotted my boat after I'd been adrift for several days . . . I'd lost track of time by then and was delirious. That ship was enroute to the Bahamas, so they took me there. It has, unfortunately, taken me from then until now to make my way back here. I managed to secure passage by way of inter-island shipping to Haiti, much as I'd arranged for Mr. Comstock and his two companions when I encountered them on Abaco Island. From there, our consul helped me get aboard a merchant ship bound here to Charleston."

"You met Lieutenant Comstock after he was marooned?"

"Yes sir, that was when I learned of what Captain Dangerfield was doing, of just how much danger he was putting the ship and crew in."

"One last question, lieutenant, why did it take you so long to return home?"

"As I said, sir, I was delirious from exposure to the elements. My recovery took many months. Furthermore, I'd been put ashore, an American naval officer in British territory. I had to hide out until I recovered, and then until I could find a safe way to depart, lest I be impressed into the British navy, or worse, be treated as a spy."

"Mr. president, I have no further questions," Morris said. "Mr. Sutterwaite, your witness."

Sutterwaite, who had been alternating between listening to Colin's story and trying to calm his client who was rocking back and forth in his chair, mumbling incoherently, was taken aback. He looked from Morris, a satisfied expression on his face, to Colin, he stared levelly back at him, to the three stern faces on the bench. He'd been a lawyer for a long time, and one thing he'd learned in all those years before the bar was when to cut his losses and admit defeat. He looked down at his client whose sanity had obviously departed.

"I have no questions of this witness, Mr. president," he said.

Chapter Forty-one

With his client tipped over into insanity, Sutterwaite had no defense to present, no witnesses to call, for he could not risk his legal reputation by putting Dangerfield on the stand. The president called a recess, and the three-judge tribunal retired from the room to deliberate.

They were back two hours later, and the grim looks on their faces told the story before the president even spoke.

"This tribunal, having carefully reviewed the evidence and testimony presented to it, finds the defendant, Beauregard Dangerfield, guilty of dereliction of duty and of conduct that reflects poorly upon the navy. He is declared unfit for command, and is hereby relieved of any and all such command. Furthermore, he is to be discharged from the navy effective this day. This hearing is adjourned."

As one, the judges rose, faced left and marched stiffly from the room. Dangerfield, a completely broken man, sat slumped in his chair, staring at the wall, while Sutterwaite, looking at him with an expression equal parts pity and disgust, began stuffing his papers in the small attaché case he carried.

The officers and men of *Intrepid*, happy to be rid of a tyrannical commander and even happier to see one of their favorites still among the living, began spilling into the corridors outside the courtroom, each vying for a chance to shake Colin's hand or pat him on the back.

Albert Comstock, uncharacteristically bold, pushed his way through the crowd, and stood in front of Colin, his hands on his hips and a half-smile on his face.

"You cut it awful close, Colin," he said. "I was beginning to think you wouldn't come."

"Now, Albert, you know I'm a man of my word. I make a promise, I keep it."

Pettigrew punched Comstock lightly on the shoulder. "Yeah, Albert, you know that, Colin's never gone back on his word. By the way, old boy, you looked really good in there. I've always thought you were the shy and retiring type. You really stood up to that pompous lawyer."

Comstock smiled shyly. "I reckon working on the docks for a few weeks will beat the shyness out of you, that's for sure."

The sergeant in charge of the marines stepped forward. He could not look Colin in the eye.

"Sir, I'm hopin' you'll be Christian enough to forgive me for my role in what happened to you," he said.

"Sergeant," Colin said. "You were only following orders. Stupid, illegal orders, but orders nonetheless. I hold no grudge against you for that."

"Thank you, sir. Do you know where you'll be goin' now? I mean, will you be comin' back to *Intrepid*?"

"I don't know, sergeant, I—"

"Lieutenant Worth," Morris's voice cut him off. He was coming out of the courtroom. "Might I have a word with you?"

"Yes, sir." Colin followed him along the corridor, around a corner, and into a small office with one small desk, three chairs, and four bookcases piled high with books and documents.

Morris indicated the chair to the left side of his desk, and sat in the one behind it. "Forgive my office, lieutenant. I'm afraid the best offices here go to officers of the line. Those of us performing . . . other duties must make due."

"This is much bigger than my space aboard ship, sir," Colin said.

"You're probably wondering why I asked to speak to you, Lieutenant Worth."

Colin was afraid to venture a guess, so he only nodded.

Morris regarded him thoughtfully for a moment.

"I notice that the officers and men think very highly of you," Morris said. "At the same time, I sense a great respect as well."

"It is my belief, sir, that getting men to do what you want them to do does not require harsh methods. Give them respect and a job worth doing, and they will perform well."

"That is, I'm afraid, not a philosophy that many of our ship's captains seem to follow."

Colin nodded. "Sad, but true, sir. But, I think some day, that will all change."

"In the meantime, you will make that change personally in the here and now?"

"It is a strong belief, sir. My father taught it to me, and his father taught it to him. I suppose that makes it impossible for me to ever aspire to captain a ship, but I must be true to my beliefs."

Morris smiled. "Would you like to be captain of a ship, Colin Worth?"

"Is there a navy man who wouldn't, sir?" Colin returned the smile.

"Then, how would you like to be master of *U.S.S. Intrepid*?"

Colin's mouth opened. He snapped it shut, but couldn't make himself speak, except for a gulping sound in his throat.

"I will take that as yes," Morris said.

"Truly, sir? I'm being offered command of *Intrepid*?"

"It's true." Colin nodded. "The president of the court martial is also the vice commander of the northern fleet. He was impressed with the way you conducted yourself, and the way the men responded to you. He ordered me to offer you the position just now before I spoke to you."

Colin wondered why the man hadn't done it himself, but wasn't one to look a gift horse in the mouth, or any other orifice for that matter.

When he entered the courtroom, he'd feared it would mark the end of his naval career. After all, he'd been in long enough to know that the senior officers formed a close fraternity, and tended to stick together. Had it not been for the overwhelming evidence of Dangerfield's misdeeds, and his complete psychotic break in the courtroom, it was, he knew, unlikely they would have found him guilty. As it was, they only really found him guilty of one of the charges. Nothing had been said about his attempt to murder Colin. They'd gone remarkably easy on the man. He would spend no time in prison, except in the prison of his own tortured mind. Then again, he thought, maybe that was the worst punishment they could've inflicted upon him, and all without making a public spectacle that might embarrass the navy.

No matter, he thought. I have achieved my dream. I am now the captain of my own ship. Then, another thought flitted across his mind. Not my only dream. There is one other, and it has now been forever put out of my reach.

He shook himself, shook hands with Morris, and went in search of his officers and men, thinking that it was a good thing he still had a goodly amount of the gold coins Elizabeth had given him just before his departure from Lost Island.

Charles Ray

Chapter Forty-two

June 1812, *U.S.S. Intrepid* in Boston Harbor

The first eight months of Colin's new job went by in a blur. He'd formally promoted Albert Comstock to the position of executive officer, and put Pettigrew in charge of the gun crews. The grizzled old marine sergeant, when he learned that Colin would be the new captain, had offered his resignation, which Colin refused.

They sailed from Charleston three days later, with a fully-repaired ship and a shipload of hangovers from having spent two of those three days closing every tavern within walking distance of the wharf.

Colin had run daily ship drills during the voyage to Boston, from cannon drills to man-overboard drills, so that by the time they arrived at Boston Harbor, his crew was functioning like a well-oiled timepiece, and given his habit of singling out those who did particular good jobs, and commending them in front of the whole crew, was happier than any of them had ever been.

The drills had been a good thing in another way;

upon arrival, Colin had gone directly to fleet headquarters, where he was congratulated on his assignment, promoted to lieutenant commander, and told to proceed forthwith to his assigned patrol, a swath of ocean from the northern tip of Maine to the southern tip of Delaware and the mouth of Chesapeake Bay. His orders were to patrol and keep on the lookout for British ships entering American waters, or any other hostile action by foreign vessels, but not to engage unless he had no other choice. If he saw anything resembling an aggressive move by the British, he was to make for the nearest American port and report it.

While patrol duty can be boring, the men had practiced the basics during the journey from Charleston, and most of the senior enlisted had many years of experience at sea. Nonetheless, during the many months of patrol duty, he continued to drill them, and when they made port on occasion to renew ship's provisions, he only allowed a third of the crew to go ashore, and threatened severe punishment for anyone who got drunk, became involved in an incident, came back late, or came back unfit for duty. Needless to say, his announcement when they were a day out of Boston, that he would allow all but a skeleton duty watch to enjoy the liberties of the port— again reminding them of the standard of behavior he expected of them—was met with cheers so loud he had to cover his ears.

Yes, as he stood on the quarterdeck, watching the wharf belonging to the navy come closer, things were finally as they should be. He wondered if he shouldn't perhaps take a few days off and allow Comstock to command the ship while he went to visit his family in Philadelphia. He could reboard there, and it would be good to see his mother and father again, and to show his father that going to sea had not, after all, been such a bad move for him to make.

His ebullient mood was dampened when he saw the officer, a lieutenant commander like him from the insignia, standing near where the *Intrepid's* gangplank would come to rest. The man was wearing the full-dress uniform, something that only those working in fleet headquarters did other than on special occasions. *This cannot be good. They don't send high ranking messengers to deliver good news.* He kept his expression impassive as his men expertly brought the ship into the wharf and tied it off. Near the helm, a smiling Comstock, who'd had the duty to supervise the docking, turned and saluted.

"Ship is secure, sir," he said. "Would the captain like to give the liberty order."

A sixth sense told Colin to hold off on that. "Not at this moment, exec. It appears we have a visitor from headquarters. Perhaps we should see what he wants before we allow the men to stampede off the ship."

"Aye, sir." He turned and faced the main deck. "Lower the gangplank, and standby."

When the gangway was secured to the dock, the waiting officer stepped on it and started up toward the main deck. Comstock, as the officer in charge of the ship's final maneuvers, after receiving a nod from Colin, went down to welcome him aboard as befitted his rank. Once the formalities of requesting permission to come aboard and having that permission granted, the somewhat portly officer, as Colin could now see, stepped onto the deck. He said something to Comstock that Colin could not hear, and the two men started walking toward the quarterdeck where he stood.

On the quarterdeck, the lieutenant commander stopped in front of Colin and saluted. "Captain Worth, I'm Lieutenant Commander Alistair Mooney, executive officer to the northern fleet commander," he said.

Colin returned his salute, a bit confused at the formal introduction. While it was appropriate for the man to address him as 'captain,' as he was the ship's master, it seemed far too formal. He would have expected a more informal, though still correct, greeting. He also wondered why the fleet commander's executive officer would come to the dock himself rather than send an ordinary seaman clerk, or at most, one of the marine infantrymen who did ceremonial guard duties at the headquarters. Warning bells began to clang in his mind.

"Welcome aboard, Lieutenant Commander Mooney," he said. "To what do I owe the honor of such an august welcome committee?"

Mooney looked around at Comstock and the helmsman, both of whom were standing at attention and affecting not to be listening to the conversation.

"Captain, I must speak privately with you. May we go to your cabin?"

"Of course. Please follow me."

Still with troubling thoughts whirling through his mind, Colin led the way down the ladder to his cabin just under the quarterdeck. Once inside, Mooney insisted on closing the door, after looking to make sure no one was lurking in the passageway. Colin looked on curiously. Finally, he took a seat behind his desk and nodded for his visitor to take the chair at the right side.

"Now, Commander Mooney, just what is it that's so secret that we couldn't discuss it in front of my second in command, or any other crew aboard for that matter?"

"I'm sorry for the cloak and dagger routine, Colin," Mooney said. "But, I was instructed to pass you your new orders, and that they were for your ears only."

The warning klaxon in his head was as loud as the bell hanging in the State House Tower in Philadelphia, and just as discordant.

"And, just what are those orders?"

"I regret to have to inform you that your liberty here in Boston must be cancelled. You must set sail immediately for Charleston. Once there, you are to contact Captain Llewelyn Morris who will give you the details."

Damnation, the men aren't going to be happy to hear they don't get to sample the delights of North End. He shrugged off the thought. Orders were orders, and he was sure that his crew, while disappointed, would comply with the alacrity he'd witnessed over the eight months he'd been in command.

"Can you give me some idea of what the mission is?" he asked.

"No, I'm afraid not. I can, however, tell you this; as of four days ago, on the 18th of June, we are at war with Britain. President Madison convinced Congress to declare war."

Colin felt a chill go through his body. After several years of nipping at each other's heels, America and Britain would finally stage a repeat of the events of the late 1700s. But, he surely misheard. Would it not be the English who first declared hostilities?

"Did I hear you correctly? *We* declared war on Britain? For what earthly reason?"

He noticed the dark rings around Mooney's bloodshot eyes. The man was exhausted.

"I only know what I've heard," he said. "The president, apparently tired of the English kidnapping men from our ships, and there's the matter of English officers stirring up the Indian tribes on our western border. Whatever the reason, the president is taking us to war with full congressional approval."

"Wouldn't it then make more sense for *Intrepid* to remain with the north fleet? After all, the threat from Canada is greater than that in the south, and there is Washington to consider. We'll need every ship we have up here to fight the damn English off."

"Come, Colin, you that ours is not to reason why. You and your ship are needed in the south. I know not why, and it's not my place to question."

He stood and adjusted his trousers.

"Very well," Colin said. "We'll get underway immediately after we reprovision. I'll escort you off the ship."

"Thank you, Colin, and Godspeed."

As he took the man back up to the deck and to the gangplank, watching him as he walked, slump-shouldered, down the steep incline. His mind was racing with thoughts of what he would say to his disappointed crew, and wondering what awaited him in Charleston.

Chapter Forty-three

June 1812, *U.S.S. Intrepid* in harbor at Charleston, South Carolina

There were looks of disappointment when Colin announced that shore leave was cancelled, but no one said anything, not even a murmur of discontent. To make up for it, he eased up on the shipboard drills during the voyage south.

They hugged the coastline all the way south to minimize the chance of encountering an English ship, and Colin noticed that word of the war must have spread, because they also noted very few merchant ships or fishing boats, especially in the area around Chesapeake Bay which was usually heavily populated with fishermen, until they were approaching the entrance to Charleston's harbor. Along the Atlantic coast, lined with stately old mansions belonging to the rice, tobacco and cotton plantation owners, the only signs of the war were the coastal batteries along the shore that hadn't been there the last Colin was in Charleston.

As soon as they passed the low island that sat almost dead center of the mouth of the harbor, and which Colin thought would make a good defensive position against a navel assault upon the port, he saw that Charleston harbor was filled with ships, some of them navy.

After they were well past the entrance, he again allowed Comstock to take responsibility for maneuvering the ship, and again the young man did a capable job, finding them an empty slot at a pier on Smith's Quay at the mouth of the Copper River, fortunately, not that far from the navy headquarters.

"Mister Comstock," he said, just before leaving the ship. "I don't know how long I'll be gone, or how long we'll be in Charleston, so allow one-fourth of the one hour of liberty in rotation, and let's hope it takes me four hours to conclude my business.

"Aye, sir," Comstock replied.

Colin was impressed. Not once had his number two asked about the strange mission, or why they were not allowed to remain longer in Boston. Now, he also didn't question the strange liberty procedures, even though Colin knew he must be aching with curiosity.

He could have taken a carriage for the half-mile walk to the headquarters building, but decided to walk, which turned out to be a mistake. By the time he arrived at the two-story stone building nestled between two larger buildings on a busy street, his uniform was soaked through with sweat.

It wasn't much better inside the building. The air was heavy with moisture and had a moldy odor that tickled his nose.

He paused for a few seconds, trying to recall where

Captain Morris's office was, and after remembering, he made his way to the second floor and down the narrow hallway, where he found the unmarked door at the end. He knocked.

"Come in," a muffled voice said.

He entered. Morris sat behind a desk piled high with papers. His face was sallow from lack of sun and his eyes bloodshot from lack of sleep. He looked up as Colin entered, and when Colin stood at attention and opened his mouth to speak, waved a hand lazily through the air and pointed at the chair to the side of his desk, which was also piled high with papers.

"Forget the formalities, Colin. Push those papers onto the floor and take a load off. Looks like you walked. Hot outside, is it? I haven't been out of this damn building for nearly a week. How was the voyage down?"

As Colin moved the papers, placed them neatly on the floor near the chair, and sat, he looked worriedly at Morris, whose rambling indicated just how exhausted he was.

When Morris just sat there looking at him through bleary eyes, and saying nothing, Colin cocked his head and spoke, "Sir, I was told you would tell me why I had to cancel liberty for my crew and come here."

Rubbing at the stubble covering his cheeks, Morris continued to look at him. Finally, he leaned forward and rested his chin on his cupped hands.

"I can, Colin, and I will. First, though, I need to give you some background . . . put you in the picture as it were."

"If it's about the war, sir, I already know about that."

"Of course, you were in Boston, you would have heard. Sorry, son, I'm just tired." He turned and picked up a tin coffee pot from the table behind his desk. "Would you like a cup of coffee?" Colin shook his head. "I shouldn't. I've been living on this stuff for a week, and it's eating my stomach away, but it keeps me awake, and that's important right now." At Colin's look of impatience. "Sorry, there I go, rambling again." He shuffled through the papers on his desk, found what he was looking for, and peered at it for a few seconds. "Ah, here it is. We have reliable information that the British are placing the bulk of their naval and army forces in the north, in Canada, and poised for attacks along the coast as far south as here. They're also planning, have already implemented, a blockade of our ports from Maine to Louisiana to prevent the French from coming to our aid, as if they would."

"That makes sense," Colin said. "I imagine they'll go after the capital, and try to cut off our main ports."

"It's also where we pose the greatest danger to them. Our army has already made a move toward Canada. If we should defeat their armies there, they'd be hard-pressed to provide logistics to any land force. It would be a repeat of the war of independence all over again."

"So, given that, sir, why am I here. I should be with the fleet in the north, giving the English a bloody nose."

Morris smiled and shook his head. "I think I know how you feel, son, I really do. I was not always a fat, deskbound lump of wasted flesh. I too miss the smell of the ocean and feeling of salt spray in my face. But, someone has to do jobs like this, and I seem to have a

. . . particular talent for it, as do you, my friend, which is why you're more valuable here than sinking British warships in the North Atlantic."

"What kind of job are you talking about, captain?"

"Tell me, what do you think would happen if the British divided their forces, land and sea, in half, and then attacked us with those two forces, one from the north and one from the south?"

Colin shuddered at the thought. "We would be hard-pressed, sir. The navy is stretched thin as it is, and what we have in land forces is really a joke. I imagine with the congress declaring war, the states are raising militia, but they will take time to become trained and battle-hardened."

"Precisely. It is to our advantage that the British not press us from the Gulf of Mexico until we've built the forces to face them appropriately."

"And, what role would I play in such a strategy? This sounds to me a job for someone experienced in espionage." Then, it hit Colin; why Morris, a captain, was sitting in a nondescript, windowless office rather than prowling the deck of a ship. He was a spy. "Uh, sir, I have no experience in—"

"You have *just* the experience we need, Colin," Morris said. "The key to tying the English up in the south is to occupy them in the Bahamas, and you have more experience in those islands than any other officer in the navy."

Colin shuddered at the thought, but kept his lips pressed tightly together. He hadn't told anyone the details of his stay in the islands, not even Albert Comstock, who, in addition to being his executive officer, had become his best friend. He wondered, though, if Morris, a navy spy, knew anything of his activities with Elizabeth and her crew.

"Uh, most of my experience in the islands, sir, consisted of scrounging for food and avoiding English colonial officials and their navy. I don't see how that is of any value to this operation you talk about."

"Now, Colin, you're being too modest. You survived for months in a hostile environment, some would even say thrived. You were able to get Comstock and his men out, and you got yourself out. I would think that an enterprising young man such as yourself had to have developed a good network of friends and acquaintances to be able to do all that."

"Well, yes sir, I did become friendly with some of the locals. There are those there, especially the former slaves, who have no great love for the English."

"Just so. It is just such relationships that are of value to us. Tell me, what happens when a mosquito bites you?"

"You slap at it, of course."

"Yes, you do. I want you and your . . . friends in the islands to be our mosquitos. I want you to bite at the English. Make them stop what they're doing to slap at you. If they're doing that, at least a few of them won't be available to attack us in the south. It might just be enough to give us the time to prepare."

It made sense, but Colin still worried about how much the man knew.

"I suppose I could get some small resistance started, sir," he said.

"Oh, I think you can do better than a small resistance, in fact, I have a feeling you'll make the bloody English worry that they have a whole swarm of mosquitos on them."

Morris smiled, and in that moment Colin knew—he knew what had happened in the Caribbean. How he knew, and how much, he couldn't be sure, but the knowing smile on the captain's face told Colin that he knew a *lot*.

"I'll do the best I can, sir."

"I'm sure you will, commander. I've looked at your record. You have a reputation as a hard but fair officer, and you've demonstrated the ability to think on your feet, which is why you were the very best man for this job." He searched the pile of papers again, pulling a brown envelope from the very bottom, which he slid across the desk to Colin. "In there, you'll find the information you'll need to start your mission; contact information and procedure and the like. Your main contact will be George Hoskins, our consul in Haiti. He's a bit bombastic, but don't let that put you off. He has a sharp mind, and can be quite helpful in getting information from you to us and from us to you.

He waited while Colin quickly scanned the three sheets of paper in the envelope.

"I would suggest that you allow your crew two days liberty before departing," he continued when Colin had put the papers back. "That will keep from drawing attention to you and your ship, and will also give you time to start planning how you will operate. Any questions?"

Of course, Colin had a hundred questions, none of which he dared ask. All he could do was shake his head, and say, "No, sir. I think I have enough here to get started."

"In that case, good luck, and Godspeed."

Morris went back to studying the papers in the mess on his desk, ignoring Colin. *So, this is the spy business. At least, though, I might get the chance to see Elizabeth again.* He almost smiled at the thought, realizing that she had been in his thoughts often over the past months, and wasn't surprised that he was excited at the prospect of seeing her again.

When it was clear that Morris was truly finished with him, he saluted hastily, which was also ignored, rose and left. Only outside Morris's office did he allow himself to smile.

Chapter Forty-four

June 1812, Lost Island

Elizabeth was fuming. She wanted to hit something or someone, but the only convenient person was M'nondo, who sat across the table from her with an enigmatic look on his dark face. When she glared at him, he lifted the corners of his fleshy lips in a half smile, which only infuriated her more.

"You sit there like some mahogany statue of a wise man," she said, her voice growling. "While we have not been able for three months now to find an unescorted merchantman to raid. Stop smiling and start thinking how we shall deal with this situation."

"Calm yourself, little sister. There are some situations that cannot be dealt with. They must simply be endured."

"Would you tell the sick children, the women great with child, or the elderly, all in need of their medicines, to simply endure?" She slapped the table with the palms of her hands, rattling the china cup sitting near her. "How can you sit there and tell me to

345

endure it? We need to find a way to overcome it."

For a moment, he closed his eyes. He looked weary, and she felt a twinge of guilt. She knew that, despite enjoining her to endure their present situation, he'd been laboring day and night to find a solution. And, now *he* was enduring her wrath without complaint, wrath that was wrongly directed at him simply because there was no other target available.

"I know that you feel responsible for everyone on this island, little sister, and I know how you suffer when they suffer. They are like family to you, and that makes them family for me as well." He leaned forward, propping his elbows on the table, and resting his chin on his fists. "But, we cannot control the sailing routes of merchant ships. With so many English warships in these waters, and rumors of war between them and the Americans, most of the southern merchants are avoiding the Caribbean Sea. And, can you not blame them? How many times in the past two months have we had to dodge an English ship?"

She picked up the cup, which was half full of coffee and put it to her lips. As the dark brown liquid touched her tongue, she made a face and spit it back into the cup. "Ugh, the coffee's cold, and it tastes like caulking tar." She put the cup down. "I know, big brother, and truly, I don't really blame you. I am just frustrated. And, it's not just the problems on the open ocean that bother me. Have you noticed that the English officials have been much stricter lately? It's becoming almost impossible to find one to bribe. It's getting so it's hard for a self-respecting pirate to make a living."

He smiled more broadly at her bit of levity at the

end. "Ah, it is good to see my Elizabeth has returned. For a while, there was this evil witch in her place."

"Hah! The witch had to deal with an unfeeling ogre."

They both laughed. It felt good to her, falling back into the habits of her childhood, bantering with M'nondo, trading verbal jabs, and just enjoying each other's company. If only things weren't getting so desperate. She hadn't been joking about the need for medicines, which they normally procured from doctors or pharmacists on the larger islands of the Bahamas. But, the English colonial officials had started cracking down, and many of her former sources were suddenly 'out of stock.' She worried that they might have to sail to Haiti, or even Mexico, to get what they needed, which would mean running a gauntlet of English warships, risk being thought English by the French warships that still lurked near the few colonial possessions they still maintained, or even being attacked by the Spanish who still maintained a foothold in Cuba and on the mainland of the southern continent. Worse, with merchants avoiding the Caribbean because of the rumors of war, her hoard of gold coins was diminishing.

"I have been thinking about our situation, little sister," he said, turning back a serious topic. "And, I must confess that I am unable to come up with any useable plan to improve our condition."

"Nor have I, big brother, nor have I."

He lifted his head, and reached across the table, placing his large, dark hand on hers. She enjoyed the warm, dry touch, and marveled at the contrast of his ebony skin against her slight tan.

"We must not give up, though," he said. "The people do depend on us."

"I know, I know." She gazed at a point above his head. "If only Colin were here. He would come up with something."

Her gaze dropped, and she saw how he looked at her with the lopsided smile and narrowed eyes he used when he'd caught her at some mischief. Her cheeks felt hot. She knew, of course, she hadn't truly hidden her feelings from him. He was her big brother. He could read her thoughts. And that made her cheeks feel even hotter.

Chapter Forty-five

July 1812, *U.S.S. Intrepid* at *Cap Haitien*, Haiti

Keeping close to coastlines by day and making a mad dash south after dark, often without any running lights aboard, making it extremely hazardous for those working on the decks, it took *U.S.S. Intrepid* eighteen days to sail from Charleston, South Carolina to *Cap Haitien*, the island nation of Haiti's main seaport. Because they'd gone around the southern tip of the Florida peninsula, and then west toward Mexico before turning south and east, and sailing around the south side of Cuba, they approached the port from the west rather than the northeast, which Colin hoped would be missed by any British warships lurking in that area, on the lookout for American warships.

George Hoskins, the American consul in Haiti, an obese man with a fringe of brown hair, tending to gray, ringing a sun-burned bald top, and intense blue eyes, took a pilot boat out to meet them as they entered the harbor. He remembered Colin from having helped him get back to America previously, and had obviously been informed of his arrival.

When he climbed aboard *Intrepid,* his white suit gray from sweat and the effects of salt air and perspiration, he greeted Colin like a long-lost relative, congratulating him profusely on his promotion, and in general making small talk. Colin, though, didn't fail to notice that the pilot who came aboard with Hoskins was guiding them to a remote section of the harbor, to a pier that was out of sight of the main harbor, in the event any English ships should come calling. It was something he had thought of, but hadn't figured out an answer, so he was grateful that Hoskins was apparently experienced at the spy game.

Once the ship was secured to the pier, Hoskins pulled Colin aside and leaned in close to him.

"Captain," he said. "You and me, we have to have a little private talk, if you will. I've taken the liberty of arranging a table at a local inn, not far from here."

So, the spy briefings begin, Colin thought. "Very well, sir." He turned to Comstock. "Exec, set up watch and liberty schedules. I think we'll be in port here for a bit, so be liberal. I should be back in . . ." He turned back to Hoskins.

"Oh, I think we only need about two hours," the fat man said.

"I'll be back in two hours," Colin said. "We'll discuss long term plans at that time."

"Aye, sir," Comstock said, saluting smartly.

As they departed, Hoskins said, "You got yourself a right smart buncha men, captain. I seen lots of ships come and go since I been consul here, but never have I seen a more disciplined, but happy, crew."

Colin nodded acknowledgement, but remained

silent. He wanted only to get about his mission.

The inn, *L'etoile Polaire*, was a five-minute walk from the ship's berthing place, on a side street populated by some of the most unsavory types Colin had seen, even in the port at Tripoli, where a man's throat might be cut for a purse containing two gold coins. Men of all shades, from pasty white to the deepest ebony, lurked in alleys, or stood outside questionable looking establishments, watching passersby through narrow slits, and keeping a hand concealed, a hand that Colin knew probably contained a knife. Hoskins didn't seem to notice or mind, and no one appeared to take any notice of them as they passed. *L'etoile Polaire* was an out of place jewel among its neighbors. The modest looking two-story building looked recently painted, there were no broken windows, and no thuggish looking type stood at the door to welcome those wanted within and discourage others.

They entered a well-lit room that had a dozen tables scattered about, and a large wooden bar in back. Next to the bar was an ornate stairwell leading to the second floor. A mulatto bartender wearing a white linen shirt wiped at the top of the bar with a red cloth, and ignored them as they crossed the floor to the stairs. A waitress with milky-white skin and hair the color of straw, wearing a shimmering blue dress without shoulder straps, and that barely contained her large breasts, stood at the end of the bar. She gave Colin an appraising look, but said nothing. There were no customers, but it was still early in the day. From the look of the waitress, if indeed that was her job, Colin felt sure that there was far more than food on the establishment's menu.

Hoskins led him upstairs, down a long, carpeted hallway, to a door, which he opened by manipulating a board in the wall. They stepped through into a dimly lit hallway that ended at a set of wooden steps leading down to another door.

Through that door, Hoskins had a windowless room with a large table in the center, upon which was a map of the Caribbean and the Gulf of Mexico, and numerous pins with colored labels attached. A small desk and chair sat in one corner, and in the other was a bookcase filled with leather-bound volumes that looked like the logbooks ships' captains were required to maintain.

Hoskins ushered Colin to a chair in front of the desk and squeezed his bulk into the chair behind it.

"Well, Mr. Hoskins," Colin said. "What do you have for me."

"Just call me George. I don't stand much on formality." He opened the top drawer of the desk and extracted a piece of paper. "This is a list of my contacts around the region. You need to commit it to memory. If you have messages for me, or you need something, get in touch with one of them. They have their ways of getting in touch with me."

Colin perused the list, names and addresses on several islands scattered about the Caribbean, a total of ten. *Shouldn't be too hard to remember this.* Then, one name caught his eye, *Lillie St. Clair, Cat Island.* He was at first shocked, but then remembered that Mama Lillie had originally come from Haiti. That she would still have contact with her old home came as no surprise, but one of Hoskins' contacts?

"So, Colin," Hoskins said. "What's your plan?"

As soon as he saw Mama Lillie's name, he knew what he would do, and where he would go.

"I'm going to Cat Island," he said. "I think I can mount quite an effective campaign against our English friends from there."

Hoskins chuckled, nodding his head so vigorously his several chins quivered.

"I was told you were a hellion. I see they weren't far off the mark. You're gonna hit the bloody limey from right in the middle of his own home. I love it. You need anything from me, you know who to contact."

"I do, George. And, I have one thing I need you to do. I'm leaving my ship here under the command of my executive officer, Mr. Comstock. He's a capable man, but young and a bit inexperienced. Keep an eye out, will you>"

"I'll stick as close to that youngster as a tick on a dog, so don't you worry."

Charles Ray

Chapter Forty-six

July 1812, *The Vixen* at Cat Island

Out of desperation, Elizabeth decided to take her chances with the British, and sail to Cat Island. If there was anyone who could help her get through the difficult times they were facing, it was Mama Lillie. Mama Lillie knew everyone, never seemed to be affected when economic times were hard, and most importantly, even with the English officials and their new stringent regulations, maintained her regular clientele.

To avoid contact with British ships, and minimize the chance of encountering any of the colonial officials on Cat Island, Elizabeth had the ship anchor off a secluded cove at the north end of the islands. She had herself, accompanied by M'nondo, rowed ashore, and gave instructions for the boat to return to the ship and relay to Garcia, who she'd left in command, to leave and return in two days, when she and M'nondo would be waiting for them at their landing point.

She wore the dress she'd purchased on her last trip

to Abaco Island, and M'nondo was dressed in the livery of a house servant. They hired a local to transport them into the town in his cart, pulled by a single, sway-backed roan that appeared barely able to pull the cart with just the driver. Their entry into town wasn't as fancy as she would have preferred, but no one they passed gave them any notice.

She had the driver drop them off a quarter mile from Mama Lillie's place, and they walked the rest of the way. M'nondo, with a sour look on his face, walked a step behind her, holding a parasol over her head. She couldn't suppress a smile at his discomfort at being placed in the role of a common servant.

Mama Lillie's was empty of customers when they entered. Mama Lillie sat on a stool behind the counter, looking as content as Elizabeth always remembered, seemingly unaffected by the lack of paying customers.

"Elizabeth, *ma cherie,* it is so good to see you. It has been a long time since you visit Mama Lillie." Her eyes widened when she saw M'nondo struggling to close the parasol. "M'nondo, *mon ami,* I must say, you look *tres elegant.* You should dress like that more often."

His response was a deep-throated growl. He tossed the partially closed parasol onto the nearest table.

"How have things been, Mama Lillie? I notice that you have no customers," Elizabeth said.

"*Ah, oui, c'est tres desole.* It is this talk of war with the *Americains,* it has dampened the mood of the people for fine dining. Now, people are staying close to home."

"So, it's true. The Americans have declared war on England?"

Mama Lillie nodded her head, her jowls quivering,

and frowned. "Yes, *cher*, the Americans, I hear, finally tired of the British treating them as if they were still a colony. Unfortunately, while they bark and bite at each other, it is small places like this that must suffer. Already, the number of merchant ship arrivals have been cut in half."

"It is so true," M'nondo said. "When the elephants fight, the grass gets trampled."

Elizabeth stomped her feet to get their attention. "That's all well and good," she said. "But, we have people on Lost Island who need their medicines, war or no war. What am I to do about that?"

Mama Lillie ran a pudgy finger over her chin and, with her head cocked to one side, seemed deep in thought.

"Ah, *mais oui*, that is a problem." Then, she snapped her fingers. "I just might have a solution, but it will take some time."

"As long as it does not take too much time, Mama Lillie," Elizabeth said. "What can you do for us?"

"I have a . . . friend coming from Haiti. He is due to arrive in two weeks. I might be able to get a message to him. If you will give me a list of the medicines you need."

Elizabeth rushed to the woman and threw her arms across her shoulders. She wanted to pull her close and enfold her, but Mama Lillie's girth prevented that. It did not, however, prevent Mama Lillie from wrapping Elizabeth in a warm embrace.

"Oh, Mama Lillie, what would I do without you? If this works, I owe you more than I can ever repay. The people of Lost Island owe you . . . we'll be forever in your debt."

"Oh no, *ma cherie*, Mama Lillie will think of a way you can repay this, how you say, debt. Never fear."

Elizabeth, her face snug against the big woman's shoulder, didn't see M'nondo and Mama Lillie look at each other and wink.

Chapter Forty-seven

August 1812, from Haiti to Cat Island

Colin's journey from Haiti to Cat Island was slow, much slower than he would have liked, but necessary to avoid the English. He backtracked almost his journey from the islands almost a year previously, riding in the hold of merchant vessels, or dressed as a crewman on some of the few fishing boats rash enough to brave the English warships that patrolled the waters between Haiti and the Bahamas, stopping frequently at islands along the way to receive communications from Hoskins, and check in with people from the man's list of contacts.

He also left messages for Lillie St. Clair at each stop, letting her know of his arrival on Cat Island. At his third stop, to his surprise, there was a response from St. Clair, welcoming him, giving contact instructions, and strangely, asking that he procure certain medicines, giving the names and quantities. Hoskins had given him an obscene amount of gold coins and gold dust, and at that particular stop, purchasing the requested items presented no problem. He left the port, a few ounces of gold dust lighter, carrying a new leather bag of significant weight.

He also received news of the war at each stop, and as expected in such turbulent circumstances, and, as far removed as he was from the actual events, what he heard was contradictory.

At his stop on the island of Mayaguana, as he sat alone at a table in the corner near the bar, dressed as a humble merchant seaman and hunched over a flagon of ale, he heard a pompous-looking dandy in a green waistcoat at the other end of the bar bragging about a British victory over American ground forces in Canada just a few days before.

"Aye, Sir Isaac chased that bounder Hull out of Canada, he did," the dandy said. "Forced him to surrender Detroit without a shot being fired. The bloody colonials who weren't captured are probably still running."

The statement was greeted with half-hearted cheers throughout the room, but Colin noticed that some of the drinkers merely stared morosely into their mugs.

Amazing, he thought, how fast bad news travels, although, he wasn't surprised to hear that the army was having such a bad time. At the beginning of June, the month that James Madison was pressured by the war hawks in the American Congress to declare war on England, the regular army was a mere 10.000 men, over half of whom were green recruits with no field or battle experience. Before leaving Charleston, he'd heard of recruiting efforts, but with the pay of a private only five dollars per month, less than half the wage of a skilled laborer, it was a slow, laborious effort. The low pay and danger was further compounded by the fact that soldiers often went months without pay. Roped into a five-year enlistment, and led by sergeants and officers with no more experience than they had—and, who were also poorly and belatedly compensated—it was a wonder that William Hull's force had even managed to cross the Canadian border in the first place. If such disasters as Detroit continued, he thought, the 'Second War of Independence,' as the militant congressmen from the south and west called it, would be short, and the country's independence would be in jeopardy.

His attention was caught by a swarthy man at a nearby table, who leaned toward his companion, a tow-headed young man with a scraggly beard, and said, "Bloody poof," he said in a gravelly voice. "Beatin' a rag tag army ain't gettin' ye nothin', unless you can resupply and move in new troops. I hear'd that the feckin' English navy ain't havin' it so easy."

"Oh yeah," his companion replied. "They got them damn ships blockadin' American ports from Maine to Florida."

"Aw hell, they ain't got but less'n thirty ships to do that, 'n the bloody Americans been givin' Letters of Marque to privateers what been runnin' blockades 'n raidin' English merchant ships at will."

"I s'pose that do present a problem."

"Damn right it do, 'n even with a navy what ain't got as many ships, them damn Americans been givin' the bloody poofs a go for it at sea. I hear'd the English done lost two ships to Americans, *Alert* and *Guerriere*. Now, that done give the poofs a bloody nose for sure."

That information brightened Colin's mood. If his

navy comrades were able to thwart the English armada in the north, and privateers, along with whatever force he could muster, could keep the English occupied, it might just give the army time to get itself together. Even though it was badly outnumbered, the English were preoccupied with their war against France's Emperor Napoleon, making their war against the upstart Americans a low priority. Yet again, despite their own arguments with the Americans, the French were providing the balance that could give them breathing room.

It was with mixed emotions that he left Mayaguana, dressed as an itinerant crewman on a produce boat heading north. The boat's final destination was San Salvador, and from there he would have to find a way to get to Cat Island, where the mysterious Lillie St. Clair awaited him.

Soon, very soon, he thought, his heart racing, he would see Elizabeth.

Chapter Forty-eight

August 1812, *Mama Lillie's*, Cat Island

The two weeks had dragged on interminably for Elizabeth. She'd spent most of the time secluded in her house, pacing the floor and wondering if Mama Lillie would come through with the medicines her people needed. M'nondo, sensing her mood, had left her alone.

When the day finally came, she dressed in a green dress befitting the English lady she was pretending to be, and once again, M'nondo grudgingly put on his servant's attire, and *The Vixen* set sail for Cat Island.

This time, they managed to acquire the services of a more suitable conveyance, a surrey belonging to one of the wealthier native landowners at the relatively isolated north end of the island. Again, they had their driver drop them off some distance from their final destination, not wanting anyone to associate Mama Lillie with pirates should their disguises be penetrated.

Elizabeth was surprised when she pushed through the beaded curtains into *Mama Lillie's* to see her old friend dressed, not in her usually gaily colored dresses, but in a dark blue dress with a white, ruffled collar. The sleeves came down to just past her elbows. On her feet, she wore a pair of men's boots, of brown leather and highly polished. She had a serious expression on her face, and her smile when she saw Elizabeth was not the normal bright-as-the-sun beaming smile, but a weak, almost hesitant lifting of the corners of her mouth.

"*Bon jour, cherie*," she said. "You are early. That is good."

Elizabeth rushed across the room and embraced her, Holding the big woman by the shoulders, she leaned back and peered into her eyes.

"Yes, *maman*, we had good winds today. Is everything all right? You look worried."

"Oh, little one, it is nothing. I was expecting a . . . business associate, but he is late."

"Is he involved in bringing the medicines you promised me?" Elizabeth's brow wrinkled.

"*Oui*, just so. I suppose his ship is late. You know how these small boats are."

Elizabeth nodded. She knew, and she also knew that Mama Lillie's 'business associate' was probably a smuggler, required to travel by circuitous routes to avoid customs officials and patrolling warships.

"Was he able to get everything?" she asked.

Mama Lillie frowned and shook her head. "I do not know, *cherie*, I have not been able to contact him for two day now."

The thought that her much-needed medicines might not arrive sent a shiver of worry through Elizabeth.

"Is it possible he might have been stopped by the English authorities?" she asked, coming as close as she dared to about the true nature of her old friend's contacts.

Mama Lillie, though, didn't seem to notice. "Oh no, if such had happened, I would know about it. It is probably nothing. The boats that run between the islands do not keep a regular schedule. I am sure he will be here soon."

Her words were reassuring, but Elizabeth couldn't help but notice that her expression belied those reassuring words. She saw that even M'nondo had a concerned expression. That two of the most important people in her life, two people who didn't usually show worry, were worried, was beginning to cause her stomach to knot up. It was all the worse because she had no idea why they were worried.

"Is there anything I can do, Mama Lillie?"

"Oh no, my child. We must just wait. I guess I am worried because of this stupid war between the Americans and the English. It is bad enough that the English and French are always fighting, but we had adapted to that here in the islands. This new war, though, it is different somehow. It is too close to home."

Something in Mama Lillie's tone set off alarm bells in Elizabeth's head, but before she could say anything, she was distracted by the rattling of the bead curtain over the entrance. Along with everyone else, she turned toward the noise, and received the shock of her life.

Standing just inside the door, dressed as an itinerant seaman, with several days' growth of beard on his face and a tatty sea bag over his shoulder, stood the last person she expected to see—but, the one person she knew deep in her heart that she *wanted* to see.

As their gazes locked, Colin's eyes went wide. His gaping expression quickly transformed into a smile that threatened to undo her.

M'nondo broke the silence. "Colin, you are the last person I expected to see right now."

"Nice seeing you, too, M'nondo, old friend," Colin replied in that insolent, but endearing tone that Elizabeth remembered so well. "Elizabeth, Mama Lillie, nice to see you as well."

He stepped forward and placed the sea bag on a table.

"Colin Worth," Mama Lillie said. "What are you doing here?"

He looked at her, that half-smile still on his sun-darkened face.

"It was a long voyage, but the seas were calm," he said.

Mama Lillie's eyes went wide, and she put a hand over her mouth.

"You? You are the . . . one?"

"That's not exactly what I was told to expect," he said.

Mama Lillie looked flustered for a moment, but quickly regained her usual composure. "Yes, the seas are usually calm this time of year," she said.

Colin pointed at the sea bag.

"I have the items that you requested, although, I don't understand why you needed medicines. Are you ill?"

Vixen

Before Mama Lillie could reply, Elizabeth stepped forward, and planted herself in front of Colin, almost close enough to touch; close enough to feel the heat from his body and smell the tangy odor of his sweat. It was all she could do to keep from trembling.

"Those are for me," she said. "They are for the children and old people on Lost Island." She turned to Mama Lillie. "*Maman*, you didn't tell me that Colin was your contact."

"That, my child, is because I did not know."

"But, you said you'd been in contact with him."

"Only through, how do you say it in *anglais* . . . intermediaries. I did not know his name."

She turned back to Colin, a confused look on her face. "Can *you* explain it?"

He smiled at her, again causing a flutter in her chest. "I can, Elizabeth, and I will, but first, I must speak with . . . Mama Lillie along."

"Yes, I thought you would," Mama Lillie said. "Come, we will go in the back. *Mes Enfants*, please excuse us for a few moments, then all will be explained."

She turned and headed for the back of the restaurant, behind the beaded curtains that led to the kitchen. Colin smiled at her, and reached out and gently caressed her cheek.

"I'll be back shortly, and all will be explained."

He then followed Mama Lillie to the back.

When they were gone, Elizabeth turned to M'nondo.

"Do you have any idea what's going on here?"

He had a look on his face that she was all too familiar with. He knew something that she didn't, and he was holding it back.

"I have a good idea," he said. "But, I believe it best if I let Colin tell you himself."

"M'nondo, we are family, and families do not keep secrets from one another."

"That is wrong, little sister, and you know it well. Everyone has secrets, sometimes secrets that they keep from themselves."

"And, just what is that supposed to mean?"

"That, too, will come clear in time. For now, it is best if you exercise some of the patience I have tried so hard to teach you since you were a rebellious child."

"I am not a child now, M'nondo, and I *am* your captain. I order you to tell me." She stamped her foot for emphasis.

"I am sorry, Elizabeth, but I am not able to do that. It is not for me to do. Soon, you will understand."

She stamped her foot again. Well she knew that ordering him, getting angry with him, yelling at him, none of it would do one whit of good. He was as stubborn as the hard wood he sometimes resembled. She hated waiting, but was left with no choice but to wait. She didn't, however, have to like it, and the pouting expression she knew had come involuntarily to her face made that abundantly clear.

Just when she thought her patience had reached its limit, the rattling of the beads behind her announced the return of Colin and Mama Lillie, both of whom were smiling broadly.

"Well, are you two ready to tell me what's going on here?"

Colin crossed the room in long strides, reached for her, and pulled her into his arms. As angry and frustrated she was at being kept in the dark, it felt good. She relaxed in his warm embrace, but wasn't ready to completely surrender.

"I'm waiting," she said.

Colin eased his embrace, and stepped back to stare into her eyes.

"I'll tell you and M'nondo everything during the voyage to Lost Island," he said. "For now, I have a question for you."

She looked hard into his eyes. She wasn't sure what she saw there.

"Very well, as long as you do tell me everything, what's your question?"

"Are you up for a little adventure?"

Charles Ray

Vixen

Author's Note

I've played a little fast and loose with history in *Vixen*, although I have tried to remain fairly true to the events of the War of 1812, one of America's forgotten wars. If that sounds like a cop-out, it probably is. While a few actual historical characters' names appear in this book, the events are entirely fictitious.

Pirates were common along the Atlantic seaboard and in the Caribbean during this period, and contrary to what you might think, there were actually a few women pirates as well. As for behind-the-lines operations by the Americans, I can find no records to substantiate them, so that part is purely imaginary. What both sides did do, however, is use privateers, a form of contract pirate, against each other, by issuing *Letters of Marque* to private citizens and ship captains, in effect, hiring them to conduct a form of piracy against the other side. It's easy to believe, therefore, that an operation such as the one described here, just might have happened.

This is not the end of Elizabeth and Colin's adventures, or their relationship for that matter. At some point, when I've done a lot more research on sea battles and the war itself, I'll bring them back and allow them to create havoc in the Caribbean, and in each other's lives.

If you liked this book, I would appreciate it greatly if you'd leave a short review, just a few words will do, on Amazon, Goodreads, or any other site that carries reviews. Independent authors can only be successful if their books are read, and reviews help readers find those books.

Charles Ray

Books by this author:

Al Pennyback mysteries

Color Me Dead
Memorial to the Dead
Deadline
Dead, White, and Blue
A Good Day to Die
The Day the Music Died
Die, Sinner
Deadly Intentions
Death by Design
Till Death Do Us Part
Deadly Dose
Dead Man's Cove
Dead Men Don't Answer
Deadly Paradise
Kiss of Death
Death in White Satin
Death and Taxis
Deadbeat
A Deadly Wind Blows
Death Wish
Deadly Vendetta
A Time to Kill, A Time to Die
Dead Ringer
Death of Innocence
Dead Reckoning
Murder on the Menu
Over My Dead Body

The Buffalo Soldier series:

Buffalo Soldier: Trial by Fire
Buffalo Soldier: Homecoming
Buffalo Soldier: Incident at Cactus Junction

Buffalo Soldier: Peacekeepers
Buffalo Soldier: Renegade
Buffalo Soldier: Escort Duty
Buffalo Soldier: Battle at Dead Man's Gulch
Buffalo Soldier: Yosemite
Buffalo Soldier: Comanchero
Buffalo Soldier: Range War
Buffalo Soldier: Mob Justice
Buffalo Soldier: Chasing Ghosts
Buffalo Soldier: The Piano
Buffalo Soldier: Family Feud

Ed Lazenby mysteries
Butterfly Effect
Coriolis Effect
The Cat in the Hatbox
Negative Side Effects

Other fiction
Angel on His Shoulder
She's No Angel
Child of the Flame
Pip's Revenge
Wallace in Underland
Further Adventures of Wallace in Underland
Dead Letter and Other Tales
The White Dragons
The Dragon's Lair
Dragon Slayer
The Last Gunfighters
The Culling
*Frontier Justice: Bass Reeves, Deputy
    U.S. Marshal*
Angel on His Shoulder-Revised Edition
Battle at the Galactic Junkyard

Mountain Man
Devil's Lake
Wagons West: Daniel's Journey (from Outlaws Pub.)
Dead Letter and Other Tales: Revised and Expanded
Vixen

Nonfiction
Things I Learned from My Grandmother About
  Leadership and Life
Taking Charge: Effective Leadership for the
  Twenty-first Century
Grab the Brass ring
African Places: A Photographic Journey
  Through Zimbabwe and southern Africa
A Portrait of Africa
There's Always a Plan B
In the Line of Fire: American Diplomats in
  the Trenches
Advice for the Insecure Writer
Looking at Life Through My Lens
Ethical Dilemmas and the Practice of Diplomacy
Making America Grate Again

Children's books
The Yak and the Yeti
Samantha and the Bully
Molly Learns to Share
Where is Teddy?
Catie and Mister Hop-Hop
Tommy Learns to Count
Catie Goes to School

Charles Ray

ABOUT THE AUTHOR

Charles Ray served 30 years in the Foreign Service (from 1982 to 2012), after completing a 20-year career in the U.S. Army. His first Foreign Service assignment was as a consular officer at the U.S. Consulate General in Guangzhou, China. He then served as the sole consular officer at the newly-opened consulate general in Shenyang, China, where he achieved tenure and was reassigned to the Consulate General in Chiang Mai, Thailand, as the administrative officer and acting deputy principal officer.

After three consecutive overseas tours, he returned to Washington where he served as the Special Assistant to the Director of PM Bureau's Office of Defense Trade Controls. After Washington, he went to Freetown, Sierra Leone as Deputy Chief of Mission.

In 1998, he became the first American consul general in Ho Chi Minh City, Vietnam, with consular responsibility for Vietnam from Hue to Phu Quoc Island. In 2002, he became ambassador to Cambodia, serving for three years. During the 2005-2006 academic year he served as diplomat-in-residence at the University of Houston. After leaving that job, he was appointed deputy assistant secretary of defense for Prisoners of War/Missing Personnel Affairs in the Office of the Secretary of Defense, responsible for the recovery, repatriation and identification of personnel missing from World War II to current conflicts.

His final assignment before retiring from the Foreign Service was as ambassador to Zimbabwe, from 2009 to 2012.

He holds a B.S. in business administration from Benedictine College, Atchison, KS; an M.S. in systems management from the University of Southern California; and an M.S. in national security management from the National War College. Ray is also a graduate of the U.S. Army Command and General Staff College (resident/non-resident program), the Army War College's Land Forces Commander Course, and the Defense Intelligence School's Postgraduate Intelligence Course.

His military awards include two Bronze Stars, the Joint Service Commendation Medal, Army Commendation Medal, National Defense Service Medal, Armed Forces Reserve Medal, and the Humanitarian Service Medal among others. He received a Superior Honor and a Meritorious Honor Award from the Department of State, and the Distinguished Civilian Service Award from the Department of Defense.

A native of Texas, Ray now leaves in suburban Maryland, just outside Washington, DC, with his wife, Myung.

www.ingramcontent.com/pod-product-compliance
Lightning Source LLC
Chambersburg PA
CBHW060346260626
47160CB00006B/2224